KERRY BARRETT was a bookwor[m]... did a degree in English Literature, then trained as a journalist, writing about everything from pub grub to EastEnders. Her first novel, Bewitched, Bothered and Bewildered, took six years to finish and was mostly written in longhand on her commute to work, giving her a very good reason to buy beautiful notebooks. Kerry lives in London with her husband and two sons, and Noel Streatfeild's Ballet Shoes is still her favourite novel.

Also by Kerry Barrett

The Could It Be Magic? Series
Bewitched, Bothered and Bewildered
I Put a Spell on You
Baby, It's Cold Outside
I'll Be There for You
A Spoonful of Sugar: A Novella

The Forgotten Girl
The Girl in the Picture
The Hidden Women
The Secret Letter

Readers Love Kerry Barrett

'A thoroughly enjoyable read!'

'Fantastic book, really loved reading it'

'Loved it! The best yet!'

'Gripped from start to finish'

'It's definitely worth a read'

'I devoured the story it's a real page turner with a great twist'

A Step in Time

KERRY BARRETT

ONE PLACE. MANY STORIES

HQ
An imprint of HarperCollins*Publishers* Ltd
1 London Bridge Street
London SE1 9GF

First published in Great Britain by
HQ, an imprint of HarperCollins*Publishers* Ltd 2020

Copyright © Kerry Barrett

Kerry Barrett asserts the moral right to be
identified as the author of this work.
A catalogue record for this book is
available from the British Library.

ISBN: 9780008389239

MIX
Paper from
responsible sources
FSC   FSC™ C007454
www.fsc.org

This book is produced from independently certified FSC™ paper
to ensure responsible forest management.

For more information visit: www.harpercollins.co.uk/green

Printed by CPI Group (UK) Ltd, Croydon CR0 4YY

Prologue

Afterwards I realized I was far, far drunker than I thought I was and that's probably why it all went so badly wrong. But at the time, I thought it was a great idea. Matty, my boyfriend, was out at the opening of a new club and I wanted to see him. So I left the hotel where I was oohing and ahhhing over a fancy brand of hairbrush, jumped in a cab and headed to the West End to catch up with my man.

I posed for the photographers outside the club, giving them a beaming smile and a cheeky look over my shoulder so they captured the back of my mini dress, and then I trip-trapped down the stairs in my super-high heels to find Matty.

At first, I couldn't see him. It was dark in the club and the flashing lights on the dance floor meant I took a while to get my bearings. But then I spotted his best mate, TJ, chatting to a girl I didn't recognize, and Matty's broad back in a tight white T-shirt, his head turned away from me, his tongue firmly stuck down another woman's throat and his hands all over her bum.

People talk about a red mist descending, don't they? I never knew what they meant until that moment. All I could think about was that some two-bit reality TV starlet was snogging my boyfriend. The man I loved. The man I intended to marry – just as soon as we agreed terms with *Yay!* magazine for the engagement photo shoot that would cover the cost of the huge rock I had my eye on.

Shrieking with rage, I launched myself at the girl. I took a fistful of her hair extensions in my hand and pulled her face away from Matty's.

'Get your lips off my man!' I screamed. And then – and believe me, I'm not proud of this – I pulled my arm back and punched her. Right in the nose. I honestly didn't know there would be so much blood.

Everything stopped. I couldn't even hear the music any more. It was like the whole room was suddenly in slow motion.

'AAAAAMMMMMYYY!' Matty was yelling. 'Whaaaat have you dooooonnnne?' He had blood all over his white T-shirt.

The girl he'd been kissing was squealing as TJ shoved napkins at her, and out of the corner of my eye I could see other clubbers filming the whole sorry escapade on their phones.

Sounds bad, doesn't it? Really bad. But that's not even all of it.

Realizing I'd gone too far, I turned to leave. But like I said, I'd had quite a lot to drink at that hairbrush launch (honestly, it's the only way to get through things like that – the free booze) and I was wearing really high heels.

As I spun round, my foot caught on the edge of the dance floor and suddenly I was face down in a puddle of pina colada with my super-short dress up round my hips and my Hello Kitty knickers on display.

Lying there, my cheek stinging from the pineapple juice, I watched two men compare photos on their phones' screens and high-five each other. And then firm hands lifted me up.

'Out!' said one of the two bouncers who were either side of me. They were both twice as tall as me and seemingly three times as wide. They'd lifted me so high that my feet weren't even touching the floor.

'Don't worry, I'm going,' I muttered to the bouncer on my left. 'I just feel a bit …'

And then I puked. All over his trousers.

Chapter 1

'Get your lips off my man.' My boss, Tim, threw the paper down on his desk and glared at me. 'Amy's meltdown. Full story continues on pages three, five, seven and nine.'

I glanced down at the photo on the front of the paper and winced as I saw the now familiar shot of me face down on the dance floor, bum in the air, as a blood-splattered Matty gazed on in horror.

'Today's news, tomorrow's fish and chip paper,' I said hopefully.

Tim rolled his eyes and turned his computer screen round so I could see it.

'You are the only person who's ever made every single thumb-nail on the *PostOnline*'s Sidebar of Shame,' he said. Sure enough, the column of pics down the side of his screen replayed each moment of that awful night in full technicolour glory. It was like a flipbook animation of the punch, the blood, the fall and the vomit.

'I'm sorry,' I whispered. 'I just really loved him, you know?'

Tim's face softened.

'I know you did, sweetheart.'

'So what happens now?' I asked, scared to hear the answer. Tim was the producer of *Turpin Road*. It was the biggest soap in

Britain and I was arguably its biggest star – at least I liked to think so. I played Betsy, a damaged but sparky barmaid at the Prince Albert pub. I'd been on the show for three years and I absolutely loved it. And Tim loved me. I'd had some brilliant storylines and I was tipped as the next big thing. At least I had been, until I punched a reality TV star called Kayleigh and showed my knickers to the world.

I gave Tim a sheepish grin.

'Suspension?' I suggested. 'I'll go to my mum's in Spain for a month, stay out of everyone's way, and when I get back all this will have blown over and the tabloids will have a new victim. Just write me out for a bit.'

I was wearing a scarf round my neck – I'd hidden my face with it when I'd come into the studios earlier to avoid the paps waiting at the gate. Now I wrapped it round my head like Dolly, the actress who played my on-screen granny, and picked up the phone on Tim's desk.

'Oh, hello, Betsy,' I said, in what I thought was a pretty good impression of Dolly's shrill cockney voice. 'Oh, your uncle's broken his leg, has he? Of course you should stay and look after him. About a month, you say? We'll miss you.'

I put the phone down again, pulled the scarf off my head and stared at Tim, waiting for the axe to fall.

I knew how these things worked. One of my co-stars had sent a photo of his willy to a fan via Snapchat, she'd screengrabbed it, shared it, and it was all over the internet about thirty seconds later. He'd been suspended for a while but he was back now and it was like nothing had happened. Tim adored me. The *Turpin Road* viewers adored Betsy. Surely my punishment would be similar?

Tim shook his head and my heart sank.

'Longer?' I whispered. 'Two months?'

'You assaulted her, Amy,' Tim said. 'You broke her nose.'

'She was kissing Matty,' I pointed out.

'You were given a caution. You were lucky not to be charged.'

'I wasn't charged because her nose was full of coke and she didn't want to make a fuss,' I said.

Tim shrugged.

'That's as may be,' he said. 'But she doesn't work for me and you do.'

He paused.

'At least, you did.'

I went cold. I buried my face in my scarf and looked up at Tim in horror.

'What are you saying?'

'Don't give me those puppy dog eyes Amy,' Tim said. 'You know what I'm saying.'

'I'm out?'

He nodded.

'My hands are tied, love,' he said. 'You punched someone, your pants are all over the *PostOnline* and there's bound to be more. They'll be after anything and everything. Ex-boyfriends, girls you fell out with at school, hairdressers you were rude to – it's all fair game now.'

I closed my eyes.

'Build them up, knock them down,' I said.

'Exactly,' Tim said.

'No,' I said. 'No. The viewers love Betsy. They love her and they love me.'

I jumped to my feet.

'Look,' I said, pointing to a framed photo of me gripping a gold statue that had pride of place on the office wall. 'Do you think the show would have won this BAFTA without Betsy's mental health problems?'

Tim shrugged.

I picked up a pile of magazines that were on his bookshelf and went through them one by one.

'Amy wins big,' I read, showing him a photo of me with an armload of statues at last year's soap awards.

'Steal Amy's summer style.' I opened *Hot* magazine at a fashion shoot I'd done and waved it at him.

'Amy bares all?' I fake-gasped, then giggled as I showed Tim the cover of *Cosmo* featuring a make-up-free me. 'I was in make-up for an hour before that shoot.'

'Don't,' Tim said. 'Don't do this.'

But I was on a roll. I picked up *Yay!*

'Amy and Matty: Our plans for the future,' I read. My voice shook as my bravado deserted me.

'I've lost him, Tim,' I said, hugging the magazine close. 'Don't make me lose this, too.'

'No one's bigger than the show,' Tim said sadly. 'But you'll be okay. You're very talented.'

'I can come back, right?' I said, still gripping my magazine. 'Betsy will come back?'

Tim looked down at his feet.

'We're killing you off,' he said.

I couldn't speak.

'It's going to be huge,' Tim carried on. 'The biggest whodunnit since "who shot JR?". People will be talking about it for years.'

I bit my lip. I didn't want him to see me cry.

'We're rewriting some stuff,' Tim said. 'And we'll film your last scenes this afternoon.'

I felt sick. This afternoon? How could my entire life change so fast? But I pasted on a smile, took a deep breath and stood up, throwing *Yay!* down on the desk.

'Okay then,' I said briskly. 'Let me have the script A-sap, yes? Thanks for everything.'

I air-kissed him on both cheeks and legged it out of his office, down the corridor and into the safety of my dressing room. And then I started to cry.

Chapter 2

I never let myself cry for too long because I hated when my face got all puffy and my eyes swelled up. So after about ten minutes sobbing into the cushions on my dressing room sofa, I forced myself to get up and face the rest of the day. At *Turpin Road* we shared our dressing rooms, though I'd heard that on other soaps they got their own. I shared with two other actresses, which I quite liked, actually. They were nice enough and generally I enjoyed having someone to hang out with. Not today, though. Today I was relieved that they weren't around and I had the place to myself so I could wallow in gloom alone.

I knew that I'd be called on set soon, so I dragged myself into the shower, trying to think about anything and everything apart from the fact that in the space of twenty-four hours I'd gone from being TV's hottest star to a jobless, homeless, boyfriendless nobody. I stifled another sob as I shampooed my hair. Crying wouldn't solve anything.

By the time I got out of the shower, I had thirteen missed calls – mostly from my agent, Babs, who'd been phoning me non-stop since the story went viral this morning – and a script pushed under my dressing room door. That was it then, the end of Betsy. I picked up the envelope – it was very thin, so obviously the script wasn't very long. Poor Betsy. I took a deep breath before I opened the flap and scanned the text.

Interior: The Prince Albert
Betsy is clearing empty glasses after closing time. A noise makes her jump and turn.
BETSY: You! What are you doing here?
A hand reaches out and whacks Betsy on the head. She falls, motionless, to the ground.

Disgusted, I threw the papers to the floor. I'd given this show three years of my life, and this was how they repaid me? I was their biggest asset. In my head I heard Tim's voice in my head saying: 'No one is bigger than *Turpin Road*, Amy.' I winced. What a way for him to prove his point.

Well, at least I didn't have any lines to learn really. I could just lie on the sofa and feel sorry for myself until I got called on set.

I slumped down and had had my eyes closed for about thirty seconds when my phone rang. Listlessly I looked at the screen. Babs. Again. I supposed I couldn't avoid her for ever, so I swiped the screen to answer.

'Hi Babs.'

'Bloody bollocking hell, Amy. What the flaming arse have you been doing?'

I held the phone away from my ear as she continued her foul-mouthed tirade. Babs swore like a trooper at the best of times, so when faced with a crisis – like now – she was really filthy. Eventually she calmed down a bit and I cautiously put the phone back to my ear. Her voice softened.

'How are you?' she said. 'Are you holding up?'

I felt close to tears again.

'Don't be nice,' I warned. 'I am barely holding it together and if you're nice I'll crumble.'

10

'Chin up,' Babs said in her no-nonsense Glasgow tone. 'I've got good news and bad news. Which do you want first?'

'Bad,' I said, bracing myself.

'The catalogue's pulled your fashion line,' she said. I groaned. That was the end of my wardrobe full of free clothes then.

'And the good news?'

'Hold on, I've not finished the bad news yet,' Babs said. 'Your nail varnishes are on hold but it's not looking good, and I've had a call asking you not to come to the premiere tonight.'

'I'd forgotten all about it,' I said. 'And all my clothes are at Matty's flat anyway.'

'Where are you staying?' Babs asked.

'Phil's,' I said, sitting up on the couch and picking up a cushion to hug. 'He's looking after me, like always.'

'Every girl needs a gay best friend, eh?' said Babs.

I laughed without any real humour.

'Yeah, well, it's not quite so fabulous when your gay best friend's boyfriend hates you,' I said. 'I can't stay there for long.'

'Where will you go?'

'Not sure,' I said. 'Maybe to my mum's for a while. Get some sun.' And a whole lot of grief, though – I was trying not to think about that. Another thought struck me.

'What's the good news?'

'What good news?'

'You said there was good news'

'Oh, yes,' Babs said. 'I just want you to know that this is not a disaster. I've got people out of worse scrapes than a small punch-up in a nightclub.'

I smiled despite myself.

'It wasn't really a small punch,' I said. 'More of a wallop.'

Babs made a dismissive sound.

'And my knickers are all over the internet,' I added, feeling another wave of self-pity.

'Ach,' said Babs. 'It's fine.'

11

'It's not fine,' I said. 'It's awful. I really just want to go away for a while. Disappear for, like, six months, longer even. I can get off the bloody media roller coaster and lick my wounds, then come back revitalized and ready for a new challenge.'

'Absolutely not.'

'Babs, I can't do this,' I wailed. 'There are paps everywhere. And Tim's right – they're going to dig up every tiny bit of dirt they can. This story will go on and on and on. Unless I disappear and give them nothing.'

'Oh, get over yourself,' Babs said. 'You're not bloody Greta Garbo. If you disappear now, everyone will forget you. Your career will be over.'

'Ouch,' I said. 'That's harsh.'

'It's true,' said Babs unsympathetically. 'But don't worry. I've got a plan.'

'You have?' I said, feeling marginally more cheerful.

'We need to make the most of this interest in you. Use it to our advantage and take control.'

'And how do we do that?'

'Oh, it's easy. We just need people to know how lovely you are,' she said blithely. 'Not Betsy – Amy. Your adoring public need to remember why they adored you in the first place.'

'Right,' I said, doubtfully. 'I'm not sure that's the most straight-forward idea you've ever had. How would we do it, anyway?'

'Reality TV, baby,' she said.

I took the phone from my ear and scowled at it.

'No,' I said. 'No.'

'Don't dismiss it, Amy,' Babs said. 'It can work wonders.'

'And it can destroy careers,' I said.

There was a pause.

'From where I'm standing, it looks like you don't have much of a career left to destroy,' Babs said. 'When you've hit rock bottom, Amy, the only way left is up.'

'I'm not doing *Big Brother*,' I said.

'Fine.'

'And only major channels.'

'Fine.'

'And I get to choose which show.'

There was silence.

'Babs, I get to choose.'

'Fine,' she said, grudgingly.

'And minimal publicity,' I said. 'I'll do what I have to do, but not too much. I've got to get away from all this.'

Babs made a huffing sound.

'You can't hide away,' she said.

I wished I could, but I knew she was right really. I bit my lip.

'I've got contacts everywhere – I'm sure we can get you into something,' Babs went on, oblivious to my misgivings 'Have a think and let me know what you want me to focus on. But do it soon. We need to strike while the iron's hot.'

'Okay,' I said, suddenly feeling very tired. 'I'll have a think.'

'Amy,' Babs said. 'It's going to be okay, you know.'

I tried to smile but it was more of a grimace.

'Yeah, we'll see,' I said. 'We'll see.'

Chapter 3

'Was it awful?' Phil said, giving me a sympathetic look as he adjusted the hat on a mannequin.

I flopped dramatically over the low table where he showcased his most exclusive designs to his poshest customers.

'So awful,' I said. 'I can't even tell you how bad.'

'Don't put fingermarks on that table,' Phil warned.

I gave him a fierce look but sat up anyway.

'Well, it's done now,' Phil said. 'You've filmed your last scenes. Betsy is no more.'

He paused.

'So who killed her then?'

I shrugged.

'Not a clue,' I said. 'It was just one of the props guys who dealt the fatal blow – they only filmed his hand. They'll add in someone later, when they decide who the killer's going to be.'

Phil made a face.

'It's not a great ending,' he said. 'Still, onwards and upwards.'

Phil's relentless cheeriness was what had brought us together at school. I loved him because, like me, he was always up for a party, because he understood what made me tick, and because he adored me. And we all need a bit of adoration in our lives, right?

14

Our friendship had lasted through several boyfriends (his and mine), broken hearts (his and mine), career highs (his and mine) and career lows (mostly mine), and he'd obviously been the person I'd run to when the shit hit the fan with Matty. The only fly in the ointment was Phil's boyfriend, Bertie, who thought I was a bad influence (he was probably right) and who had not been pleased to see me when Phil brought me home, hungover and tear-stained, after spending hours in a cell.

Now Phil gently lifted my arm and extracted a fabric swatch from beneath my elbow.

'What happens now?' he said. 'Where does Amy Lavender go from here?'

Self-pity overwhelmed me again and my throat began to ache with the promise of more tears.

'Oh, Phil,' I said. 'I don't know. What am I going to do?'

He put his arm round me.

'You'll bounce back, sweetie,' he said. 'You always do.'

But that made me feel even worse.

'Everyone dumps me,' I said quietly. "Eventually, everyone gets fed up with me and they dump me.'

'That's not true,' Phil said.

'It is true.' I sniffed and Phil thrust a tissue box in my direction.

'Matty dumped me,' I said. Phil opened his mouth, probably to tell me I was well shot of Matty – he'd never been a fan – but I gave him a look and he closed it again.

'Tim dumped me from *Turpin Road*,' I went on. A tear ran down my cheek. 'Even my own mum, Phil. She dumped me.'

'She didn't dump you,' Phil said, wiping my tear away with a folded tissue. 'She just took a chance to make a better life for herself.'

'In Spain,' I pointed out. 'Hundreds of miles away from me.'

'You could have gone with her,' Phil said. 'She asked you to go.'

'Only because she knew I wouldn't,' I said.

15

'Have you spoken to her, since all this happened?'

'God no,' I said. 'She's only interested in me when things are going well. I bet she's taken that photo of me down from the wall in her bar already. "My daughter the screw-up" isn't half as impressive as "my daughter the soap star".'

Phil chuckled, ruefully.

'You've still got me, honey,' he said. 'You'll always have me.'

I forced myself to smile at him.

'I know,' I said. 'PhAmy for ever, right?'

'Right,' he said, kissing my nose.

But I wasn't convinced. Phil had been my rock for years. My best friend, my support network, everything. But since he'd met Bertie I felt like I had to fight for his attention and I wasn't sure I liked sharing him.'

'So what are you going to do?' Phil asked again. 'Can I help?'

'Would you?' I asked, flashing him my best, most beseeching smile.

'What do you need?'

'Well, first I need to go and get all my stuff from Matty's. The only clothes I've got are what I had at work – and I'm running out of knickers. But I can't face him on my own, so will you come with me? Please?'

Phil put his arm round my shoulders again.

'Of course,' he said, kissing the top of my head. 'I've got a few things I'd like to say to Mr Matthew actually.'

I grinned. Phil was always fighting my corner.

'And then, I need you to help with one more thing,' I said. 'I need to choose a reality TV show. Babs reckons that's the best way to get the public back on my side.'

Phil, who, if he ever went on *Mastermind*, would choose the specialist subject Reality TV 2000–2015, gave a deep, satisfied sigh.

'She's right,' he said. 'She's completely spot-on. Ooh, she's clever.'

'She should be,' I grumbled. 'I pay her enough.'

'So which show?' Phil said.

'I convinced her to let me choose,' I told him. 'Babs reckons she can get me on anything. You know what she's like – she knows all the right people. I'm just not sure it's the right thing to do.'

Phil looked at me appraisingly, his head tilted to one side. Then he nodded.

'Of course,' he said in delight. 'It's perfect.'

'What?' I said, suspicious of his gleeful expression. 'What are you thinking? Not *Drag Race*?'

Phil gave a chuckle.

'No,' he said. He pushed his thick-rimmed glasses (just for show – they had clear lenses but he thought they gave him a geekish charm, and he was right) up his nose and pulled me to my feet.

'I'm thinking you in a tiny bikini, tanned, skinny, bravely carrying on without Matty, perhaps flirting a little with another similarly tanned young, male TV star, and showing the legions of Amy fans – and those who dared to be Amy doubters – what a game old bird you are.'

'Ohhhh,' I breathed. 'You mean the jungle?'

'The jungle,' Phil said. 'It's perfect.'

I thought about it.

'I'd be away for weeks – so no paps chasing me the whole time,' I said. 'Lots of time to think, to work out what I want to do next …'

'And you look smoking hot in a bikini,' Phil said.

I made a modest face. I knew he was right.

'You're strong because you work out, like, all the time, you're sporty and adventurous, you're funny, you're kind … you're bound to win.'

'What about my hair extensions?' I said, holding up a strand of the brunette locks that were my pride and joy.

17

'They'll have to come out,' Phil said, grim-faced. 'Better to do it now, so people get used to seeing you without them.'

I nodded.

'I can do that,' I said. 'New hair, new start.'

'So ring Babs and tell her,' Phil said. 'Do it, do it now.'

'Okay, okay,' I giggled, pulling my phone out. 'I'm doing it.'

I found Babs in my contacts, and waited for her to answer.

'Voicemail,' I said. 'She must be on the tube ... Babs, it's Amy. The jungle. I want to go to the jungle. Call me back.'

As I ended the call, there was a ring on the doorbell of the shop.

'I thought you were closed,' I said to Phil.

He frowned.

'I am,' he said. 'Oh, balls. I'd forgotten about her.'

'Who?' I said. 'What?'

'Natasha Lucas,' he said. 'She's a fashion editor.'

'A journalist,' I shrieked, diving off the chair and under the table so she wouldn't spot me through the glass door.

'Relax Princess Di,' Phil said with a smile, waving at the woman and going to open the door. 'She works for *Society* magazine. She only cares about toffs. She won't have a clue who you are.'

'She might,' I said frostily, crawling out from under the table. 'You'd be amazed how many people watch *Turpin Road*.'

'Darling Natasha,' Phil said, throwing open the door. 'Come in!'

In came a tall, willowy blonde woman in her early forties. She had her hair in a neat twist, and she was wearing a classic tan mac, cropped white trousers, nude sandals and a striped blue-and-white scarf. I instantly felt cheap and scruffy in my baggy jeans and hoodie.

'God, Phil,' Natasha said, throwing her oversized bag onto the chair next to me. 'I am having such a day. Sorry to be so late – and looking such a mess.'

I raised an eyebrow and Natasha noticed me for the first time.

'Hi,' she said, sticking out a hand for me to shake. 'I'm Natasha.'

'Amy,' I said, hoping my hands were clean. 'I'm Phil's best friend.'

'Lovely,' said Natasha, sounding like she didn't really care. 'Anyway, can I have a root around, darling? We've got this blasted photo shoot first thing and I need at least three, probably four, hats and the stylist's pulled out so I'm organizing the whole thing on my own. Plus my nanny's gone AWOL, my buggering husband's sodded off to Hong bloody Kong, the baby's got chicken pox, my grandmother isn't well, and basically everything's gone to shit.'

I grinned at her. It was nice to meet someone who was having almost as rotten a time as I was.

'Cup of tea?' I said.

Chapter 4

When I came back into the shop from the tiny kitchen out the back, Natasha was wearing one hat, holding another, and had her phone balanced between her shoulder and her ear.

'No, no, no,' she was saying. 'There's simply no point in sending another inexperienced nanny. I've got four horrible children and they will break her. I need someone tough ...'

'She's hilarious,' I said, putting down the tea tray.

Phil nodded.

'She juggles about a million things, but she's always in control,' he said. 'Her fashion spreads are gorgeous and believe me it's worth my while to be a bit flexible for her.'

He sat down on the sofa and patted the cushion next to him.

'Listen, Amy,' he said, his voice serious. 'I need to tell you something.'

'About Natasha?' I said, in a whisper. 'What?'

Phil gave a faint smile.

'No, not about Natasha,' he said. 'About Bertie.'

I tried to look sympathetic.

'Not going well?' I said. 'I'm not surprised. You're very different people, you and boring Bertie.'

Phil laughed.

'Nice try, Miss Lavender, but yes, it's going very well, thank you. In fact, Bertie's parents are coming over from France next weekend and I'm keen to make a good impression on them.'

'Ohmygod you are adorable,' I said, taking his face in my hands. 'Of course you'll make a good impression.'

Phil took my hands from his cheeks and held them tightly.

'Amy,' he said. 'Please try and understand what I'm telling you.'

Realization dawned.

'You're kicking me out?' I said. 'You don't want me in your flat when Bertie's parents are there?'

Phil screwed up his nose.

'Sorry, darling,' he said. 'You know I wouldn't see you on the streets, but this is really important to me.'

I took a deep breath.

'It's fine,' I said. 'Honestly. I can easily find somewhere to live. No problem. I'll go and stay with Mum perhaps.'

'Really?' said Phil. 'I'm not sure that's a very good idea.'

Slumping against the sofa cushions, I bit my lip.

'Nah, probably not,' I admitted. 'There are more paps in Marbella than there are here nowadays. It'd be a nightmare. Don't worry, I'll find somewhere.'

'Sorry to interrupt,' said Natasha, who'd come to stand in front of me. 'I couldn't help overhearing.'

I narrowed my eyes.

'It was actually a private conversation,' I said.

Natasha waved her hand as if there was no such thing, her huge blinging engagement ring catching the light.

'You're Amy Lavender, right?' she said.

I threw Phil a triumphant look. See! She did know who I was.

'Yes,' I said cautiously. 'That's me.'

'So I'm guessing you need somewhere to live that's cheap and quiet and available right now?'

'Yes,' I said again, sitting up a bit straighter. 'Do you know somewhere?'

'I certainly do,' said Natasha. She sat down in between me and Phil.

'My mother has just had something of a mid-life crisis – for the fourth, or perhaps the fifth time. This time, she's in the throes of a passionate affair with a yoga instructor and she's headed off on a sort of old lady gap year,' she began.

I blinked at her, impressed at the idea of her mum and the yoga teacher, but not knowing how this had anything to do with me.

'Okaaaaay,' I said

'So, she convinced me to keep an eye on my grandmother,' Natasha carried on. 'Which is no hardship because I adore her, but I've got such a lot on, and it's proving hard to get round to hers every day.'

She chewed her lip.

'She's quite sprightly, really, considering she's almost ninety. She doesn't need much looking after. Just someone who's there, you know, if she needs something?'

'Okaaaaay,' I said again, still not understanding. 'Oh, god. Do you mean me? I can't look after an old lady.'

Natasha gripped my hand.

'You can,' she said. 'She's fine. She can look after herself, honestly. It's not like you need to cook for her, or bathe her, or anything like that. Her house has a flat, in the basement. It's really nice – I lived there myself when I was younger. One bedroom, lounge, blah, blah. So you wouldn't even be living with her, not really. She just needs someone who's there in case she has a fall.'

'No,' I said. 'I'm not the right person. I'm too selfish to be an old woman's companion.'

Natasha gripped my hand tighter.

'Ow,' I said. 'Where is it?'

'Clapham.'

I screwed my nose up.

'I don't like South London,' I said.

22

'It's perfect,' Phil commented. 'There won't be any paps down there. You'll be left alone.'

He had a point, but that wasn't enough to change my mind.

'The rent's cheap.'

'How cheap?'

Natasha named a tiny figure that I could easily afford even if I didn't work for the next six months, and Phil widened his eyes.

'So I won't need to bathe her?' I said.

'You probably won't even see her,' Natasha said. 'She's got loads of friends. I just need to know you're going to be there overnight and that she can call on you if she needs to.'

'I can only stay for a few weeks,' I said, checking my phone to see if Babs had called back. 'I'm going into the jungle, and who knows what could happen after that.'

'My mother should be back by the New Year,' Natasha said. 'The timing is perfect.'

I knew when I was beaten.

'Fine,' I said, throwing my head back against the sofa. 'Fine. Yes, I'll move in.'

'Tomorrow?' Natasha said hopefully. Phil clapped his hands and I glared at him.

'Tomorrow,' I agreed wearily.

My phone rang and I snatched it up, hoping it was Babs with good news about the jungle. But it was Josie, a TV presenter who lived in the flat below Matty's. She was probably calling for the gossip, I thought, cancelling the call. Immediately she rang again. I rejected the call once more. There was a pause, and Josie started calling again. I sighed.

'I should take this,' I said to Natasha and Phil. 'Hi Josie.'

'Amy, you need to get here,' Josie said. 'Matty's putting all your stuff outside in the street. There are loads of tramps wearing your dresses and the paps are going crazy.'

'WHAT?' I shrieked. 'Which dresses?'

'I don't know,' Josie said. 'Does it matter?'

23

'I suppose not,' I admitted. 'I'm on my way.'

I ended the call and stood up, tossing my hair over my shoulders.

'I have to go,' I said, trying hard not to cry. 'It seems that, not content with breaking my heart, Matty's determined to make a fool of me in the papers too.'

Natasha delved into her huge tote bag and pulled out a piece of paper. She scribbled something on it, then delved again and found a set of keys.

'Here,' she said, shoving them at me. 'This is the address and these are the keys. You can move in tonight if you like?'

Relief flooded me. And Phil, by the look on his face. Clearly he didn't want to think about taking me – and all my belongings – back to his pristine flat for another night.

'Thank you,' I said, meaning it.

'Will you be okay on your own?' Phil said.

'Oh, I'll be fine,' I said. 'How much worse can things get?'

Ready to face the world – and the paparazzi – I twisted my hair into a ponytail, pulled on my baseball cap and picked up my sunglasses. Then I grabbed my bag and gave Phil a kiss.

'Thanks for everything, buddy,' I said. 'I'll give you a call later.'

Chapter 5

I found a cab without any trouble and soon I was on my way to my old flat in Camden, feeling sick with nerves about what I'd find when I got there.

What I found was worse than I could have imagined. Matty had stuffed all my clothes into bin bags and then, by the look of it, chucked them all off the balcony of our – sorry, his – first-floor flat. Some of the bags had burst and so clothes were scattered across the drive. Pyjamas, underwear, jeans, dresses – they were all strewn on the paving stones and on the neighbours' cars. One of my bras swung jauntily from the handlebars of Matty's motorbike.

It was raining so everything was slightly soggy and, like Josie had said, word had obviously spread around Camden. Some giggling schoolgirls were rooting through the bin bag squealing in delight as they pulled out all my gorgeous clothes and shoved them into their backpacks. And the old bearded man who hung out at the tube station dancing to the music from the buskers was wearing one of my favourite dresses.

Aghast, I pushed my face up against the window of the cab.

'That's my soap awards dress,' I wailed.

I opened the window a fraction and was wondering if I should shout something at someone when I heard a yell.

Matty was hanging out of the bedroom window. I gasped when I saw him. He was so handsome. I'd spent the last two days thinking of him as some kind of monster so it was strange to see him now looking so good. Seriously, seriously good. I almost wanted to rush over to him, kiss his beautiful face, tell him how sorry I was and beg him to take me back …

'Take everything you want,' he was yelling. 'Help yourselves.'

Oh.

Of course there were three photographers busy capturing everything, plus a camera crew, obviously filming for Matty's fly-on-the-wall show.

'Keep driving,' I shrieked. 'Keep driving!'

The cab driver met my eyes in the mirror and nodded briskly. Next to me, on the pavement, the teenage girls dug into another bag, pulling out what seemed to be my favourite jeans and trainers.

I made a split-second decision.

'Stop!' I shouted. The cabbie jammed on the brakes and I was out onto the pavement in a flash, leaving the taxi door open. As skilfully as any rugby player I swerved round the group of girls. Then, catching them unawares, I yanked the bin liner from one of the girl's hands, pulled my prized Marc Jacobs clutch from an outstretched arm, and scooped up a pair of battered Converse. Then, before the photographers even had a chance to notice I was there, I dived back into the cab and slammed the door.

'Drive!' I yelled, feeling like Thelma. Or was it Louise? 'Driiiiive!'

'Where to, miss?' the cabbie said politely, flooring the accelerator and speeding away from the flat.

I took a breath.

'Clapham,' I said. 'Take me to Clapham.'

I looked down at the Converse I had clasped in my trembling hands.

'I don't think these are mine,' I said in surprise.

The cabbie let out a snort of laughter.

'I reckon you deserve them,' he said

'I reckon I do.' I looked out of the back window of the cab at the window where Matty still stood. We were going pretty fast so it was hard to see but I liked to think he looked a bit forlorn and I felt glad. After all, he had smashed my heart into tiny pieces.

'You that Amy Lavender?' the cabbie asked as we hurtled south. I thought about denying it but there wasn't much point given what he'd just witnessed. Instead I nodded.

'That's me,' I said.

'He's an idiot that fella,' he said, winking at me in the mirror. 'You're well shot of him.'

I smiled. That was nice to hear.

'I messed up,' I said.

'Had a drink, had you?' the cabbie asked.

'More than one.'

'Well, we've all been there,' he said. 'Things get a bit tasty when you've all had a few. But the way I see it, you had good reason.'

He grinned.

'Mind you, probably should have belted him – not her.'

I laughed for what seemed like the first time in days.

'Want him back?' he asked.

'Nope.'

'Nice one,' he said, indicating and pulling into the kerb. 'Find someone who's worthy of you, that's my advice. Here we are then.'

He had stopped outside a beautiful house facing a huge expanse of grass – Clapham Common, I guessed.

I widened my eyes in surprise.

'Is this it?'

It was. It was a stunning house. One of the Victorian double-fronted villas that lined the edges of the common like sentries. It had wrought-iron railings, flowers in pots either side of the enormous front door, and a black-and-white tiled path. And to the left some stone steps led down to a second front door, this one painted a smart grey, at basement level. My new home. For now.

I handed over a bundle of notes and scrambled out of the car, clutching my handbag, bin liner and the stolen Converse. The cabbie waved cheerily at me as he drove off and I blew him a kiss – he'd been a real tonic – and gazed up at the house. I saw a movement at the window on the ground floor and wondered if the old woman was watching me. Maybe she was planning to phone the papers and tell them where I was, I thought, slightly hysterically. Or perhaps she was going to be a nosey old trout who made my life a misery. I squinted at the window again but I couldn't see anyone, so I made my way carefully down the steep stairs.

The flat was actually really nice and surprisingly light for a basement. It had one bedroom with a double bed and fitted wardrobes – not that I had much to put in them – and when I lay on the bed to test it I could see people's feet and ankles as they walked along the road.

There was a basic bathroom and a large sitting room, with an open-plan kitchen area at one end. It was a lovely room with wooden floors, an original tiled fireplace and French windows that opened onto a tiny paved backyard. There was a sofa and a squishy armchair, a small TV and DVD player, and empty bookshelves. It was all a bit unloved but it was okay. For now, I thought again.

My phone rang and I dived for it. Babs.

'Hit me with it,' I said. 'When do I fly out to Oz?'

There was a pause.

'Ah,' said Babs.

'What do you mean, "ah"?' I said, hysteria mounting. 'What does "ah" mean?'

'Jungle's not a goer, I'm afraid,' Babs said. 'But don't be down-hearted. I've come up with something really special.'

'Really?' I said, curiosity overtaking my disappointment. 'What is it?'

'I've called in just about every favour I've ever been owed, and pulled a lot of strings,' Babs said.

'Yes,' I said.

Babs made a noise that I thought was supposed to be a drum roll.

'Babs,' I said. 'What is it?'

'Strictly. Stars. Dancing,' she said triumphantly.

I sat down heavily on the sofa.

'What?' I said.

'*Strictly Stars Dancing,*' Babs said again. 'It's glittery, it's fabulous and it's going to make you the nation's darling once more.'

I felt sick.

'Babs,' I whispered. 'I can't dance.'

Chapter 6

Cora

I watched as the girl stumbled down the steps to the basement flat, carrying bin liners that spilled their contents over the concrete stairs. She was very pretty, though her eyes were swollen and red, from crying, I assumed. And she was very thin. Her legs in her skin-tight jeans were like twigs. She reminded me of my Ginny, back in the sixties, when she was fashionably little-boy thin and wore her ravishing red hair in a pixie crop that made her look like a street urchin.

The girl looked up at my window and I drew back slightly, not wanting to be spotted spying.

She looked, I thought, like someone in trouble, as she stood at the front door of the flat, gripping the keys so tightly her knuckles gleamed white. Someone in need of a friend. Her shoulders slumped as she plucked a bra from where it had dropped onto one of the plants next to the door, then she turned the key in the lock and went inside.

Disappointed, I gave up my vantage point and settled down on the sofa. My new tenant interested me. There was something in the set of her shoulders, in the haunted look in her eye, that reminded me of the girl I'd once been – frightened, heartbroken, but, in my case, not alone. My eyes rested on a photograph of Audrey and me that stood on the mantelpiece. It had been taken in the fifties and we both wore clam-digger trousers and fitted blouses. I remembered how sassy we'd thought ourselves in those outfits. We were grinning like the kids we were really. Audrey had a cigarette dangling from her lips and I was laughing, with my head thrown back.

'I hope she's got a friend like you, Aud,' I said aloud, wondering if I was finally turning into a batty old woman. 'And I hope, if she does, she listens to hers.'

I picked up my half-drunk G&T and raised it towards the ceiling.

'I should have listened to you, Audrey,' I said. 'I should have listened.'

1944

I peeked through the gap in the curtains and hugged myself in delight. He was here. Just as he'd promised he would be. Sitting bang in the middle, about three rows back. Worried he'd spot me spying, I let the curtain drop, but then couldn't resist taking another look. Donnie was smiling widely and looked wonderfully handsome, every bit as handsome as I remembered. I had a churning excitement in my stomach and I couldn't wait to talk to him after the show. To hold him and kiss him.

'Is he here?' Audrey stood on her tiptoes to see through the curtain above my head.

I gave her a shove.

'I'm trying to be discreet,' I giggled. 'Don't make it so obvious that we're looking.'

'Girls,' Henry, the entertainment officer, hissed at us from the side of the stage. 'Places, please.'

The band struck up and, still laughing, Audrey and I ran to get into position for the opening number.

I loved being on stage. I liked everything about it – the costumes, make-up, the applause from the audience. I enjoyed singing, though I knew I wasn't a natural singer, not like Audrey was. I did short skits with Nigel, a rotund actor who everyone adored and I liked those, too – it was fun making people laugh. But it was dancing that was my real love. I heard music in my head all the time, and so I danced all the time, when I was queuing for breakfast, or making my bed at whatever digs we were staying in that week. Sometimes I wondered how other people stayed so still.

And on stage – oh, that was where I really came alive. I didn't care if I was dancing a solo or part of the chorus line, I loved it all. And frankly I was so glad to finally have been allowed to become part of the Entertainment National Service Association, now I'd turned eighteen, and to shake off the shackles of my overbearing mother, that I always made the effort to enjoy every single part of a performance.

But not tonight.

Tonight, I was distracted. I barely registered the first few numbers, I performed my solo – which was my favourite part of the show – as if in a dream, and though I tried to throw myself into my comic scenes with Nigel, I knew I wasn't really firing on all cylinders. Because of Donnie. He was all I could think about, and for the first time since I'd joined up, I just wanted the show to be over.

As soon as the curtain fell on the grand finale, I scarpered. I raced to the tent the girls in the company used as a dressing room and stripped off my costume. It was an adapted showgirl outfit commandeered from a London theatre and, though it looked wonderful under the lights, up close it was shabby and losing its sheen.

I pulled it off and instead put on my uniform, wishing I had something else to wear. I brushed my blonde hair until it shone, and pinned it up, then I pinched my cheeks to give them some colour, thanking my lucky stars that, unlike some of my friends back home, who were working in factories and kitchens and hospitals, I still had make-up. I spat on my mascara and slicked it onto my lashes and smoothed on a tiny amount of red lipstick. I may have had make-up but who knew how long it would last? Then I checked my appearance in the mirror and grinned.

'Not bad, Cora,' I said.

Audrey appeared in the doorway of the tent.

'Blimey, you were off that stage at a fair old whack,' she said. She straightened my skirt over my hips and kissed me on the cheek.

'You look beautiful,' she said. 'I hope he's bloody worth it?'

I gave her a poke.

'I think so,' I said. 'Which is all that matters.'

Audrey rolled her eyes at me.

'Just be careful, Cora,' she said. 'The one thing blokes are good at is lying.'

I poked her again.

'Don't be so miserable,' I said. 'Have you seen him?'

Audrey scowled at me, then her face softened.

'He's waiting for you out the back, you soppy cow. I saw him just now. Go on, if you really have to. Go!'

I gave a small squeal and rushed off to find Donnie.

He was waiting exactly where Audrey said he would be, behind the mess hall where the performance had been. He was watching some bags being loaded onto trucks and he had his back to me.

Suddenly shy, I paused, but he turned and saw me, and opened his arms, and all my shyness was forgotten as I ran to him.

We walked round the edge of the camp, hand in hand. It was dark there and away from the shouts and engine noises. You could even hear the wind in the trees on the other side of the fence, if you listened hard enough. It wasn't the most romantic location but just being with Donnie made it perfect.

'How long are you staying this time?' Donnie said as they strolled. His soft American accent made me shiver with pleasure. I'd found myself forgetting his voice over the months since I'd seen him last and so it was wonderful to hear him again.

I groaned.

'Only a few nights,' I said. 'Nothing like as long as last time.'

When we'd been at the camp before we'd stayed for a month, doing shows on a rotation to the GIs stationed there. With so much time together, my romance with Donnie had blossomed and our letters had kept things going while I toured Britain with the ENSA.

But there weren't many troops left now. Donnie would be headed back to France before too long, and this time we only had a few days.

'Tell me again,' I said now. 'Tell me the plan.'

Donnie had mapped out our future while we'd been apart, spelling it all out in his letters. But I'd never heard him actually say the words.

'When this damn war finally ends, and the Americans send those Germans packing,' he began.

I giggled and pulled his arm round my shoulders, grateful of his warmth on this cold, clear night.

'Not just the Americans,' I said.

Donnie chuckled.

'Whatever you say, honey,' he drawled in an over-the-top accent.

'So when the war is over …' I prompted, giving him a fake-stern look.

'We'll ship out of England and head back to the States,' Donnie said. 'Soon as we can.'

'And where will we go?' I said, knowing the answer but wanting him to say it.

'Well, I guess we should call in on my folks,' Donnie said. 'Mom's desperate to meet you.'

'She is?'

'Sure she is. I got a letter from her just the other day asking to know more about you.'

I blinked. This was all news to me.

'More?' she said. 'What have you told her already?'

'That you're beautiful, funny, talented and you've made me the happiest man in England,' Donnie said.

'Sounds about right,' I said, striking a pose.

'Have you told your mom about me?' Donnie asked.

Up ahead was a parked jeep. Not wanting to answer Donnie's question, I saw my chance to distract him, so I bounced over to the car and climbed up onto the bonnet.

'Come on,' I said. I lay back against the windscreen and looked up at the stars, bright in the clear December sky. Donnie climbed up next to me and gripped my hand.

'So we'll call in on the folks in Connecticut and then we'll get on a train,' he continued.

'A train,' I said. 'That's good. I like trains.'

'We'll go all the way cross country. We'll go to Chicago – I love Chicago. And to Las Vegas – take in a few shows.'

I was getting impatient.

'And where then?' I said.

'And then we'll go to Hollywood,' said Donnie, propping himself up on his elbow and looking down at me. 'And you'll be snapped up by some big movie producer and you'll dance in films and become the superstar you were born to be.'

I reached up and rubbed his buzz cut with the palm of my hand.

'What will you do?' I asked, looking deep into his blue eyes.

'I'll devote my life to making you happy,' he said, bending his neck to kiss me. 'That's all I care about.'

Chapter 7

'This is a very bad idea,' I said to Phil as we went up the stairs to the theatre.

'Oh, get over yourself,' he said, giving me a delicate nudge. 'You can't shut yourself away for ever.'

'It's hardly for ever,' I said. 'It's only been a week.'

'One week and two days,' Phil said. 'And one royal pregnancy announcement, one pop star falling off the stage at an awards ceremony, and one fabulous dress worn by Beyoncé. The gossip mags have moved on. Everyone's moved on. It's time you did, too.'

'I'm moving on,' I said, sulkily. 'But unfortunately, I'm moving on to a bloody dance show when I've got two left feet and I'm going to be a laughing stock.'

'You're not that bad. I've seen you throwing some magnificent shapes on the dance floor after a few drinks.'

'Yes, but I can't get hammered before every rehearsal, can I?' I said, wondering if, in fact, I could.

'Relax,' Phil said, taking my hand. 'You'll love this show and I guarantee it'll give you the dancing bug.'

We were at a West End theatre to watch the opening night of a revival of a classic Broadway musical. Phil had promised me old-school Hollywood glamour and lots of dancing to get me in the mood. I wasn't convinced, but he was right that I needed a night out. A week rattling round in my empty flat had made me stir crazy.

'You look fabulous, by the way,' Phil said as we found our seats.

I bobbed a curtsey to him.

'Well, thank you, sir,' I said. 'I had to go shopping because sodding Matty virtually gave away all my clothes and this dress just fell into my basket.'

Phil raised an eyebrow.

'Sure it did,' he said, looking at the Gatsby-style beaded shift dress appraisingly. 'Don't forget you're not earning at the moment.'

'Shh,' I said, not wanting to hear his words of wisdom right at that second. 'It's starting.'

Phil was right. It was a gorgeous, gorgeous show and it did make me want to get up and dance. Though I wasn't sure I could pull it off with quite as much style as the leading lady. It was glitzy and sparkly and wonderful and as the curtain went down I clapped until my hands stung.

'Sooooo,' Phil said, hopefully. 'Did you love it?'

I nodded.

'Yes, I loved it.'

'And is Phil always right?'

I made a face.

'About this,' I admitted. 'But I wouldn't say always.'

'What about this?' Phil said. He produced two tickets to the opening night party and I groaned.

'A party?' I said. 'Really?'

'Really,' he said, grabbing my hand. 'It's fine. You need to get back out there and this is a good place to start. It's going to be quiet, classy, and there's absolutely no chance Matty will be there.'

'Okay,' I said, letting him lead me up the stairs to the bar at the very top of the theatre where the party was. 'Let's go and party.'

Phil was right. It was indeed a quiet party. But it was kind of nice, and knowing it was Matty's idea of a nightmare made it easier for me to relax. There was a barbershop quartet in the corner, singing songs from musicals, and groups of people stood together chatting and drinking glasses of champagne.

'It's very sophisticated,' I said to Phil. 'Not sure I belong here.' Phil took two glasses from a passing waiter and stuck his tongue out at me.

'Of course you do,' he said. 'We both do.'

I shook my head at the glass he offered and swapped it for an orange juice when the waiter passed us again.

'I'm off booze,' I said. 'It just gets me into trouble.'

We stayed for a while, chatting about mutual friends and eating as many canapés as we could get our hands on. But it wasn't the most exciting party in the world and, eventually, Phil looked at his phone.

'Do you mind if we call it a night?' he said. 'Bertie's round the corner with his parents and I said I'd go and meet them. Do you want to come?'

I shuddered.

'God no,' I said. 'I'll head home.'

'Do you want me to find you a cab?' Phil said.

'Nah,' I said, picking up my bag. 'I'll pop to the loo first and then head out. Call me tomorrow?'

Phil gave me a quick squeeze.

'Will do,' he said. 'Stay safe.'

I blew him a kiss as he headed for the stairs, then I went to find the loo.

I was still in the cubicle when I heard two women come in, chatting in that slightly too loud way that told me they'd had rather a lot of champagne.

'I just hope this is it,' one was saying. 'I've fucking had enough of being in the chorus line. If this isn't my big break, then I don't know what else I can do.'

'You could get your boobs done,' the other one said. 'Everyone does it.'

'How would that help?'

'Dunno,' the second one said, giggling. 'I have no idea.'

I went to flush the toilet, then stopped as I heard them say my name.

'… like Amy Lavender,' the first one said. 'She was here earlier, did you see her?'

Great. I couldn't burst out of the cubicle now, could I? Surprise! Quietly I put the seat down and sat on it.

'Do you know what I heard about Amy Lavender?' the other one said, lowering her voice to a quiet shriek.

Oh, this would be good.

'Her name's not even Amy Lavender. It's Amy Brown.'

'Nooooo,' said the first one.

Sitting on the loo, I rolled my eyes. That was hardly a state secret. My real name was, in fact, Amy Lavender Brown, so I'd simply dropped the boring Brown when I started acting. It had been my mum's idea, actually – in fact, it was the reason behind my unusual middle name. She'd hoped I'd be a star one day, even before I could talk. Pressure, much?

'I feel a bit sorry for her, you know?' one girl said. 'Everyone knew her fella was cheating on her, for months and months before she found out.'

Oh, really? I thought. People were always so wise after the event.

'True,' the other one said. 'He slept with Casey. And he was all over Felicity at that album party.'

My mind raced. What album party? Not the one Matty went to when I'd been doing that week of night shoots? Surely not …

'He tried it on with me once,' the first one said. 'He was quite persistent. I had to get Greg to have a word with him in the end.'

'What a sleaze,' said the other girl. Then she giggled. 'You had

39

a lucky escape, though. That Amy Lavender could have whacked you instead.'

Laughing, they both left the toilets and I heard the double doors back into the bar bang shut.

I sat there for a while, trying to process what I'd heard. Matty had cheated on me before? It just didn't make sense. I had to speak to him, to find out if it was true. I pulled my phone out of my bag and scrolled to his number, then paused. No, I was giving too much weight to silly gossip. It wasn't true.

Feeling more settled, I flushed the loo, washed my hands and made for the stairs. Then I changed my mind and headed to the bar instead. I needed something to calm my nerves.

'Champagne, please,' I said to the barmaid, all my intentions of staying teetotal abandoned. 'Quick as you like.'

Chapter 8

'Celebrating?' said the man next to me at the bar. He was sitting on a bar stool, slumped over his own glass of bubbles.

I downed my glass in one mouthful and turned to look at him.

'Well, I just found out my ex-boyfriend was actually cheating on me for a lot longer than I thought, with more women than I thought, and that just about everyone else in London knew about it and was laughing at me behind my back. Do you think that sounds like a reason to celebrate?'

The man laughed.

'Sure it does,' he said. He had a soft American drawl that I liked. 'Sit down.'

I perched on a stool next to him and he topped up my glass and then his own.

'What are you celebrating?' I asked. He didn't look particularly joyful, gazing into the bottom of his champagne flute like the answers to all the world's problems were there.

'Oh, nothing much,' he said. 'I got offered the job of my dreams this afternoon.'

'Well, that's good,' I said, encouragingly.

'Yeah, it is,' he said. 'But when I called home to tell my parents, my dad wasn't interested because I'm not in his line of work.'

'What's that?' I said, draining my glass again.

'He sells cars,' the man said. He ran his fingers through his blond hair. 'And my mom was more interested in telling me my high-school girlfriend just got married.'

'Do you care that she got married?' I asked.

'Nope,' he said. 'Not really. I've not seen her for years. But then I came here to support my flatmate – he's the lead. And he's abandoned me to go off with some girl.'

He looked into his glass again.

'I just felt a bit lonely.'

I grinned at him.

'It sucks, doesn't it?'

He nodded.

'So why don't we get drunk and drown those sorrows?'

He smiled back at me, showing straight white teeth in what was, I now realized, rather a handsome face.

See, I told Philip in my head, I am moving on.

While my companion ordered another bottle from the barmaid, I studied him. He was about as different from Matty as it was possible to be. Matty was swarthy with finely styled dark hair and – at the moment, at least – a beard. This guy was clean-cut with messy blond hair and a sprinkling of freckles across his nose. He looked like an overgrown and – I cast a sneaky glance at his arms – very buff teenage surfer.

'Do you surf?' I asked him suddenly.

He smiled wistfully.

'Of course,' he said. 'I grew up in California. Everyone surfs.'

'Really?'

'Nah, not really. But I do. I miss it when I'm here.'

'You should go to Cornwall,' I said. 'There's brilliant surfing down there. I used to go on holiday there with my best friend's family when we were kids. Maybe I'll take you one day.'

'I'd like that.'

Our eyes met for a fraction of a second too long, and I felt

42

slight butterflies in my stomach. Moving on could be fun, I thought.

It didn't seem nearly as much fun when I woke up the next day.

My head was banging, and there was sun pouring through the window, which seemed to be in the wrong place.

Cautiously, and without lifting my painful skull, I opened one eye. Yes, that window definitely hadn't been there yesterday. I opened the other eye. Man, that sunshine was bright – it had to be late morning, possibly even lunchtime. I felt on the bedside table for my phone to check the time – but the table wasn't there. Hold on. What was happening? I sat up, trying to ignore the hammering in my head and looked round me.

I was in a smallish attic room, with a fitted wardrobe and white walls. It had one large window – the one the sun was streaming through – and two smaller ones on the opposite wall. My Gatsby dress was draped over a chair but I couldn't see my underwear. I had a quick check under the duvet. Nope. No undies there. I squinted in the sunshine and saw my knickers poking out from under the bed. Next to me, snoring loudly, was the blond surfer.

'Shit,' I whispered. 'Shit, shit, shit.' This was not staying under the radar. I was so desperate to get off the endless treadmill of courting the showbiz media one minute, then having to avoid the inevitable press interest when things went wrong – and this was not the way to go about it. I tried to remember leaving the party and if there were any photographers there. I couldn't recall being papped, but that didn't mean it hadn't happened. Judging by the horrendous hangover I was developing, there were bound to be bits of the evening I didn't remember exactly.

I did remember telling Surfer Dude how Matty had cheated on me over and over and I'd lost the upper hand by whacking poor Kayleigh. I also recalled him telling me that Matty was an idiot and that he didn't deserve someone as nice as me. Which

I'd thought was just the most lovely thing anyone had ever said to me, so I'd rewarded him with a kiss. And then another one. And we'd carried on kissing all the way to Surfer Dude's flat. Which must be near the theatre because we'd definitely walked there, but I had no idea where I was exactly.

And then we'd kissed all the way to his bedroom. And it had been really very nice. My head may have been banging but I had no trouble remembering that part of the evening. Carefully, I peeked under the duvet again. Surfer Dude was starkers as well. And rather magnificent he looked, too.

Focus, Amy.

So we'd had sex. That was fine. Perhaps not my classiest moment, but a completely understandable reaction to being cheated on. Best way to get over one man was to get under another, Phil always said. But now I had to get out of there without being spotted by anyone – I couldn't risk more pics on the *PostOnline*'s Sidebar of Shame; I'd never work again. And I definitely had to leave before the whole awkward 'I'll call you' thing happened. I felt a small pang of regret. He was really nice, Surfer Dude. If I'd met him at a better time, who knew what could have happened? But right now, I had to focus on saving my career. Sleeping with someone new wasn't the best start.

Carefully I slid out of bed, picked up my dress and pulled it over my head. Then I went in search of my bag and shoes. They were in the lounge. I sat on the sofa – where I remembered sitting last night – and pulled on my heels, wishing I had my stolen Converse to put on instead. I was just checking I had my phone, my door keys and my purse when Surfer Dude appeared at the bottom of the stairs wearing a pair of shorts.

'Doing a runner?' he said with a grin. 'I thought maybe we could hang out today.'

Don't be nice to me, I thought. Please don't be nice.

'I've got stuff to do,' I lied, trying to look apologetic. I blew him a kiss. 'Thanks for a lovely night.'

I turned towards the front door, but Surfer Dude was too fast.

'Was that a brush-off?' he asked.

I paused.

'I think it was,' I said honestly. 'Sorry.'

He grimaced.

'Wow,' he said. 'You British girls are brutal.'

I felt a bit embarrassed.

'Look,' I said, knowing I was about to sound completely up myself and hating it. 'I'm on TV – at least I was – and I've got an image that I need to protect. This was a mistake. I can't be here.'

Surfer Dude winced.

'It was a lovely night,' I said. 'Really. And I'm sorry.'

I pulled my dress down a bit so my walk of shame wasn't quite so shameful (who was I kidding – everyone I passed was going to know what I'd been up to) and opened the front door.

It was only when I reached the street that I realized I didn't even know his name.

45

Chapter 9

Cora

The sound of a car door slamming stirred me from my doze in the armchair. I found that increasingly these days I woke very early then snoozed in my chair whenever I sat down. This morning I'd risen before six, made myself a cup of tea, and settled down to read a book. But I'd fallen asleep almost immediately. My tea was still warm, though, I thought, touching the back of my hand to my mug, so I hadn't been dozing for long.

Ever the nosey neighbour, I rose from the chair to see who was slamming doors at this early hour. It was my new tenant – Amy. She was leaning into the window of a taxi, paying a fare. I watched as she handed over the cash, then turned away to go down to her flat. She was wearing a sparkly 1920s-style dress and in her hands she had a pair of high heels and a similarly sparkly clutch bag. She looked very beautiful, I noted, but very overdressed for a Sunday morning in Clapham. She'd obviously been out all night and I hoped she'd had some fun – she'd struck me as someone who was in need of fun when I'd spied on her the other day. I smiled as she tiptoed down the stairs to her front door. She definitely reminded me of myself, I thought once again. At least, she reminded me of the old me. The one I'd once been …

1944

I hurried through the camp, stopping anyone I recognized to ask if they'd seen Donnie. I had no idea where he'd gone. His friend, Paul, had told me he'd had a letter from home and had seemed upset. So now I was worried he'd had some bad news and I wanted to find him to see if I could comfort him.

I skirted the edge of a garage and came face to face with another of Donnie's friends, Rog.

'Have you seen Donnie?' I asked.

Rog nodded.

'Saw the back of his head,' he said, pointing to a storage tent. 'He was going in there.'

'Thank you,' I said, giving his arm a squeeze.

I dashed into the tent and let the heavy canvas door drop behind me. It was dark in there and it took a while for my eyes to adjust.

'Donnie,' I whispered. 'Donnie, are you in here?'

There was a noise from the back of the tent, so I carefully picked my way towards the far end. The tent was full of bags of uniforms, piles of boots, sandbags – anything and everything. And at the back, sitting on a pile of scratchy grey blankets, was Donnie. He was holding a letter and crying, and when he saw me he turned his face away so I wouldn't see his tears.

My heart ached for him so much I felt his pain like it was my own. I sat down next to him and gathered him into my arms and he cried and cried onto my neck.

'What is it?' I whispered, kissing his tears away. 'What's happened?'

Donnie gave a sort of hiccupping sob.

'Gene,' he said.

I knew who Gene was. He'd been Donnie's best friend since they started school. They'd gone all the way through school together but joined up separately – Gene into the navy and Donnie the army. Donnie talked about him a lot and had told me how much he wanted us to like each other. Now my stomach twisted with sadness.

'Is he ...?'

Donnie wiped his face with the heel of his hand and handed me the letter.

'Torpedo,' he said. 'The ship sank. No survivors.'

I scanned the letter – it was from Donnie's mum and broke the bad news in such a sweet, sad way that I felt tears pricking my eyelids, too.

'Oh, darling,' I said, pulling him closer to me. 'What a sad, sad loss.'

'This damn war,' Donnie said. 'You know, sometimes I don't even know why we're fighting.'

I didn't know what to say. I'd been a schoolgirl when war broke out, and it was so much a part of my life that I couldn't remember what it was like before. But I was lucky. I had no brothers to lose, and my dad, who'd seen action in the Great War, had passed away before war broke out this time.

Donnie was crying again.

'I just want it to be over,' he said. 'I just want it to end.'

'I know,' I said, kissing him again.

'I don't want to go to France,' Donnie said. 'It's awful there. It's really, really awful. I'm scared, Cora.'

Now I was crying, too.

'Oh, my darling, darling boy,' I said. 'I'm scared, too. I'm so scared. But we've got this time together. We need to make the most of it.'

Donnie nodded.

'And when you're in France, I want you to think about me all the time,' I said, kissing his face all over. 'I want you to think about the hours we've spent together, and the way you make me laugh more than anyone else, and the way you make me happier than anyone else ever has.'

Donnie kissed me deeply and I shivered in pleasure.

'And the way your kisses turn my legs to jelly,' I said weakly.

I began unbuttoning his shirt. Donnie stopped my hand with his and looked at me.

'Are you sure?' he said.

'Anything can happen,' I said, hearing my voice tremble a little bit. 'Gene thought he had his whole life ahead of him and he didn't. There are bombs dropping, and guns, and all sorts of horrible things. Anything can happen to anyone and I don't want to regret not doing something when I had the chance.'

Afterwards we lay curled up together, under one of the scratchy blankets.

'No regrets?' Donnie said to me, his face close to mine.

'Never,' I said. 'I will never regret today as long as I live.'

A shout from outside made us jump and I suddenly remembered where we were and what a risk we were taking.

'I have to go,' I said, kissing Donnie and then wriggling out from under the blanket. 'Audrey will cover for me, but she can't keep pretending I'm in the privy.'

I pulled on my skirt and buttoned up my shirt, while Donnie watched me, smiling.

'What?' I said.

'You're beautiful.'

I threw my hat at him, then had to retrieve it.

'You soppy old so-and-so,' I laughed.

'I love you,' he said.

I blew him a kiss.

'I love you, too,' I said.

For the next three days we met up in the tent whenever we could. We couldn't get enough of each other. I wanted the smell

49

of Donnie on my skin, the feel of his breath on my face. I just wanted to be near him all the time.

I knew that emotions were heightened because of the war, and that in peacetime our romance probably would have taken months, or even years, to get to this stage, but I didn't care. Gene's death had shown us how important it was to live in the moment and to make the most of every single day.

Our unit was going to London after Christmas – we had a six-month stint entertaining troops in the capital and I was looking forward to settling in one place for a while. But Donnie knew he'd be leaving for France soon. I tried not to think about how he'd be forced to live. The things he'd see and do. The danger he'd be in.

As Audrey and I were packing up our costumes and getting ready to hit the road, Donnie came to find me.

'I have some good news,' he said, grinning widely.

'The war's over?' Audrey said, putting a feathery headdress into a box.

Donnie chuckled.

'Not that good,' he admitted. 'But good for me. We're going to be in London for a couple of nights before we leave for France in the spring.'

I was delighted.

'Really?' I said, throwing my arms round him. 'So we can meet?'

Donnie looked down at me and kissed the end of my nose.

'Oh, better than that,' he said. 'I thought we could get married.'

Chapter 10

I was having fun. Lots of fun, actually, much to my surprise. It was my first day on *Strictly Stars Dancing* and so far it had been brilliant.

I'd arrived at the studios early that morning, bracing myself to face photographers but there was no one there.

'We'll do all the publicity shots today in costume,' the director explained. 'Then we'll release your names to the press one by one, starting tomorrow. We've not confirmed anyone yet – it creates a buzz.'

I'd felt a shiver of excitement when she mentioned costumes. I may have had misgivings about *Strictly Stars Dancing* but the fabulous outfits weren't one of them. And I definitely wasn't disappointed. As soon as we arrived we were hurried into the enormous costume department, where there were rails and rails of frothy material in every colour of the rainbow, racks of shoes, and wonderful headdresses. I'd never seen so much glitter. I let out a small whimper of joy; it was absolutely amazing.

I was whisked away by a dresser who took me to a rail with a sign saying AMY. It was filled with lots of very sparkly, very small costumes. I swallowed.

'There's not much to them,' I said.

51

She grinned.

'There's not much to you,' she said. 'You'll wear long dresses for ballroom and whatnot, but for the pics we wanted to make the most of that gorgeous bod of yours.'

The outfit she chose was a gold mini skirt and fitted crop top. Both the top and the skirt were completely covered in fringing and shimmered under the lights.

'Really?' I said, holding up the tiny scraps of material.

'You'll look fabulous,' she said. 'Trust me.'

At the risk of sounding big headed, she was right. Good genes – my mum still had the figure of a twenty-one-year-old despite three kids and a fondness for sangria – combined with years of controlling my diet and working out every day had made sure I didn't have an ounce of blubber. The costume showed off my tight abs and my toned legs.

The hairdresser kept my brunette locks loose and gently waved. Instead of having my extensions taken out like I'd planned to do if I went into the jungle, I'd had them redone and I was very pleased with them. My hair fell over my boobs and halfway down my back and it was thick and lush. The *Strictly Stars Dancing* make-up was way over the top, but it worked with the costume and all, in all, the final result was pretty good.

I looked at my reflection in the mirror, turning from side to side to see every bit of the costume. I didn't look like the normal me, but I quite liked the effect.

'Smoking,' said my dresser in admiration as she looked at me. 'You look like the real deal.'

'Except I can't dance,' I said, looking at my back view over my shoulder. 'So as soon as I start to move, everyone will realize I'm not the real deal at all.'

She gave me a nudge.

'Every single contestant I've ever dressed has said that,' she said. 'And they've all had a ball. The professional dancers are amazing – they'll soon whip you into shape.'

Oh, God. I'd been trying to forget that, as well as having our photos done, we'd also be meeting our dance partners. I already felt sorry for whoever landed me. I was a lost cause.

I didn't have long to wait. We gathered together in the main studio. I looked at the dance floor and imagined dancing there in front of millions of viewers and a lively audience and felt a bit sick.

'Nervous?' said one of my fellow competitors. He was a rugby player – absolutely enormous with broad shoulders and ripped abs.

'So nervous I can't even think about it,' I confessed.

He laughed.

'It'll be fun, I reckon,' he said.

'Definitely,' said the woman to my other side. She was a newsreader who must have been in her late forties but looked a lot younger.

'You'll be fine,' she assured me. 'You actors always do well. Didn't you have dance training at drama school?'

'I did,' I admitted. 'Until the day I made my dance teacher cry because I was so awful and she chucked me out of the lesson.'

'Ah,' said the newsreader.

The rugby player chuckled.

'Stick with me,' he said. 'I'm so rubbish I'll make anyone look good.'

I smiled widely. I was having such a lovely time my nerves were beginning to recede. All the other contestants seemed very nice. They were a mixture of celebs from all walks of life – I'd met the rugby player and the newsreader, of course, but I'd also said hello to an older actor who'd starred in a rival soap for years and who I knew from various awards ceremonies. He'd greeted me like a long-lost friend, and I realized everyone was just as nervous as I was. There was also a beautiful actress who'd been a model in the sixties, then moved into films and now made documentaries in which she travelled round the world. She was

53

one of my heroes and I was too starstruck to even speak to her. There were a couple of pop stars, an Olympic swimmer who was wearing her gold medal round her neck, and a few TV presenters. Even if I got nowhere in the competition, I thought, it would be nice to meet all these people and find out more about them.

There was a buzz of chatter from the back of the studio and I turned to see the two presenters come in. They were both women and always amazingly, astonishingly glam when I saw them on TV. But today they were both wearing jeans and vest tops. The blonde one – who I knew was called Melissa – had her hair piled on top of her head in a messy bun, and the other one – Vicky – had a blunt, dark, Mary Quant bob and wasn't wearing any make-up.

'Oh, God, you all look so beautiful,' Melissa squealed. 'Are you all raring to go?'

Vicky grinned.

'The dancers are all out there,' she said, pointing to the studio exit. 'They can't wait to find out which of you they've got to train.'

'I pity whoever gets me,' I muttered and the rugby player laughed again. He really was a lovely chap.

'Right then,' Melissa said. 'Let's get cracking.'

She and Vicky explained that we'd meet our partners now and do all the publicity shots and so on. Then later in the week we'd film the launch show, and be introduced all over again, pretending it was the first time we'd met. Then, we'd have a month or so of rehearsals with our partner before the first live dance show. They made it sound so much fun and so straightforward that I suddenly felt really excited about this new challenge I was taking on.

I watched and clapped as one by one the dancers filed in and met their partner. And then they called my name. I went up to the front and said hello to Melissa and Vicky.

'Excited?' Melissa asked.

I nodded.

'You should be,' Vicky said. 'Your partner is gorgeous.'

Melissa gripped my arm.

'Amy,' she said. 'Meet Patrick Walker.'

The doors opened and in came my partner, twirling and dancing his way towards me. He was definitely gorgeous – there was no doubt about that. But I'd met him already.

He stopped in front of me and our eyes met.

'You,' he said.

It was Surfer Dude.

Chapter 11

We looked at each other for a beat too long then Surfer Dude – Patrick – picked me up and spun me round, just like all the other male dancers had done to their partners.

'Great to meet you, Amy,' he said as he put me down. 'We're going to have a ball.'

'A glitter ball,' I said fake-brightly. God, this was excruciating. Most people managed to have drunken one-night stands without being forced to spend the next ten weeks with the object of their ill-advised affection.

'Do you guys know each other?' Melissa asked. She'd obviously seen the glimmer of recognition when we were introduced.

'No,' I said.

'Yes,' said Patrick.

'We were introduced very briefly at a party last week,' I lied. 'Though I didn't know Patrick was a dancer.'

'And I didn't know Amy was the famous Amy Lavender,' Patrick said, flashing his broad grin at Melissa and giving me an accusatory glance over his shoulder.

'How funny,' said Melissa. 'Enjoy getting to know each other better!'

But I was too embarrassed to enjoy anything.

The photo shoot was fine, actually. I'd done enough of those things over the years to be able to switch it on at will. I smiled, posed, spun and shimmied my way through all my solo photos, then escaped to the canteen for a (horrible) coffee so I didn't have to watch Patrick do his. He was really very good looking and seeing the muscles working in his back – which was barely covered by a sheer shirt – was very off-putting.

To keep my mind on the task ahead, I hid in the loo and took a close-up selfie of half of my made-up face, eye closed and false eyelashes brushing my tanned cheek. I sat on the closed toilet seat and added many filters so it was as flattering a pic as possible. Then, knowing I was risking my place on the show when we weren't really supposed to tell anyone we were competing until the press were told tomorrow, I sent it to Matty.

'Guess what I'm doing?' I typed.

There was no reply. But I didn't expect him to reply immediately. I had no idea what had possessed me to message him. After all, the last time I'd seen him he'd been throwing my belongings onto the street. All I can think is I was feeling unsettled and guilty about my night with Surfer Dude – Patrick – and I wasn't thinking straight. Plus, I had to admit that I missed Matty. We'd been together a long time and it was weird being alone. I wondered if he was missing me, too. It was doubtful considering there were always girls throwing themselves at him when we were together – he was bound to have even more now we'd split so publicly and I was sure he was making the most of it

I tossed my hair back. All the more reason to make a success of this ridiculous dancing show, I thought. I would throw myself into it, learn to cha-cha like a pro. I'd learn to live without Matty, Babs would be thrilled and my career would surely be back on track.

Filled with new-found enthusiasm and vigour for the task in hand, I wandered down the corridor towards the room where I knew Patrick was. He was sitting on the floor of the room, beating out a rhythm on his long outstretched legs, and a camera crew was recording what he was saying. About me.

'I'd read all the stories, of course,' he was saying. 'And I'd heard people say she was a bit shallow – you know like some of these reality TV stars can be.'

I bristled. I was an actress. Who happened to have appeared in occasional episodes of my boyfriend's fly-on-the-wall TV show. I was NOT a reality TV star.

'So is Amy how you expected?' one of the camera crew said. 'What are your first impressions?'

'She's beautiful, of course,' Patrick said. 'But she also seems fun and genuine and a good laugh.'

Well, that was nice. Quickly I planned what I'd say when they asked me the same question about Patrick – welcoming, friendly, friendly.

But Patrick was still talking.

'I really like her,' he said, a funny look on his face. 'And that kind of surprises me.'

Oh man, he wasn't falling for me, was he? My whole life men had been harbouring crushes on me. I wasn't stupid enough to think they really wanted to be with me. I knew it was my pretty face they were interested in – and even then it was just the face I showed the world. Very few people had ever seen the real me – the one who slobbed out in leggings and a vest top with greasy hair and no make-up; the one who watched *Pitch Perfect* then went back to the beginning and watched it all over again straight-away. The one who loved to laugh but had a bit of a temper. Phil knew the real Amy, of course. We'd been friends since we were fourteen and I couldn't ever fool him. But even Matty had seen a carefully edited version – until I let my mask slip that night in the club.

Patrick having a crush on me could be awkward, I thought. I should probably put him straight as soon as I could. I really just wanted time to myself to get my head together and learn to be me again, instead of being part of Brand Matty and Amy. I was too bruised, too broken, to risk another relationship right now. Plus I'd totally had it with high-profile romances and being fodder for the showbiz gossip columnists. I didn't want any saucy stories damaging my hopes of getting more acting work in the future.

But for now I had to get on with this photo shoot so I plastered a huge smile on my face and pretended I'd just walked into the room.

'Hi guys,' I said. 'Are we ready for the next lot of photos?'

Patrick stood up.

'Amy,' he said. 'Great. Let's get cracking.'

Doing our photo shoot together was strange. We weren't dancing, obviously – our rehearsals hadn't started yet. Instead, we just posed as though we were. I quite enjoyed looking like I knew what I was doing, even when I clearly didn't have a clue. But what I didn't enjoy was being so close to Patrick. The feel of his tight muscles under my hands, the smell of his skin and the rasp of his stubble against my face brought back lots of memories of the night we'd spent together. Memories that were really too nice …

'Stop it, Amy,' I told myself sternly, smiling at the camera as Patrick lifted me up in his strong (stop it), ripped (seriously, enough) arms. 'No more stories for the *PostOnline*.'

When we had a break I wandered over to get some water and checked my phone to see if Matty had replied to the photo I sent, but there was nothing. I scrolled through the pictures, intending to resend it.

Patrick followed me.

'Who are you messaging with such a serious look on your face?' he asked.

'My boyfriend,' I said without thinking. Patrick's smile slipped just a little bit.

'You're back together?' he said.

'Oh, well, no,' I said. 'I just thought …' Feeling silly to have been 'caught' messaging the man who cheated on me, I pressed 'send' firmly, then looked up at Patrick from under my eyelashes, the way I made Betsy do when she was apologizing for something. Like murdering the pub's sleazy landlord or sleeping with her best friend's bloke. Anyway, I channelled my inner Betsy and focused on Patrick.

'Listen,' I said softly. 'I had a really great time with you the other night. But things are complicated with me right now and I don't want this …' – I waved my arm wildly, taking in me, Patrick, the camera crew, everything – '… this thing to get in the way. We're professionals, right? We can do this.'

For a second Patrick gave me a look like I'd kicked his puppy. Then he straightened up and gave me a smile. The kind of smile I recognized because I'd used it myself so often. A fake it until you make it smile.

'Sure,' he said. 'You're not really my type anyway.'

I narrowed my eyes.

'What is your type?'

'Oh, you know. Bit more wholesome. Less concerned with appearance and more about what's inside.'

I stared at him. I hadn't really expected a character assassination.

'More real,' Patrick said. 'More like a human being.'

My phone beeped with a message and I leapt on it, grateful for the distraction.

It was from Matty. Finally. My heart thumping, I swiped to open the message.

'Who is this?' it said.

I burst into tears.

Chapter 12

Cora

1945

I tugged at the top button of my uniform skirt. No. There was no way that was going to do up. I'd have to pin it. Trying not to think about what my swelling shape meant, I rooted around in my sewing box for some safety pins and secured my skirt. Thankfully my jacket was long enough to cover it for now, but I couldn't keep doing this. Plus my costumes had very little give in them and the seams on one outfit were already stretched to their maximum.

I threw myself onto the narrow bed and stared at the ceiling, trying to muster up the energy to go to rehearsal. I glanced at the clock on the wall. I still had half an hour, thank goodness. I could lie here for a few minutes longer …

'Cora, wake up.' Audrey shook me gently by the shoulder. 'Rehearsal in five minutes.'

I blinked wearily. Audrey was sitting on my bed, while Fat Joan – the other occupant of our cramped attic bedroom in the boarding house that was our home for now – leaned against the door. She wasn't fat, Joan. In fact she looked like a film star, with long blonde hair and deep brown eyes. Now she narrowed those eyes at me.

'Have you been sick again?' she said. 'I heard you this morning.'

I sat up.

'I think it was last night's tea,' I said. 'Corned beef has never agreed with me.'

Fat Joan tossed her hair over her shoulder, looking decidedly lacking in concern for my innards.

'Want me to tell Henry that you're ill?' she said.

I shook my head.

'No, I feel better now,' I said. 'Could you just say I'll be there in five minutes and apologize?'

Languidly Joan straightened up.

'Fine,' she said. 'Make sure it is only five minutes.'

I forced a smile.

'I'll be right there,' I said.

As soon as Joan's footsteps died away, Audrey jumped off the bed and locked the door; then she turned on me.

'What is going on?' she hissed. 'Are you ill?'

'No,' I said slowly. 'Not ill.'

Audrey looked at me, realization growing in her grey eyes.

'Oh, Cora,' she said. 'Oh, Cora.'

'Do not breathe a word of this to anyone,' I said.

'Have you told Donnie?'

I swung my legs off the bed and stood up.

'No,' I said in horror. 'Of course not. I can't tell him in a letter – Dear Donnie, I'm pregnant, Yours, Cora.'

Audrey shrugged.

'Can't imagine it'll be less of shock to hear it out loud,' she pointed out.

'I'll tell him when he comes to London,' I said. 'He'll be here soon.'

As planned, Donnie's division was off to France and they had some time in London before they left for the coast. We'd planned to meet up as soon as we could and Donnie was still talking about getting married if we could arrange it.

Audrey came over to me and helped me arrange my hat on my head.

'So what are you going to do?'

I closed my eyes.

'I have no idea,' I admitted. 'I'm not going to Africa with the rest of you, that's for sure.'

A glimmer of a smile crossed Audrey's face.

'Well, that will please your mum,' she said.

She was right. My mum had been desperate to keep me at home in Worthing, dancing in the end-of-the-pier show and teaching toddlers. But I'd been equally desperate to join up, to see the world, and as soon as I'd turned eighteen I'd been off. So far we'd only done the rounds of the bases in Britain with a short trip over the sea to France, but we were scheduled to leave for North Africa in the summer, when our time in London was done. I had been giddily excited at the prospect – until I met Donnie. And now this.

'How far along are you?' Audrey said, staring at my stomach.

'Don't,' I said, nudging her. 'Don't make it obvious.'

'How far?' she said.

'About three months, I think,' I said. 'I'm not sure exactly.'

Audrey looped her arm through mine.

'I can ask around,' she said. 'See if anyone knows anyone.'

'What do you mean?' I said, naively.

'You know,' she said. Audrey was from London and since we'd been in her hometown her accent had become more pronounced. 'My sister knows someone in Camberwell. I can find out how much it is?'

'No,' I said. 'No. Not yet.'

'Have you tried a bath and gin?' she said. 'I've heard that does the trick.'

I grimaced with the frustration of trying to make her understand.

'No,' I said again. 'It might be all right. Donnie might …'

Audrey gave me a pitying look.

'He might still want to marry you?' she said. 'Yeah, and I might be queen of bloody England.'

'We've got plans,' I said, thinking of our trip across America. 'He's going to take me to Hollywood.'

'What, with a great big bump or a babe in your arms? I don't think so, sweetheart.'

Her face softened as tears filled my eyes.

'Look,' she said, putting her arm round me. 'Donnie's a lovely bloke but that's all he is at the end of the day, isn't it? A bloke. Look at you. You're gorgeous. Nice hair, good tits, great legs. You're young. You're lively. You're a catch. No wonder he's full of talk now. But will he still be so interested when you're fat, and your legs are puffy and you've got a nipper hanging off your breast?'

She sucked her lips.

'Unlikely, I'd say.'

'Audrey,' I said, appalled. 'Not all men are like your dad, you know? Donnie loves me whatever I look like. He wants to marry me.'

Audrey squeezed me tighter.

'It's not their fault,' she said. 'It's the way they're made – to only see pretty faces and long legs. And it's just a shame we're left to pick up the pieces. I'll write to my sister, see what she says. It's best to be prepared.'

I felt overwhelmed with exhaustion. I'd been terrified when I realized I was expecting, but I'd assumed everything would be fine. I'd tell Donnie, and we'd just get married a bit ahead of when we'd planned. I'd stay in London, or go to the country with the baby – anywhere as long as it wasn't going home to Worthing and my mother – until the war ended, then we'd go to America.

But now Audrey had made me wonder if I was just being naive. Maybe she was right. Perhaps Donnie would run a mile when he heard.

I slumped against Audrey, tearful and tired.

'I really don't feel very well,' I said. 'I feel awful, in fact. I think I need to go back to bed. Can you tell Henry that I'm poorly?'

Audrey nodded.

'Of course,' she said. 'Have a rest and you'll feel better tomorrow.'

Like a mum – not my mum, but how I imagined mothers to be – she helped me take my uniform off and slipped my nightie over my head. Then she tucked me into bed and pulled the curtains closed.

'Rest up,' she whispered.

I cried myself to sleep.

Chapter 13

It was safe to say that *Strictly Stars Dancing* was a nightmare. An absolute, complete bloody nightmare. We were two weeks into the month of training we had before the live shows began and I was hating every single moment.

After that first day when we did the photo shoots, the sparkly costumes were put away and the hard graft began. Patrick and I trained in a gym in a basement in Shoreditch. Which is a surprisingly long way from Clapham. After three days of tutting, whingeing cab drivers, I admitted defeat. No one was going to recognize me in my training gear anyway, so I did the whole hair-tucked-into-a-baseball-cap, sunglasses, jogging-bottoms thing and got the tube in every day.

Each morning I'd get off the tube and go into the little Italian cafe next to the gym where I'd buy two coffees – one for me, one for Patrick – and some pastries.

Patrick never drank his coffee and he never ate the pastries. He never thanked me for either In fact, he barely spoke to me at all unless it was to say things like: 'No, the other foot.' Or: 'Left, left, LEFT.'

Because, as I suspected, I was a terrible dancer. I mean, really, really terrible. If I was meant to be going left, I'd go right. If

Patrick said quicker, I went slower. If he said up, I went down. I was awful. Phil had been right when he said I loved dancing in clubs and at weddings – I did. But I found that without the comforting support of a lot of alcohol I couldn't let myself go enough to be able to do it.

I got the impression Patrick thought I wasn't trying. But I was. Mostly. It was just really annoying not to get it straightaway and sometimes I thought it was easier to be a bit silly rather than try – and fail – again. Sometimes I complained that I didn't want to mess my hair up, or get too sweaty. I didn't mean it but I said it anyway. It was like now I knew Patrick thought I was shallow, fake and only concerned with my looks, that was how I had become.

And to be brutally honest, I felt like he wasn't trying either. He kept me at arm's length – literally – like he didn't want to touch me too often, too closely, or for too long. Despite our night together it was obvious that we just didn't click.

I'd had that sort of thing before, on *Turpin Road*. Sometimes you'd start a scene with someone new and every line would feel laboured and unnatural. I'd had it the opposite way round, too, where things just fell into place. On *Turpin Road*, though, I had Tim watching and listening and swooping in to swap scenes round or change storylines that weren't working. On *Strictly Stars Dancing* I had to struggle on regardless.

The other dark cloud over my head was the fact that I'd not heard anything more from Matty. He'd clearly deleted my number from his phone, just like he'd deleted my clothes from his flat, and me from his life. It was hard not to feel hurt and humiliated. I'd heard he wasn't seeing Kayleigh, the reality TV star, any more, but still he didn't call.

Even when the contestants on this year's *Strictly Stars Dancing* were announced and my photo was all over the papers and showbiz mags he didn't call. I spent ages looking at my promo shots, and comparing them to the selfie I'd sent Matty. It was fairly obvious it was me, even though you couldn't see my full face. I had to accept that he knew the message was from me, and he'd just chosen not to respond. Deep down I knew it was for the best – he'd cheated on me and broken my heart and I knew I was better off without him. But I couldn't help thinking that was another reason my failure at dancing was so annoying. I wanted to be good so he'd watch me sashaying down those steps on the first week's show and be overwhelmed with longing and regret. Sadly, it didn't look like I was even going to be able to walk down the steps without going arse over tit, let alone sashay anywhere.

So I had all this angst going on in my head when Patrick and me fell out – big time.

We'd been working on our cha-cha. It was the first dance we were doing and according to Patrick it wasn't too hard. But when I turned away from him instead of towards him for the twentieth time that day, then lost my footing, stumbled and fell, Patrick didn't help me up. Instead he sighed heavily and looked at his watch.

'Oh, I'm sorry,' I said, my voice laden with sarcasm. 'Do you have somewhere you'd rather be?'

Patrick looked down at me as I sat on the floor rubbing my ankle.

'Frankly,' he said, 'I'd rather be anywhere than here right now.'

That stung a bit, I had to be honest.

'Yeah? Well, it's not much fun for me either.'

'You're not even trying, Amy,' Patrick said. 'You can't even remember the simplest steps.'

'You're not helping me,' I said, furious that he was blaming me for something that was clearly the fault of both of us. 'You won't come near me, you won't talk to me – this is horrible.'

Patrick rubbed his nose. Then he gave a resigned shrug.

'You're right,' he said. I felt a small surge of triumph that I'd made him see things my way.

'It is horrible.'

Oh.

That just made me even angrier. I stood up, wincing a bit at my sore ankle and picked up my bag.

'I'm sorry that I'm not a natural dancer and I'm sorry I'm finding this so hard,' I said, adopting the voice Betsy used when she was sorting out fights in the Prince Albert. 'I'm going home now and hopefully we can start afresh in the morning.'

Calmly, I walked to the door but just as I stepped through I heard Patrick mutter: 'If I'm here tomorrow it'll be a damn miracle.'

Annoyed that he'd had the last word, I whirled round, flicked him the Vs – childish, I know – then stomped off, slamming the studio door behind me.

I got a cab all the way back to Clapham – I couldn't be bothered with the tube today. It was bad enough going back to that flat, miles away from all my friends, with hardly any belongings. I hadn't even unpacked the few possessions I did have. There didn't seem to be any point. I hadn't met the old woman who lived upstairs either – even though I was supposed to be looking out for her. I'd heard the front door opening and closing a few times and I'd heard voices but I'd never seen her. I supposed I should have gone up to introduce myself but that seemed like accepting my fate, so I hadn't.

It was a lovely day. My bare front room had double doors at one end, leading out to a paved yard. The sun was streaming in and it was stuffy in the room so I threw the doors open and then threw myself on the sofa and stared at the blank walls.

How dare Patrick say I wasn't trying? How dare he say it was all my fault when he was acting so weird? I'd show him.

Chapter 14

After a while I got bored lying there feeling sorry for myself, so I went in search of food. I poured myself a glass of wine, then I dug around in the fridge and I found some olives and cheese. I couldn't find any crackers in the cupboard but I did find half a bag of crisps. That would do. I drained my glass then poured myself another one and wandered back into the lounge.

'Right,' I said. Still holding my wine, I pushed the sofa back against the wall with my bum and rolled up the rug, so the wooden floor was bare. Then I scrolled through Spotify until I found the Bruno Mars track that we were dancing our cha-cha to.

'I'm going to show you, Patrick,' I said out loud. 'I'm going to be the best damn cha-cha dancer *Strictly Stars Dancing* has ever seen.'

I drained my glass again and topped it up. Then I pressed play on the laptop and started trying to cha-cha.

Bruno started singing about her eyes. I swayed slightly and stepped on the wrong foot.

'Bollocks,' I said. I took another gulp of wine and started again.

Bruno was singing about her hair now, but I was still on the wrong foot.

70

'This is a nightmare,' I said. 'It's a complete bloody nightmare.'

I should never have signed up for *Strictly Stars Dancing*. I should have said no when Babs phoned. I should have gone to America, or Australia. Actually, Australia wasn't a bad idea – maybe Babs could get me an audition for one of their soaps? Sun, sea, sand – and the added bonus of knowing that my knickers hadn't been seen by just about everyone I walked past in the street.

Then I thought about Patrick's annoying face and thought about how shocked he'd be if I went in tomorrow knowing how to cha-cha. Maybe I'd stick it out for now.

I took another swig of my wine, dumped the glass on the side and restarted the song.

Bruno was back to her eyes again. I stepped on the wrong foot. Again.

'Other leg,' said a voice.

I span round in surprise and there, standing in the double doors that led outside, was an old woman. A really old woman. Possibly the oldest woman I'd ever seen in my whole life. She was wearing long white linen trousers, a pink wrap-around top, and sparkly ballet pumps, and her pure white hair was swept up in a bun.

'Who the bloody hell are you?' I squealed. I grabbed my phone and held it out like a weapon, which was slightly overdramatic given that my would-be assailant was a tiny old lady, but it had been a tough few weeks.

'I am two seconds away from calling the police. What are you doing in my house?'

'You're in my house, my darling,' she said in a throaty voice that sounded like late nights and smoky jazz clubs. 'And you're starting on the wrong leg.'

I looked down at my legs and then back at the old woman, realization beginning to dawn.

'Are you Mrs Devonshire?' I said. 'You're Natasha's grandma?'

71

'Call me Cora,' she said. She came into the room properly, walking in a very upright way, like a ballerina, despite her advanced years. She was really elegant and I could see where Natasha got her looks from.

Cora looked me up and down and I shifted uncomfortably under her stare, aware that I had mascara halfway down my face, my hair piled on top of my head like a pineapple and a hole in my leggings.

'You must be Amy Lavender,' she said.

I nodded, not sure what to say.

'Pleased to meet you,' I muttered.

'Start again,' Cora said. 'Left leg.'

I looked at her in confusion.

'Shut your mouth, darling,' she said. 'Start again. Go on.'

Not wanting to argue, I restarted the song and began my cha-cha – on the left leg this time.

'That's right,' Cora said encouragingly. 'Carry on.'

She lowered herself onto the sofa and tilted her head.

'Carry on.'

I stopped.

'I can't,' I said. 'I can't do it.'

I burst into tears.

'I can't do it,' I said. I looked at Mrs Devonshire – Cora – sitting on the sofa, a concerned look on her face and something inside me burst.

'It's all gone wrong,' I wailed. I could hardly get my words out because I was crying so hard. 'Matty doesn't want to know, and Patrick hates me, and I can't dance, and those girls took my dreeeeessss,' I sobbed. 'I can't work out which leg I should start on, and I lost my job. I've been killed off.'

Cora blinked at me.

'Killed off?' she said.

'Killed off,' I said. 'I'm in a soap. I was in a soap. But I punched a reality TV star and I lost my job and I can never go back. Ever.'

I dug a tissue out from the waistband of my leggings and blew my nose.

'And Matty was cheating on me the whole time, and I sent him a picture of myself and he didn't recognize meeeeee.'

It was like all the trauma of the last few weeks had been unleashed and all I could do was cry.

I sobbed and hiccupped and snorted for a few minutes, but eventually I managed to control my tears. I wiped my eyes with my very soggy tissue and was overwhelmed with a huge wave of embarrassment instead. I looked at Cora, who was still sitting on the sofa regarding me with a mixture of confusion, amusement and – to my relief – sympathy.

'Oh, God,' I said. 'Oh, I am so sorry. I don't know where that came from.'

Cora stood up, slightly shakily but still with more elegance than I could ever hope to have.

'I came down to see if you could help me open a window,' she said, a small smile on her lips. 'But I think it's you who could do with a hand.'

'You're not wrong there,' I said. I was drawn to this woman with her sparkly shoes and her chic hair and I was suddenly desperate for her to like me.

'I'm so sorry that this is how I introduced myself. Can we start again?'

Cora stuck her hand out and I shook it.

'Cora Devonshire,' she said. 'Old but not infirm and definitely not incapable, despite what my fusspot of a granddaughter may have told you.'

I grinned. Cora was funny.

'Amy Lavender,' I said. 'Washed-up soap star, newly unemployed, newly single, newly homeless and ...' – I hiccupped – '... a bit tipsy.'

We smiled at one another and I felt like I had an ally. Someone who was stable and secure in among the chaos that my life had become. Which was ridiculous, given that I'd only just met her and I was the one who was supposed to be looking after her. Maybe I was like those baby ducklings who just attached themselves to the first thing they saw and decided that was their mother …

Cora clapped her hands and startled me out of my musings about ducks.

'Right,' she said. 'Shall we get on?'

I looked at her, baffled.

'On?'

'You come and help me open that window,' she said. 'I will make us both a very large gin and tonic, and you can tell me why you were dancing the cha-cha.' She glanced down at my feet. 'Badly.'

Chapter 15

Cora led me out of my back door, up the stone steps to the side of my little yard, which was sunk lower than the rest of the outdoor area, and into a bigger garden. It had a neat lawn and honeysuckle climbed all over the back of the house. There was a wooden table and four chairs with spotty cushions on the grass. It wasn't a huge garden – we were still in London, after all – but it was obviously well loved. It was still really warm, even though it had to be after seven, and I could smell the sweet scent of the honeysuckle. I breathed in deeply, and followed Cora through her kitchen, which was cool with a slate floor and tiles on the wall, and into the large lounge.

There was a piano at one end, against the wall, with piles of sheet music on top. There were lots of books, two enormous squishy faded sofas, and a thick oriental rug on the wooden floor. It was very nice and even I, philistine that I was, could see it was classy.

'It's the sash at the front,' Cora said. 'I just can't get a grip on it to push it up.'

She showed me her hands, which were lumpy and misshapen with arthritis, and I winced.

'I'll sort it,' I said. I gave the window a shove and it slid upwards.

'Thank you,' Cora said. 'I'll ask Natasha to get an extra handle put on it. Now, I think I mentioned G&T?'

'Your hands look painful,' I said, following Cora back into the kitchen and watching as she busied herself filling two tall glasses with ice.

'Sometimes,' she said, handing me a lemon and a knife to slice it with. 'But I've got painkillers. I do get frustrated when it stops me doing things, and do you know what the worst thing is?'

I looked at her questioningly.

'They look so bloody ugly,' she said, with a chuckle. 'I know it's dreadful, an old woman like me being concerned about her looks, but I was always rather proud of my elegant hands.'

I smiled.

'I'm too concerned with my looks,' I said, thinking about what Patrick had said. 'Apparently.'

Cora raised her eyebrows.

'Who says?'

I sliced the lemon carefully.

'Oh, my dance partner,' I said. 'I'm doing this competition, but I'm not very good and he doesn't like me very much. Shall I carry the drinks?'

I put the G&Ts and a bowl of pistachios that Cora had produced onto a tray and carried it out to the garden.

I helped Cora pull her chair out and sat down.

'This is such a lovely garden,' I said.

Cora smiled.

'I don't do it,' she said. 'But I like to look at it. I like things to be beautiful.'

'Oh, me too,' I said. I looked at Cora, sitting straight-backed in her chair, tilting her head up to the sun, in her lovely garden, sipping her G&T. I hoped I'd be like her when I was older.

'So tell me,' Cora said. 'What's all this about a dancing competition?'

I threw my head back dramatically.

'Urgh,' I said. 'It's not pretty. Do you really want to know?'

Cora leaned forward.

'Darling Miss Lavender,' she said, giving a very knowing chuckle. 'I am excellent at getting people out of trouble.'

'You are?' I said.

'Oh, yes,' she said. 'I got into rather a lot of trouble when I was young. But somehow I managed to wriggle out of it.'

'I can see that,' I said, amused at the thought.

'And my daughter, Ginny – Natasha's mother. Oh, she's dreadful. If there's trouble within a hundred miles, she'll find it.'

'Really?'

'Let's just say that this isn't the first time she's packed up and moved country to be with a man,' Cora said, tightening her lips but with a glint in her eye that made me think she was actually quite proud of her flighty daughter.

I giggled.

'What about Natasha?'

'Oh, that girl,' Cora sighed. 'She's never given me a moment's worry. I did wonder if she was adopted for a while. She's so sensible.'

I laughed again.

'She looks just like you,' I pointed out, taking a swig of my gin. 'She can't possibly be adopted.'

Cora gave me a wink.

'Tell me what's happened,' she said. 'Because I think I can help you.'

'You can?' I said, not believing for one minute that she could. 'Okaaaaaay.'

Slowly I told her about my time on *Turpin Road*.

'I'm afraid I don't watch a lot of television,' she said. 'But I did think I recognized you. Are you very well known?'

I shrugged modestly.

'Kind of,' I said. 'I've been in lots of magazines and stuff. But then it all went wrong.'

'A man?' Cora said.

I nodded.

'Matty,' I said. Keeping my eyes on my bare feet so I didn't have to see her expression – I found I very badly wanted her to realize I wasn't a horrible person – I filled her in on what had happened at the club with Kayleigh, the police caution, losing my job, losing my clothes and meeting Natasha.'

Cora sat in silence as I talked. I raised my head to meet her glance and was relieved to see sympathy on her face.

'And the dancing?' she said.

'According to my agent, it's a way to get my career back on track. I wanted to disappear for a while, but she says this is a way to get the public back on my side'

Cora nodded.

'It makes sense,' she said. 'Is she good, your agent?'

'She's stuck by me since I left school,' I admitted. 'I tend to do whatever she tells me to do. So she's got me on this TV show – we get taught to dance by professionals and the public vote for their favourites.'

Cora's face lit up.

'*Strictly Stars Dancing*?' she said. 'I love that. How thrilling. I didn't realize it had started.'

'It hasn't,' I said. 'Not properly. But we've started training.'

'But you're not enjoying it?'

I grimaced.

'Not at all,' I admitted. 'I'm a terrible dancer. I did warn Babs – she's my agent – that I would be awful.'

'And you don't get on with your partner?'

I closed my eyes briefly.

'Ah,' I said. 'We did get on. Too well, in fact.'

Cora gave me a look that suggested she knew exactly what I meant, but I spelled it out anyway.

'We slept together,' I said. 'Before we knew we were partners. And then I was horrible to him the next day. And he was horrible to me. And now we're really not ...' – I threw my hands out in frustration – '... not clicking.'

'It's important to trust your partner,' Cora said, nodding.

'Do you know about dancing?' I asked – she seemed to be very wise about it all.

Cora gave me that grin again.

'Did you go to drama school?' she said.

I nodded.

'In Croydon,' I said, reaching for a pistachio. 'The Rising Stars school. I only started there when I was fourteen, to do my GCSEs, but it was brilliant.'

'So have you heard of the London Academy of Theatre and Dancing?'

'Of course.' It was one of the best and most respected theatre schools in the country.

'I used to teach there,' Cora said simply.

I widened my eyes in surprise.

'OMG,' I said. 'So you're an actress?'

'Actually, no,' Cora said.

'So ...' I said.

'I'm a dancer,' Cora said. 'A dancer and a dance teacher.'

It was already sunny in the garden, but I swear everything seemed a bit shinier and just downright better at that moment.

'You're a dance teacher,' I breathed.

'I am,' Cora said, smiling. 'I'll teach you if you like.'

Chapter 16

Cora

1945

I took another deep breath and tapped my feet on the ground, marking out an invisible rhythm. Donnie was late. I was waiting for him near the bandstand in Hyde Park and he was late. Really late, in fact. I checked my watch again. Almost half an hour late.

Maybe he's not coming, a voice inside my head said. A voice that sounded rather like Audrey. *He's not coming because it's all got too serious. He doesn't want to marry you and you'd be a fool to tell him you're pregnant.*

I sighed. Maybe Audrey was right. Maybe Donnie was only interested in my looks and my love of life. Maybe he would run a mile as soon as I said the words I'd been practising over and over for weeks.

But no. I didn't believe that. Donnie loved me. I knew that as surely as I knew I loved him. He wouldn't let me down. Except he wasn't here.

I stood up and looked down the path left and right. It was a warm day for the beginning of March and the park was busy.

80

Soldiers home on leave strolled arm in arm with pretty women, and office workers stretched their legs out on the grass. On a bench opposite the one I sat on, a young mother cuddled a baby close, murmuring into her ear and reading a book with one hand. I wondered where the baby's father was and how he'd reacted when he'd found out he was going to be a dad. The mother sensed me watching her and looked up. I gave her a quick smile and moved away, not wanting to seem odd.

I'll walk once more round the bandstand, I thought to myself. Then, if Donnie's not here, I'll go.

Slowly, I wandered across the grass, deep in thought about how to break the news to Donnie.

I'd gone through various ways of telling him. There was matter-of-fact: 'I'm expecting.' Dramatic: 'I'm afraid I've some bad news …' Playing it down: '… We're getting married anyway …' And even jokey: 'We've done our bit for the war effort, darling …' None of them seemed right.

'Excuse me?' A voice made me jump. It was a young soldier. He was holding his hat in his hands and his dark hair stuck up like a schoolboy's.

'You're her, ain't you?' he said. 'Cora Cassidy?'

Despite how worried I was about Donnie and the future, I felt the thrill of being recognized. I loved performing, but I couldn't deny that I also loved that the troops we played to loved it, too. Their admiration – almost adoration – gave me the shivers.

I gave the soldier the full benefit of my best, most beaming smile.

'That's me,' I said.

'It's her,' he said over his shoulder to a group of lads sitting on the grass. 'I told you it was.'

The other soldiers all leapt to their feet and surrounded me, telling me how much they'd enjoyed it when I'd danced at their barracks. One of them had a photo of me, ripped from a news-letter, in his wallet – which was sweet – and I signed it for him, laughed at all their silly jokes and promised to come back and dance for them again soon.

'I'm terribly sorry, boys, I have to dash to meet a friend,' I said. 'It really was wonderful to meet you all.'

I blew them all a kiss and they parted like the red sea to let me past. Knowing they were watching me go, I lifted my chin and let my hips swing – just a bit – as I headed towards the bandstand.

And then a group of women who'd been walking in front of me swerved off the path, giving me a clear view of the wooden steps, and there was Donnie sitting on the top stair, smiling.

'Miss Cassidy, were you flirting with those men?' he said as I grinned at him, my heart thumping in my chest.

I nodded.

'I confess, I was,' I said. I ran lightly up the steps and he stood up, swept me into his arms, and swung me round, kissing my face over and over.

I squealed in joy, then, worried he might hurt the baby by squeezing me too tightly, squealed for real.

'Down!' I wriggled out of his grasp, but let him keep kissing me.

After we'd kissed all the kisses we'd missed over the last four months, since the last time we'd been together, Donnie held me at arm's length and gazed at me.

'Let me look at you,' he said. 'You are gorgeous as ever. More so, in fact. How is that even possible?'

I giggled, feeling self-conscious and very aware that I had a definite bump now. It wasn't so obvious in my uniform because my jacket hid it, but in my underwear there was no mistaking my rounded belly and heavy breasts.

'Donnie,' I said. 'I need to tell you something.'

'Wait,' he said, a mischievous glint in his eye. 'Good something or bad something?'

I paused, looking up at the sky where the barrage balloons floated.

'Good,' I said. 'I think.'

Donnie raised an eyebrow.

'You think?' he said. 'In that case, let me go first?'

I nodded.

'Cora Cassidy,' he said. 'I'm in London for five days. Wanna get married?'

I couldn't speak. Donnie looked alarmed.

'What?' he said. 'What is it? Don't you want to get married? I thought we'd agreed?'

I took his hands in mine.

'I love you Donald Jackson,' I said. 'I love you so much that I feel like you're a part of me. Of course I want to get married. I want us to be together for ever. I want to travel across America with you, and meet your mum, and charm your sister, and meet your kid brother, and see Chicago …'

'But,' said Donnie. 'What's the but?'

I gripped his fingers tighter.

'I'm pregnant,' I whispered. 'I'm having your baby.'

Donnie looked at me with wide eyes.

'You're pregnant?' he said, in astonishment. 'A baby?'

He took his hands away from me and I felt a lurch of fear. Was this it? Was this the beginning of him rejecting me?

But then Donnie put his hands, very gently, onto my stomach.

'A baby?' he said in wonder. 'In here?'

I moved his hands downwards a bit.

'It's more like here,' I said. 'Can you feel how it's really firm?'

'Does it kick?' he said.

I laughed, pure relief oozing out of me.

'Not yet,' I said. 'I've got a little way to go before that happens. It's only tiny.'

'But it's definite?' Donnie said. 'You're definitely having a baby?'

I took a step back, pulled up my jacket and turned to the side, so he could see the outline of my belly and my straining waistband.

'See?' I said, smoothing my skirt over my small bump.

'Ohhhh,' Donnie breathed.

'Donnie?' I said, bracing myself. 'I know this wasn't our plan, and I know we're both really young. And I want you to know that if you don't want to marry me, that's okay. I don't want to force you into anything ...' Donnie stopped me talking with a firm kiss.

'Are you kidding me?' he said. 'Are you freaking kidding me? Of course I want to marry you. You're having a baby!'

I laughed in delight.

'Oh, thank God,' I said, relaxing into his arms. Then a thought struck me. 'We have to organize the wedding. Is that even possible?'

Donnie smiled down at me.

'I have no idea,' he said. 'But I reckon so. We'll tell 'em it's urgent because I've knocked you up.'

I thumped him.

'Donnie,' I said in mock outrage. 'Don't be so rude.'

Donnie offered me his arm and we walked down the bandstand steps into the park.

'We do need to be quick,' I said, serious now. 'You're going to France, and I'm going to have to tell everyone. My mother, for instance.'

I winced at the thought of my mother's reaction.

'Maybe you should go to the States now,' Donnie said, thoughtfully. 'Go and stay with my mom. She'll love looking after you – and the baby.'

'Really?' I said. 'I like the sound of that. Is it possible?'

'Sure,' Donnie said. 'Well, maybe. We can find out. I'll send her a telegram after the wedding.'

Just the words were enough to make me excited.

'Come on then,' I said, pulling his arm. 'Let's go and find a church.'

Chapter 17

We had four days. Four days in which to plan a wedding and get married. Donnie's division was leaving for France on Thursday, but heading to the coast the night before. Today was Sunday and we'd planned to get married on Wednesday.

'It can't be done,' I said to Audrey in dismay. 'I don't have enough coupons for a dress, nor enough time to make it; we've got performances every night, and we've got to go and see the vicar to arrange everything. It's impossible.'

But Audrey, who'd grown up in the middle of a huge brood of brothers and sisters, was both wonderful at organizing, and incapable of taking no for an answer.

We were in our attic bedroom – thankfully Fat Joan was nowhere to be seen. Audrey came and sat next to me on my narrow bed and took my hand.

'Look,' she said, 'I think I owe you an apology.'

I gazed at her, not understanding what she meant.

'I was wrong about Donnie,' she said. 'I'm sorry.'

'You were wrong,' I agreed. 'He loves me, Audrey.'

She nodded.

'He's a good'un,' she said. 'And my mum always says to hang

on to the good'uns. Not that she'd know, bless her heart. She just hangs on to my useless dad, waste of space that he is.'

I waited for her to get to the point.

'Anyway, Donnie's a good'un and he loves you, and that's all that matters. Not the dress or a cake or any of those things. They mean nothing. As long as you're there and he's there, then you've got yourselves a wedding.'

A bubble of joy popped in my tummy. I gripped Audrey's hand a bit tighter.

'I'm getting married,' I said gleefully. 'I'm bloody well getting married.'

Audrey laughed.

'You are,' she said. 'And I might just have a few ideas up my sleeve to make it a day to remember.'

'Do you?' I said in surprise. 'What ideas?'

Audrey laughed.

'That'd be telling, wouldn't it?'

There were footsteps on the stairs and Fat Joan came in. She draped herself lazily across a chair and flipped her beautiful hair over her shoulder.

'Wedding plans?' she drawled.

I nodded.

'Got these for you,' she said, digging in her pocket then holding out a bundle of paper.

'Clothing coupons?' I said, bewildered. 'Whose are these?'

'They're yours,' said Joan. 'If you want them.'

I looked at the bundle in amazement.

'From where?'

'I did a bit of a whip round,' Joan said, shrugging as though it was no big deal. 'I asked everyone to hand over a coupon and everyone did.'

'You did that for me?' I said.

Joan shrugged again.

'Nice to have something to look forward to,' she said.

She uncurled herself from the chair and stood up.

'I've got practice,' she said. 'See you later.'

I leapt up from the bed and caught her arm.

'Thanks,' I said, giving her a squeeze.

Joan flashed me the smile that made grown men weak.

'Be happy,' she said. Then she spun on her heels and slunk off down the stairs.

I turned to Audrey, whose mouth was still open in shock.

'What are we waiting for?' I said, waving the coupons like a fan. 'Let's go shopping.'

Of course even with the coupons there wasn't a lot of choice, and I didn't really have any money to spend anyway, but I managed to get a length of white satin for my dress, and some pale blue cotton for Audrey. Then, giggling like schoolgirls, we got on the bus and went to see Audrey's mum in Camberwell.

I'd been a bit nervous when Audrey said her mum would help make my dress. Her huge, lively family sounded so different from my own upbringing.

My dad, bless him, had never been the same after the Great War and he died when I was six. I hardly remembered him, actually. He'd stayed in his study most of the time, or slept in his chair by the fire. I had to play quietly because noise bothered him, and he coughed a lot. Everything my mother did was for Dad.

'Don't bother your dad,' she'd say. 'Let him be.'

We never had the wireless on. And music wasn't something Dad could tolerate. So the house was so quiet and still, all the time.

When he died, Mum waited a few weeks and then went out and bought a wireless and suddenly there was music all the time. I danced, made-up steps, on the living room rug and Mum watched.

'Would you like to have dancing lessons?' she said one day when I was seven. I'd thrown my arms round her in delight.

'Really?' I said. 'Really and truly?'

So she found a teacher and I started to learn and I loved every second of it. And so did my mother. She loved music and dancing, too, so she enjoyed watching me. Enjoyed it a bit too much, perhaps. She made me practise over and over, and she was so proud of me when I was twelve and got my first job dancing in a show at the end of the pier.

I loved dancing, of course, but Mum's attention was suffocating. I was all she thought about – my costumes, and what I was eating, and what the other girls were eating, and what I could do for my next audition.

I was never short of work – there were enough shows on the pier to keep me busy – and I adored performing. But I dreamed of more. Along with my friend Betty, I spent every Saturday morning – the only time I had to myself with no school, dancing or homework to worry about – at the pictures. Betty liked all the romantic films –she loved Clark Gable and Spencer Tracy – but I liked Fred Astaire and Ginger Rogers. I'd save up and see the same film over and over, memorizing the steps and recreating them in my bedroom later.

So while Mother wanted me to become Worthing's answer to Shirley Temple – under her watchful eye, of course – I had different plans. When the war came and everything changed, I saw my chance and signed up for the ENSA as soon as I turned eighteen.

Mother tried to make me stay, but she couldn't say no really. I had to confess I did feel guilty when I thought about her alone at home, but not enough to make me give up on my dreams of Hollywood.

'Are you all right?' Audrey's voice startled me out of my thoughts. 'We're here.'

'Just thinking about my mum,' I said, as we got off the bus and walked down the road towards her house.

'Going to tell her about the wedding?' Audrey said.

I made a face.

'When it's over,' I said. 'Is that awful?'

'Will she mind?'

'Terribly,' I said. 'But once Donnie's gone to France, I'll go down to Worthing, tell her about the baby and the wedding and break the news that I'm going to America. It'll be better face to face and by then it'll be too late for her to try to stop me.'

'My mum would kill me,' Audrey said, leading me down the side passage of a row of terraced houses. 'And I'd feel dreadful, not letting her be part of my wedding day.'

'There's no time,' I pointed out, feeling the guilt I always felt when I thought about my mother begin to swamp me. 'There's no point in bothering her.'

'If you're sure,' Audrey said, with a glance that told me she wasn't convinced. 'This is it.'

She opened a tall gate into a yard that seemed to me to be full of children.

'Hello littl'uns,' she said, with a grin, as they all leapt on her at once. 'This is Cora.'

Chapter 18

It took us a while to explain why we'd turned up on the doorstep. Audrey had to peel several children – only a couple of them were actually her siblings; the rest were cousins, neighbours … I lost track – from her legs. Then, once the introductions were made, Audrey's mum – Reenie – put the kettle on and made a pot of tea in an enormous enamel pot, which she plonked on the table unceremoniously.

'Go on then,' she said, eyeing Audrey suspiciously. 'What you here for?'

Audrey reached over and took a cigarette from her mum's packet.

'We need you to make a wedding dress,' she said.

Reenie's mouth gaped. She was younger than my mum, but she looked ten years older. Although I'd not seen much of my own mother recently, so it was possible she'd aged, too. Reenie had the same dark brown hair as Audrey, but most of it was tucked under a headscarf. Her face was lined and her brow furrowed – more so now as she stared at Audrey.

'You stupid cow,' she said. Her hand shot out to clout Audrey, who ducked just in time, giggling.

'Not me,' she said. 'Cora.'

Reenie looked at me and I wilted, just a little, under her knowing gaze.

'Expecting?' she said.

I nodded, embarrassed.

'He knows?'

I nodded again.

'What's he like?'

'He's nice, Mum,' Audrey said. 'American. Kind. Handsome.'

She looked at me over the top of the huge teapot.

'He's a good'un.'

'He going to take you to America?'

'Yes,' I said.

'Believe him?'

'Yes.'

Reenie looked grim for a second, then she gave me a huge smile.

'Right then, best get cracking. Got your fabric?' she said.

I pulled it out of the bag and handed it to her. She rubbed it appraisingly between her thumb and finger.

'Not bad,' she said.

She stood up and unrolled the material so it draped over a chair, then she stood back and looked at it, and me.

'Showing?'

I stood up and turned to the side, smoothing my skirt down so she could see my small tummy.

'A bit,' I said, chewing my lip.

She gave me another smile.

'It's not the end of the world, you know,' she said, picking up a tape measure from the sideboard and gesturing for me to stand still. 'It might not be what you planned, but it's not the end of the world.'

Her kind words made me dissolve into tears and she laughed.

'I was like that with Audrey,' she said, pulling the tape measure round my back. 'Arms up. Couldn't stop crying the whole bloody

91

time. You stand there and cry darlin' and we'll do all the work.'

And she did.

She jotted down my measurements on the back of an envelope; then she and Audrey went through a pile of patterns, nodding and showing me pictures occasionally to get my opinion. And I sat at the table and cried. I wasn't sad, not really. I was overwhelmed with everything that was happening, with how kind everyone was being – when Audrey explained how Fat Joan had collected everyone's clothing coupons I sobbed even harder – and with the comfort of being in a noisy, happy, family home.

Children ran in and out as we worked, and later two neighbours came by to help, too. And eventually, after three hours, many refills of the enormous teapot, and lord knows how many tears, I had a dress.

It was knee-length, with little cap sleeves and small buttons – donated from the neighbour's button box – down the front. It had a pale blue belt – another donation from a different neighbour – that sat above my swelling stomach, and helped disguise it. Round the bottom of the skirt was a frill that I could swirl round my knees if I danced.

'It's like the one Ginger Rogers wore in *Swing Time*,' I said in delight, waltzing round the small room and watching the dress flow this way and that.

'It's beautiful.'

'Well, mind it stays that way,' said Reenie, giving me a grin that was at odds with her stern words. 'Take it off before you get it dirty.'

I did one last twirl and then reluctantly took off the dress and put my uniform back on.

Reenie wrapped it in paper, tied it with string and handed it to me. I gave her a hug.

'Thank you,' I said. 'I can't tell you how much this means to me.'

She squeezed me a bit tighter.

'Will you come?' I added. 'To the wedding? It's at St Giles's, tomorrow at two o'clock. Please come. All of you.'

'It was nice of you to ask them,' Audrey said, when we were on the bus home. 'Mum was really chuffed.'

'Well, there aren't going to be many people there,' I said. 'Be nice to have some guests on my side of the church.'

'It'll be packed. Fat Joan's invited everyone,' Audrey said with a chuckle. She took my hand. 'It's going to be a lovely day.'

I nodded.

'Do you know what? I think it is going to be lovely,' I said, feeling a swell of excitement once more. I looked out of the window at the river, as we crossed Waterloo Bridge.

'Did you imagine your wedding day when you were a little girl?' I said.

Audrey nudged me.

'Not really,' she said. 'My mum and dad were enough to put any girl off marriage for life.'

'I used to play brides,' I said, remembering. 'I'd put a tea towel on my head, and pick flowers from the garden for my bouquet. And I'd draw pictures of beautiful ladies wearing beautiful dresses.'

'Did they all look like Ginger Rogers?' Audrey asked, with a smile.

'Of course,' I said. I paused. 'I didn't ever imagine my wedding would be like this, though. No family there. No wedding breakfast. No cake.'

I put my hand on my growing tummy. 'And I never thought I'd be expecting when I walked down the aisle.'

'I know it's not perfect,' Audrey said. 'But you've got all of us there to wish you well. You've got a pretty dress. You've got me to stand by your side and give you a hanky if you cry. You're bound to cry. And you know what else you've got? You've got Donnie.'

'I have,' I said. 'But what if you were right. What if all men are like your dad and he'll just leave me?'

'He won't,' Audrey said calmly reaching over me to ring the bell. 'I told you, he's a good'un.'

He was a good'un, I thought, as we walked up Charing Cross Road to the boarding house. And the wedding would be perfect – or at least as perfect as it could be considering my groom would be leaving for France straight after the ceremony and we wouldn't even get a wedding night. I couldn't even let myself think about the fact that Donnie might never come back. I was just going to concentrate on the wedding day – and telling Henry that I was pregnant – before I worried about that. Not to mention breaking the news to my mother. I didn't want to go back to Worthing to have the baby – though I was convinced she'd try to persuade me. I was hoping to leave for America as soon as I could to start my new life on the other side of the world. Donnie had said he was hoping to arrange things with his mum before he left, though things weren't always easy to sort out in wartime.

'It's all going to be fine,' I said out loud and Audrey linked her arm through mine.

'Course it is,' she said.

But it wasn't.

94

Chapter 19

'Actually, he was really nice,' I said to Donnie as we strolled arm in arm through Hyde Park the next day. 'But it was rather embarrassing telling him about the baby.'

I shuddered at the memory of telling Henry that not only was I getting married, but that I was expecting.

'So did he say what you should do?' Donnie asked.

'I told him we're hoping I can go to America fairly soon,' I said. 'And he says I can stay until then. If I can't dance any more, I can sing.'

'That's great, honey,' Donnie said, pulling me closer to him. 'It's all going to work out just fine. I've written to my mom explaining everything and I'll let you have her address. Once I'm gone it'll be better for you to make arrangements with her directly.'

I nodded.

'But you're sure she won't mind?' I said, biting my lip. 'Some strange British girl turning up on her doorstep?'

'But you're not a strange British girl,' Donnie said, grinning. 'You're my wife. Or at least you will be.'

'I'll be Mrs Cora Jackson,' I said. 'I've been practising my new signature.'

'Not signature,' said Donnie. 'Autograph. You'll be signing promotional photographs for your fans before you know it.'

'You think we can still go to Hollywood?' I said. 'Even though things are going to be different now?'

'Sure we can,' Donnie said. 'Movie stars have kids all the time. And you'll be making so much money that we'll hire people to look after Junior whenever you're busy on set.'

I giggled. It sounded like the most wonderful pie in the sky idea I'd ever heard. I had no idea what looking after a baby was going to be like but, judging by Audrey's brothers and sisters, it didn't seem an easy job.

I sat down on a bench and tilted my face up to the spring sunshine, focusing on a patch of blue sky that wasn't blighted by the barrage balloons that floated above London.

'What's it like there?' I asked.

'Hollywood?' said Donnie, with a confidence that didn't for one minute give away the fact that he'd never been to California. 'Oh, it's incredible. The sun always shines. The sea sparkles bright blue. The beaches have pure white sand …'

'Sounds almost exactly like Worthing,' I said, laughing at the memory of the grey Sussex skies, murky waters and stony beach.

Donnie gave me a stern look.

'Do you want to hear about Los Angeles or not?' he said, prodding me in the ribs.

'Tell me about the trees,' I said, even though I'd heard about them so many times I could picture them as clearly as if I'd lived my whole life in the Californian sunshine.

'Palm trees,' Donnie said. 'Gently waving in the breeze. And movie producers on every street, just hanging out, waiting for the next big thing to arrive.'

'So I'll just stroll by one day,' I said. 'And one of these film chaps will be walking the other way, and he'll see me and stop me?'

'Exactly,' said Donnie. He jumped to his feet and affected

walking past me. Then he stopped and did an exaggerated double-take.

I raised my eyebrows.

'Like that?' I said.

'Like that. He'll take out his cigar – they all smoke cigars in LA – and he'll say …' He put on a drawling voice …

'Darlin,' you're exactly who I need for my next picture.'

I gasped and fluttered my eyelashes.

'Me?' I said. 'Little old me? Why, sir, I'd be delighted.'

'See,' Donnie said. 'You'll be a star as soon as we arrive.'

'I'd better start practising my speech for all those awards I'm going to win,' I said, giggling.

Donnie nodded gravely.

'That would be wise,' he said. 'You don't want to be stuck up on stage with nothing to say.'

'You're the only person I need to thank,' I said, pulling him back down to sit next to me on the bench. I took his face in my hands.

'I'd like to thank my husband, Donald,' I said. 'He's made me the woman I am today and he's always believed in me.'

Donnie kissed me softly.

'Go on,' he said, his face close to mine.

'And I'd like to thank my daughter,' I said.

Donnie frowned.

'Or son.'

'It's a girl,' I said. 'I'm sure it's a girl.'

'You think?'

'I'd like to thank my daughter,' I said, looking into Donnie's eyes. 'Donaldina.'

'Really?' he said.

'No, not really,' I said. 'But it's the best I can come up with at the moment. Stop ruining it.'

I looked into his eyes again.

'I don't care, you know,' I said. Donnie frowned.

97

'Don't care about what?'

'About Hollywood,' I said. 'It's a nice idea, of course it is. And what girl wouldn't want to be a film star? But darling Donnie, you're all I need. The films and the movie producers and the palm trees? None of that matters unless I'm with you.'

Donnie put his arm round me and pulled me into his chest.

'Honey, you're made for movies,' he said.

I shrugged.

'Maybe,' I said. 'Maybe not. It doesn't matter. I just want to be with you and our baby. I'll always be a dancer – that won't change. But I can dance anywhere. I can teach, or I can do theatre. We'll work something out.'

I looked up at him.

'Just come home, Donnie,' I said. 'Just do whatever you have to do in France and come home to me.'

Donnie stroked my hair.

'When I was in France before …' he said, a catch in his voice. 'When we were there last year, there was nothing for me to come home for.'

'You had your family,' I pointed out.

'Sure I did,' he said. 'And of course I thought about my mom and dad, and my sister. But some of the other guys, they had sweethearts, you know? Girls they wrote to, and had pictures of. And now I have you. And knowing you're here – or in Connecticut – waiting for me, is what's going to get me through.'

He kissed the top of my head.

'I love you, Cora,' he said. 'I know tomorrow isn't going to be the wedding day you dreamed of, or the wedding day you deserve, but it's going to be a wonderful day whatever happens.'

'I know it is,' I said. 'Because it'll be you and me, and we'll be husband and wife.'

'For ever,' said Donnie. 'Oh, shoot.'

'What?' I said, alarmed.

'Look at the time,' he said. He kissed me again. 'I gotta go.'

'I thought you had until four o'clock,' I said, disappointed.

'I do,' Donnie said. 'But I've got something to do before I head back.'

He laughed at my cross face.

'Don't be mad, honey,' he said. 'We've got our whole lives together.'

I was suddenly filled with a wave of pure joy that bubbled up and out of me in a delighted chuckle.

'Go on, then,' I said, giving him a good-natured shove. 'Go and do your thing. See you at the church?'

'I'll see you at the church,' he said. He stood up and twirled round, his arms outstretched.

'We're getting married,' he shouted. Two soldiers walking nearby shook his hand and he laughed.

'We're getting married,' he said again. He blew me a kiss. 'See you tomorrow. I love you, Cora Cassidy!'

'I love you, too! See you tomorrow,' I shouted.

But I never saw him again.

Chapter 20

Cora may have looked like a sweet old lady, but as it turned out she was something of a slave driver.

The day after she'd offered to teach me how to dance, I was looking forward to a relaxing weekend. It was the summer bank holiday – the very end of August – and I wasn't meant to be meeting Patrick again until Tuesday. I was free for three glorious days. Three days of doing whatever I wanted. Which was … well, I wasn't exactly sure. Phil was off entertaining Bertie and his stupid parents and while I usually spent bank holidays jetting off somewhere with Matty – and some carefully chosen photographers – that wasn't exactly an option today.

I made myself a cup of tea and went out into the garden to drink it while I thought about what to do. Maybe I could go into town and do something I'd never done before. Visit a museum, perhaps. Or an art gallery? Or I could go and see a film. London was overflowing with things to do if you were a sad, lonely spinster like me.

Grumpily, I took a mouthful of tea. Actually, it was nice just sitting here in my little patch of backyard, in the early morning sun. Perhaps I could just stay here by myself all weekend. Relax. Watch some DVDs. Read a book. And not think about Patrick or bloody dancing for days.

'Oh, good – you're up.' Cora's voice behind made me jump. 'Are you ready?'

I looked round. She was standing at the top of the stone steps that led down to my bit of garden, wearing a long black tunic and drapey yoga trousers.

'Ready for what?' I said over my shoulder.

Cora sighed.

'For your dance lesson.'

I made a face that I hoped she couldn't see.

'Now?'

'Are you busy?'

I looked at her again. She had a slight smile on her face.

'Well,' I said. 'Not busy as such …'

'Then we'll do it now.'

'But I'm not dressed.'

'Half an hour, then.'

I knew when I was beaten. I drained my mug and stood up.

'You're mean,' I said.

'Trust me, darling,' she said, spinning round and walking back towards her house. 'I've not even started.'

And so, twenty-five minutes later, I was on my hands and knees in Cora's lounge, rolling up the rug to expose the hard wooden floor, while she jabbed at my phone.

'You'll have to sort out the music,' she said. 'I can't make head nor tail of this thing.'

I laughed. I was beginning to like Cora enormously, even if she was fairly terrifying.

'Now,' she said. 'I am not as young as I used to be, and I'm afraid that, other than a few simple steps, my dancing days are behind me.'

I began to protest, but she waved her hand elegantly.

'Oh, it's fine,' she said. 'Thankfully, age hasn't withered my wisdom.'

She gave me a cheeky look.

'And you're going to get the benefit of all of it.'

'Lucky me,' I said, making a face. But I meant it really. Cora was very interesting and I was keen to get to know her better.

'So let's start with what you know already,' she said. 'You're starting with a cha-cha, yes?'

I nodded.

'An interesting choice for a beginner,' she said, shaking her head.

'I think Patrick thought I was going to be better than I am,' I admitted, scrolling through the songs on my phone until I found Bruno Mars. 'I went to drama school, you know? I'm an actress. I can sing – not well, but I can carry a tune. I think he just assumed I would be a natural dancer, too.'

'But you're not?'

'Not at all,' I said. 'Not even a bit. I can dance in a club, if I've had a drink, but having to remember steps in a certain order just seems to be beyond me.'

'Let's have a look,' Cora said.

Reluctantly, I turned on the music and started to dance. I felt massively self-conscious and tried not to look at Cora as she sat watching me intently.

I struggled through the first part of the dance, just about, thinking about Patrick and how he always got cross with me at a certain bit, and how he looked at me in a way that really made me feel like he despised me. But then, just when I thought I was doing okay, I turned right instead of left, got muddled and gave up.

'See?' I said to Cora. 'I'm completely hopeless.'

She stood up.

'You're not at all,' she said. 'Not in the slightest, actually.'

I felt a glimmer of hope.

'Really?'

'Really,' she said. 'You can hear the music, so that's a start. You've got natural timing and rhythm – that's perfect because I find it very hard to teach that to someone who can't understand it.'

I preened, just a tiny bit.

'But you're right about the steps,' she said. 'You seem to have a lot of trouble remembering what to do with your arms and legs.'

'It's doing different things with them I find tricky,' I said. 'All that opposite arm and leg stuff. It feels so wrong.'

Cora laughed.

'Walk up to the window and back again,' she said.

I wrinkled my nose up.

'Walk?' I said. 'Just walk?'

'Just walk,' Cora said. 'Go on.'

Feeling a bit silly I walked over the window, then back to Cora. She nodded in satisfaction.

'Now do it again, and tell me what you're doing with your arms and legs.'

I walked again, realizing I was swinging the opposite arm to the leg I was stepping on.'

'Oh, my God,' I said in delight. 'It's like walking.'

Cora grinned.

'See?' she said. 'It's not all that complicated.'

She came over to me and took my hands. I wasn't tall, but she was tiny. I could see the top of her scalp, showing through her fine white hair. Her hands were lined, but her nails were painted bright coral pink and she wore an enormous diamond ring on her middle finger. Her ring finger was bare.

'I think that what you're doing is a mixture of not thinking enough, and thinking too much,' she said.

'Well, that makes absolutely no sense whatsoever,' I said.

Cora chuckled.

'When you're playing a scene, are you thinking about it as Amy or are you thinking like … what's your character's name?'

'Betsy,' I said.

'Betsy,' Cora said. 'When you're saying those lines, are you thinking about what you're going to have for dinner, or what you're going to wear to a party?'

I chewed my lip thoughtfully, trying to remember.

'I'm thinking as Betsy,' I said. 'I wouldn't be able to do it if I was thinking as Amy being Betsy. I'd forget what I was meant to say next …'

'That's what you need to do when you're dancing,' she said. 'I don't want you thinking about anything other than the steps.'

'I don't,' I said.

She raised her eyebrows.

'Really?'

'Well, I try,' I said.

'Trust me, Amy,' she said. 'You need to think about the steps and only the steps. Then you'll be a dancer.'

'Okay,' I said doubtfully. 'I'll try.'

'Don't try,' Cora said. 'I'm not interested in trying. Just dance. Put that music on again and show me.'

Chapter 21

I danced all morning. Cora made me go over the same bits again and again. She made me shout the steps out while I was dancing so I couldn't think about anything else. She made me sit down and listen to the music and say the steps aloud at the right time, and then stand up and dance them, too. By midday I was exhausted but exhilarated – I felt like I'd actually achieved something – and I was slightly disappointed when Cora said that was enough for the day.

'Really?' I said. 'But we've only done the first bit of the dance.'

'I'm going for lunch and then to play bridge with some friends,' Cora said, giving me a wink. 'We don't play much bridge, I must be honest. In fact, I've never quite grasped the rules. But we have a good chat and a few drinks.'

'Sounds like Phil's book club,' I said, gathering up my phone and speakers. 'I once had to go and rescue him from some very odd club in Soho where he'd somehow ended up after a heated discussion about *The Hunger Games*.'

I turned to Cora and spontaneously kissed her on her soft, lined cheek.

'Thank you,' I said.

She waved me off as though it was nothing.

'Let's catch up again over the weekend,' she said.

I felt slightly out of sorts as I went back to my flat through Cora's garden and my little yard. Like I'd been reset or recharged. My mind seemed clear for the first time since I'd gone down the steps into that club and seen Matty kissing Kayleigh. It was like a fog had lifted.

It was still really warm and I was sweating after all that dancing. I was fit – I went to the gym a lot and I ran whenever I got a chance – but dancing was using muscles I wasn't used to using.

I downed a glass of water, then poured another and stood in the open-plan kitchen looking round the flat. It didn't really look like home.

'I need to sort this out,' I said to myself. I wiped my sweaty brow. 'After a shower.'

I showered and pulled on some denim shorts, a bright-pink strappy top and some Havaianas; then, clad in my sunglasses and a wide-brimmed straw hat, I picked up my bag and headed out to explore Clapham.

Which was very nice, actually. There were all sorts of interesting little shops, nice delis, cool bars, and a health food cafe where I stopped for an amazing lunch of the nicest Greek salad I'd tasted, outside of Greece. It was really the first time I'd eaten properly since everything happened. I always completely lost my appetite when I was stressed. But I'd found I was suddenly starving hungry. I even bought some food to make dinner. I'd not even turned on the cooker in my flat so far, surviving on mostly bananas with black coffee and the occasional cup of tea.

In a brilliant bric-a-brac shop, under a railway arch, I found a framed drawing of a flamenco dancer. Her head was turned away and she had a flower in her dark hair. Her skirt was full of ruffles and it was flying up as she moved to show her feet, which were just a blur. On a whim, I decided to buy it.

'She looks a bit like you,' the man behind the counter said, as he wrapped it up in brown paper for me. 'Can you dance like that?'

I laughed.

'I wish,' I said, handing over my cash. 'Maybe one day.'

Back home, I spent the afternoon happily arranging my flat. I unpacked all my shopping, arranged my (meagre) possessions in my bedroom and the living room, and propped my flamenco picture on the mantelpiece because obviously I didn't have a hammer, or a drill, or any of the other things you needed to put up a picture. I grilled some chicken for dinner and ate it with salad and houmous – it was so hot I couldn't bear to eat anything else, really – while I was watching old clips of *Strictly Stars Dancing* on YouTube and – would you believe – taking notes.

Later in the evening, I heard Cora moving about upstairs, so I grabbed a cold bottle of rose wine from the fridge and went to see her. She was in her kitchen, bustling about, and she smiled widely when she saw me knocking on her open back door.

'Amy,' she said in delight. 'Come in.'

'I brought you this,' I said. 'To say thank you for my dance lesson today.'

'There is no need for thanks,' Cora said. 'Teaching dancing is my great joy. But I will accept this wine on condition you stay and drink it with me.'

'Are you sure?' I said. 'Aren't you tired after your bridge session?'

'It was fairly restrained today,' Cora said. 'My friend Hazel has her son and his family staying so she had to leave early, and then we were a player short.'

'In that case, I'd love to,' I said. 'Shall we sit outside? It's still so warm.'

We sat at the table in the garden. The air was muggy and the sky was beginning to darken as though a storm was brewing, but for now it was still warm enough to enjoy the evening.

I told Cora about the picture I'd found, and how I'd spent the day.

'It's so strange,' I said. 'I feel like spending the morning with you has recharged my batteries.' I took a swig of wine and narrowed my eyes at her. 'Are you a witch?'

Cora laughed.

'It's not me who's made you feel better,' she said. 'It's dancing.'

I was sceptical.

'You think?'

'I know,' Cora said. 'My friend Audrey and I always said we could dance away our misery. It never fails.'

'That makes no sense,' I said.

'Oh, it does.' Cora looked serious. 'I've done quite a lot of reading about it and I taught some dance therapy classes for a while. It's a bit like meditation, or what I believe they call mindfulness nowadays.'

I raised my eyebrows, still unconvinced, but Cora went on.

'When you dance you have to concentrate completely on what you're doing,' she said. 'You learned that today. So it takes you out of yourself. Gives you a rest from your misery and lets you heal.'

I nodded slowly. This was beginning to make sense.

'Does it work for other things apart from misery?' I said, refilling our glasses. 'Like failure and humiliation.'

'Trust me,' Cora said. 'It works for everything.'

She gave me a sly glance.

'You youngsters thing you've got the monopoly on heartbreak,' she said. 'But you didn't invent it. Believe me, I know a few things about humiliation and broken hearts.'

She looked distant for a moment and I reached over the table and took her hand.

'What happened to you?' I asked. 'Did you lose someone?'

Cora smiled weakly.

'It was a very long time ago,' she said. 'I'll tell you all the sorry details one day.'

'Was it in the war?' I asked, trying to work out how old Cora would have been back then.

'Another time,' Cora said. 'So tell me, have you heard from that ex-boyfriend of yours?'

I gave up. She obviously didn't want to talk about it.

'I've not heard anything,' I said. 'But I'm okay about that.'

'You don't want him back?'

I shook my head.

'No, I really don't think I do,' I said. 'He was cheating on me for months and everyone knew about it. And he knew I was on my way to meet him that night so why did he choose that moment to start snogging a starlet? I can't help wondering if he set the whole thing up just for publicity, which is horrible but the sort of thing he would do. To be honest, I'm exhausted by this whole celebrity thing ...'

I paused.

'Patrick thinks I'm shallow and superficial,' I said.

Cora shrugged.

'Just because you like to look nice it doesn't mean you're shallow,' she said. 'You shouldn't have to stop wearing make-up to ensure people take you seriously.'

I grinned.

'That's exactly what I think,' I said. 'Still smarts a bit that he thinks that of me, though.'

Cora eyed me thoughtfully.

'It's very important to get along with your dance partner,' she said. 'We need to work on that, too.'

'Good luck with that,' I said. 'He hates me.'

Chapter 22

I woke up the next morning to the sound of rain battering against my bedroom window and my phone buzzing frantically on the bedside table.

I felt for it in the half-light and groaned when I saw Babs on the screen.

'Morning,' I growled. 'What time is it?'

'It's nine o'clock,' Babs trilled. 'And I want to know what you're playing at? No press attention, my arse.'

I sat up, suddenly wide-awake and filled with dread.

'What?' I said. 'What's happened?'

'Get your iPad, look at the *PostOnline* and call me back,' Babs said.

'Babs …' I began, but she'd hung up.

Feeling sick – and regretting the last glass of wine I'd had with Cora before I finally headed to bed at midnight – I slid out of bed and padded into the lounge to find my iPad. The *PostOnline* was bookmarked but the homepage was a story about benefit cheats. I sat on the sofa, balanced my iPad on my knee and phoned Babs.

'What?' I demanded when she answered.

'Top story, TV and showbiz,' she said.

110

I hit the tab at the top with my forefinger and waited for the page to load.

'Got it?' said Babs.

'Got it,' I said, looking as my face filled the screen. It was a photo of me coming out of the junk shop in Clapham the day before. I was clutching my brown-paper-wrapped parcel under one arm, grinning like a loon, and squinting slightly in the sun. My sunglasses – my trusty disguise – were propped on top of my head, and my hat – trusty disguise number two – was in my hand. It had been dark inside the shop and I'd had to take them off to see properly. More fool me for not putting them back on before I went back out onto the street.

But, I thought, looking at the picture critically. I didn't look bad. My legs were long, smooth and brown in my denim shorts. My arms were toned. My hair was a bit messy but hardly a disaster. And I was smiling.

'Moving on,' the article read. 'Shamed soap star Amy Lavender showed she was moving on with her life after being dumped by her boyfriend, reality TV star Matty Hall. Fresh-faced Amy, who's currently rehearsing for the new series of *Strictly Stars Dancing*, was spotted showing off her lean pins in tiny Daisy Duke shorts as she shopped for furniture in an antiques store in South London …'

I was a bit annoyed that I hadn't seen anyone taking a photo – and that the press were still interested in me – but I had to admit, as showbiz gossip went, it wasn't all bad. I said as much to Babs.

'You're right,' she said. 'You look amazing. Gorgeous. Happy. Healthy. We should make the most of this.'

'We should?'

'I'm wondering if this might make Matty want you back,' she said, thoughtfully. 'If he sees you looking fabulous, not missing him at all, it might make him see what he's lost.'

'Babs,' I said, in a warning tone, which she completely ignored.

'It was clever of you to be photographed like this. Like you're over him already.'

'I'm not over him,' I said, sulkily. 'At least, I'm not over the humiliation of it all. I just wanted to go shopping.'

'Well, whatever you wanted, it could be the thing that gets Matty back,' Babs said.

'I don't know if I want him back.'

'I think you're better together,' Babs said. 'You're a brand. Like the Beckhams.'

'What if I don't want to be a brand?' I said. 'What if I just want to be an actress?'

But Babs was on a roll now.

'There's a film premiere tonight,' she said. 'Lots of celebs and I'm told Matty and his crew are all going.'

'So?' I said.

'So you're going, too. I want us to capitalize on this attention.'

'Oh, Babs,' I whined. 'It's raining. And I don't want the attention. And I really don't want to see Matty.'

'You need to get out and about if you want casting directors to remember you,' she said. 'This dancing thing won't last for ever, and you'll be auditioning again soon. I need people to see you, Amy.'

I absolutely, positively didn't want to see Matty, I didn't want him to want me back, and I really wasn't excited about going to a film premiere. But Babs was the only part of my old life that hadn't given up on me, and I couldn't bring myself to argue with her. I may have been milking it a bit when I told Phil that everyone left me, but I did genuinely fear being abandoned. My mum moving to Spain had made me feel lost and alone, even though Phil's family had stepped in. Then Matty – the first man I'd really committed to – had left me in the most humiliating way. Babs had been part of my life for almost a decade and I wasn't about to risk losing her, too.

'Fine,' I said. 'Where is it?'

'Leicester Square. I'll get you a car,' she said. 'Text me your address. And bring your dance partner. He's hot, right?'

'He's really hot,' I admitted. 'But he hates me.'

'Probably wants to get in your knickers,' Babs said. I sensed it wasn't the time to admit he already had.

'Can you persuade him?'

'To get in my knickers?'

'To go to the premiere,' Babs said with a sigh. 'You'll get a lot of attention if he's with you.'

'Dunno,' I said. 'What's the film?'

'Some surfing thing, I think,' Babs said. 'Can't remember the name.'

I grinned.

'He'll come,' I said. 'But seriously, I'm not sure about Matty. I just think I'm better off without him.'

Babs tutted.

'Just trust me on this one,' she said. 'I've been in this game a long time.'

Reluctantly I agreed. She promised to email me the details of the premiere, and we said our goodbyes. I sat for a little while, watching the rain soak into the parched earth beneath Cora's lawn, thinking about Patrick. Cora had said it was important to get along with my dance partner. Maybe I should make an effort to get to know Patrick? We could go along to the film, have a laugh, and maybe get to be friends. We'd definitely clicked at the theatre that night, so we obviously had things in common. I felt like I had to apologize for being such a cow. Plus I kind of wanted to show him what Cora had taught me yesterday, too.

I took a deep breath, then I scrolled through my phone and found his number. He answered straightaway but he sounded pretty grumpy.

'Patrick,' I said, trying to be bright and breezy. 'I wondered if we could get together?'

'I thought we were having the weekend off,' he said.

'We are,' I said. 'We were. But I've got tickets to this surfing film tonight and I wondered if you'd like to come.'

There was a pause.

'The new one?' Patrick said.

'Yep.'

He paused again.

'Are you trying to decide whether how much you want to see the film outweighs how annoying you find me?' I said.

Patrick let out a bark of laughter.

'Pretty much,' he admitted. 'I'd love to come. Shall I meet you there?'

'Could you come here first?' I asked. 'I've got something to show you. About three-ish?'

'Really?' said Patrick, reluctantly.

'Please,' I said. 'Don't make me beg.'

Patrick agreed.

I spent the morning cleaning the flat (I know, actually cleaning – that was new), had a nap (cleaning was hard work) and dug out a long flowery maxi dress to wear to the premiere. I didn't have time to get someone to do my make-up and hair, so instead I just dried my hair into loose waves, stuck on a floral headband, and went for hippy chic instead. It fitted with the surfer vibe, I told myself.

As I was trying to resist painting a flower on my cheekbone with eyeliner, there was a knock on the door. Patrick.

I suddenly felt nervous. I was so desperate to make things right between us that it seemed really important that I did everything properly.

'Hi,' I said, opening the door.

'Wow,' Patrick said. 'You look great.'

I giggled.

'Do I look like I'm in fancy dress?' I asked.

He gave me a grin that showed off his white teeth, sparkling in his tanned face.

'A bit,' he said. 'But it's kind of nice.'

I showed him into the lounge and made him sit down, even though he wanted to have a nose round.

114

'Could you just sit for five seconds,' I begged.

Patrick eyed me suspiciously.

'Okaaay,' he said.

'You have to just let me talk without interrupting,' I said, standing nervously by the fireplace. 'There are some things I need to say.'

Patrick looked bewildered and ever-so-slightly annoyed.

'Fine,' he said. 'But could you sit down? You're reminding me of my dad the way you're standing up there preparing to give me a lecture.'

I perched on the edge of the sofa.

'Okay,' I said. 'Here's the thing. I don't know how much you know about me ...'

'Not much,' Patrick admitted. 'I mean, I googled you when we got put together but there was just so much, and lots of it was about that soap, and I gave up.'

I sighed.

'So, I was in a soap,' I said. 'And everything was going really great. My boyfriend Matty was a DJ and he and his friends are in a reality TV show. It kind of follows them round – it's a bit strange because it's half scripted, half not.'

Patrick nodded.

'I know the thing,' he said.

'And we got a lot of attention,' I went on. 'Magazine covers, photo shoots, endorsements, you name it. We were big business. We made a staggering amount of money just for getting engaged. Our wedding was going to be huge. But Matty cheated on me, I found out and punched the girl he was kissing; he threw me out, I lost my job and here I am.'

'Ouch,' said Patrick.

'My agent, Babs, wants me to stay in the public eye because she says it's good for my career. She pulled strings to get me on *Strictly Stars Dancing* at the last minute, to raise my profile and get the public to see the 'real Amy'. I wasn't keen – after everything that happened I wanted to disappear for a while and get away from the paps and the crazy stories.'

'Don't blame you,' Patrick said.

'So when I woke up in your flat I was furious with myself,' I said, choosing my words carefully. 'If anyone had seen me leaving your flat after we, well, you know, I'd have been back to square one. It would have been all over the *PostOnline* and I just couldn't face it.'

Understanding was dawning on Patrick's face.

'Ahhh,' he said.

'That's why I overreacted so badly,' I said. 'And why I was so horrible to you. But that doesn't excuse the things I said. I'm really sorry.'

Patrick nodded and I took that to mean I was forgiven. At least I hoped that was what it meant.

'Now Babs has got it into her head that I should get back with Matty. She says we're a brand and we're better together.'

'Holy crap,' Patrick said. 'So none of this is real?'

'Yes and no,' I said. 'I mean, I am an actress. I love acting …'

Patrick narrowed his eyes.

'But instead you're a celebrity,' he said.

'Spot on.'

I rested my chin on my hands.

'Babs says it's important to keep my profile high so that, when the dancing's over, I can start auditioning for other stuff,' I said. 'Except …'

I stopped. Patrick was very easy to talk to and I suddenly found myself about to tell him something I'd not even told Phil. I hadn't properly made sense of it in my own head yet.

'Except …' prompted Patrick.

'I've not really told her what kind of actress I want to be,' I said. 'I want to be in a BBC drama, or a crime thing, something on a Sunday night, you know the sort of stuff? But most of all I want to do *Downton Abbey*.'

Patrick nodded.

'But being a brand doesn't really work with those sorts of jobs, surely?'

I shrugged.

'Probably not,' I said. I put my face in my hands. 'I need to tell Babs what I want, but I'm terrified that, if I start changing things now, she'll stop representing me. She's really good at getting me endorsements and ads and hair-dye campaigns and magazine front covers. Now she's going to be obsessed with me getting back with Matty.'

'But do you want this guy back?' Patrick said.

'Not really,' I admitted. 'Not at all, in fact. I miss him, of course. I really miss him. I loved him so much and I never thought we'd split up. But I keep thinking about him throwing my stuff out into the street in front of all the photographers. And I'm pretty sure he made sure he was kissing that girl when I arrived, just to see my reaction …'

'He sounds really nice,' Patrick said.

I gave him a weak smile.

'Well, you might meet him later,' I said. 'Babs says he's going to be at this premiere. That's why she wants me to go.'

'I'll look forward to it.'

I stood up.

'So I just wanted to explain why I'd been such a bitch,' I said. 'And apologize.'

Patrick nodded again. Surely that meant I was forgiven?

'And I also wanted to tell you that I'm really committed to learning how to dance.'

Patrick made a face.

'Sure you are,' he said.

'Really,' I said. 'I've been practising.'

I threw him my phone.

'Put the music on and I'll show you.'

Patrick scrolled through and found Bruno Mars and I stood

117

– feeling more than a little self-conscious – in front of him, waiting. As the music began, I cleared my mind as Cora had told me, and then I started to dance. It was a bit clumpy and as I reached the bit in the middle – as far as I'd got with Cora – and stopped, I realized Patrick was staring at me, open-mouthed.

'What the heck was that?' he said. 'I mean, seriously. What the fricking heck was that?'

I felt my cheeks flame. Had I got this completely wrong?

'I've been practising,' I whispered. 'With a friend.'

Patrick leapt to his feet and grabbed my shoulders.

'That was amazing,' he said.

Relief flooded me. I looked straight at him.

'It was?' I said.

'It was.'

I threw my arms round him and squeezed and he laughed.

'Why couldn't you do that when I was teaching you?' he said.

'Embarrassment,' I admitted. 'Fear. Shame. Guilt … do you need me to go on?'

Patrick laughed again.

'So who's this friend who's taught you?' he said. 'Tell me everything.'

There was a knock on the door.

'That's our car,' I said. 'I'll tell you all about her on the way to the cinema.'

As the car stopped and started on its way into town, I filled Patrick in on Cora and her lesson.

'So she taught you all that in just one lesson?' he said in amazement.

'Well, you'd already taught me the steps,' I pointed out. 'She just told me what to do with them.'

Patrick shook his head.

'And she's old?' he said. 'How old?'

I shrugged.

'Her granddaughter said she was nearly ninety,' I said. 'But

118

she's not like some frail old lady. She's really sparky. I've never met anyone like her before.'

'Can I meet her?' Patrick said. 'I'd love to hear all her stories.'

'Oh, me too,' I said as the car got close to Leicester Square. 'I think something sad happened to her, but she didn't want to talk about it. I wondered if she'd lost someone in the war.'

'Amazing,' Patrick breathed. He looked a bit embarrassed. 'I'm a bit of a history geek,' he said. 'I studied the Second World War at college and wrote a paper on it. I've recorded all my grandfather's stories about him growing up. And I've interviewed his friends, too.'

I blinked at him.

'Really?' I said. 'I would not have predicted that.'

Patrick laughed.

'It's not something I talk about a lot,' he said. 'Is this it?'

We were pulling up next to Leicester Square.

'This is it,' I said. 'Are you ready?'

Patrick looked out of the window at the crowds.

'Shit,' he said. 'What do I do?'

I opened the car door.

'Stick with me, smile for the cameras and don't say anything other than hello,' I said.

But actually Patrick was a natural. Of course he was. He was a performer, wasn't he? Just like me.

We both turned it on for the paps, smiling and waving to the crowd. Patrick picked me up and spun me round, like we'd done in our *Strictly Stars Dancing* photo shoot and the cameras flashed madly.

We didn't see Matty or his group of hangers-on until the film had ended and we were leaving the cinema.

'There's always a party,' I was explaining to Patrick. 'But if you don't mind, I'd really rather just go home …'

I clutched his arm.

'There's Matty,' I said. He was standing in the cinema foyer on his phone. His arm was looped casually round the neck of a girl who I vaguely recognized as someone from a TV talent show. He was wearing a white T-shirt and jeans, he was tanned, and I had to admit he looked really, really handsome.

'You don't have to talk to him,' Patrick said.

I winced.

'I do,' I said. 'I'm going to be grown-up here – and it might get Babs off my back if she knows I've made an effort. Listen, I'm going to say hello. If no one from Matty's lot takes a photo, do you mind snapping a couple on your phone?'

'Seriously?' Patrick said.

I made a face.

'Seriously. I need Babs to see this.'

Patrick got his phone out and I threw my shoulders back, put on my best Betsy face and sauntered over to Matty.

Matty saw me coming. At least, I was fairly sure he saw me coming, but he didn't acknowledge me. Instead he pretended not to notice as I approached. Then he ended his call, pulled the girl towards him and kissed her.

The look of horror and humiliation on my face – which obviously three of Matty's mates captured on their phones – was real. I froze, not sure what to do next until I felt Patrick take my arm.

'Our car's here,' he said. 'Let's go.'

He steered me through the groups of people, out into the street and into our car, so quickly I barely had time to register what was going on.

I sat silently in the back seat as the car pulled away.

'So that was Matty,' Patrick said eventually.

I nodded, grim-faced.

'That was Matty.'

'Well,' said Patrick. 'He's kind of a douchebag.'

Chapter 23

Cora

1945

The wedding was at two o'clock. It was the only time the vicar could fit us in, and it worked out fine. The ceremony would be quick – only half an hour or so – and then we planned to go to a nearby pub to celebrate before Donnie had to leave. His train was departing Waterloo at six so he really had to be back with his regiment by five.

We were getting married at St Giles in the Field, not far from our boarding house on Charing Cross Road. It had escaped a lot of the bomb damage that had left London looking ragged, except for a nearby blast that had blown out one of its stained-glass windows. The vicar was a nice chap in his sixties and had been delighted to marry us. It was all planned to perfection.

But that didn't mean I wasn't nervous.

In fact, I was a wreck as Audrey and Fat Joan flapped around me that morning getting my dress ready, and doing my hair and face.

121

'Stay still,' Audrey said, jabbing me in the temple with a kirby grip while I wriggled on my chair. 'Stop jiggling.'

'I can't help it,' I said. 'I'm nervous. And I need the toilet.'

Fat Joan looked up from where she sat on my bed, examining my make-up.

'What is there to be nervous about?' she said. 'You'll go to the church, say some words, and that's it. Just like being on stage.'

I exchanged a glance with Audrey in the mirror and rolled my eyes.

'I just want it all to go right,' I said.

Audrey stood back.

'There you go,' she said. 'Like it?'

I looked at my reflection and nodded. She'd done a great job, pinning my hair up, and adding some small white flowers because I didn't have a veil.

'You're up, Joan,' Audrey said.

Joan uncurled herself from the bed and peered critically at my face.

'I'm not making any promises,' she said. 'But I'll see what I can do.'

Then she winked at me in the mirror just so I knew she was joking. Which was lucky, because I hadn't been completely sure.

Joan actually did a lovely job on my make-up, then I slipped on my dress and I was ready. Because the church was so close, we'd decided to walk. Joan went on ahead to make sure everything was set, and Audrey and I waited five minutes then followed.

As we got ready to leave, I turned to her.

'Thanks, Audrey,' I said. 'Really, thank you.'

I looked down at my dress.

'I couldn't have done any of this without you.'

Audrey gave me a gentle hug so as not to crumple my frock.

'It's nice to see someone having a bit of happiness,' she said. 'Grab it while you can, I say.'

122

'I'm grabbing it,' I said. I looped my arm through hers. 'Shall we go?'

It was a lovely walk. I had a little posy of flowers and, with my white dress, it was obvious I was a bride. People kept stopping us to wish me well, or calling out from across the street. By the time we got to the church, my cheeks were already aching from smiling.

Fat Joan was waiting outside, looking worried.

'What?' I said, as she rushed up to us. 'What is it?'

'He's not here,' she said to Audrey. 'Donnie's not here.'

Audrey sighed.

'Not here yet,' she corrected. 'It's only just gone two. He's probably been held up.'

But I was worried.

'He promised he'd be here early,' I said. 'He said he wouldn't keep me waiting.'

Audrey straightened the collar on my dress.

'Do I need to remind you that there's a war on?' she said. 'Anything could have happened to hold the poor fella up. Let's sit tight and wait a while before we start panicking.'

So we did. We went into the vestry and told the vicar what was happening. Then all three of us sat on the steps of the church and waited. And waited. And waited.

'Where is he?' I wailed as the church clock struck four. 'Oh, Donnie, where are you?'

I was bewildered. I couldn't understand how I'd gone from being so happy to sitting on the steps of a church, waiting for the man I loved, who clearly wasn't going to turn up. Had I been jilted? Had something happened to Donnie? Was he already on his way to France without being given a chance to say goodbye?

Audrey put her arm round me.

'Don't fret,' she said. 'I'm sure he's fine.'

There was a gentle cough from behind us.

123

'Sorry to bother you,' the vicar said. 'But I will need to prepare for Evensong before too long.'

Joan stood up.

'Could I speak to you for one moment?' she said, taking the vicar's arm and steering him into the church.

'She'll sort it all out,' Audrey said. 'She'll explain what's going on to everyone.'

I rested my head on her shoulder.

'Where is he, Audrey?' I said. 'Where's he gone?'

'I don't know, darling,' she said, rubbing my arm. 'But he's a good'un, remember? This won't be his doing, I'm sure of it.'

But I wasn't sure. 'You said they're all the same,' I said. 'You said men only want one thing.'

'But not Donnie,' Audrey said.

Joan appeared at the top of the steps.

'I've told all the guests what's happened but we need to go,' she said. 'The vicar's got Evensong soon.'

She bent down and spoke to me as though I were a child.

'He says you can come back any time,' she said. 'He'll marry you and Donnie whenever you want.'

Audrey helped me to my feet and brushed the dust from my dress. I shook her off, angrily.

'Don't,' I said. 'There's really no point.'

'Maybe he's gone already,' Joan said. 'To France, I mean. Maybe he's been sent away early and couldn't get word to you.'

'He could have phoned,' I said. 'Even if he phoned now, there'd be someone at the house to answer. They could have come to find us.'

'Perhaps everyone's gone out,' Joan said.

Audrey looked at her watch.

'What time's the train?' she said. 'The train he was meant to be on?'

'Six,' I said.

'I've got time,' she said. 'Joan, how much cash have you got?'

Joan dug into her bag and dropped a handful of coins into Audrey's outstretched palm.

'I'm going to Waterloo,' Audrey said. 'I'm going to find out what the bleeding hell's going on.'

She turned and ran down the steps from the church.

'He's a good'un,' she called over her shoulder. 'You'll see.'

I looked at Joan.

'What do I do now?' I said. I didn't want to stay at the church, but I couldn't bear to go back to the boarding house, either.

She looked apologetic.

'We have to go,' she said. 'We've got a show tonight.'

She took my hand.

'You don't need to go on, though,' she said. 'We can change things about a bit if we have to. We'd get by without you.'

I lifted my chin.

'I may have been jilted but I can still dance,' I said in defiance.

'Really?' Joan sounded doubtful.

I started walking back towards Charing Cross Road.

'Of course I can,' I said. 'It's best for me to keep busy. Stop me brooding.'

I threw my posy of flowers into the road and watched as it was run over by a passing taxi.

'It's just a normal day, after all.'

Chapter 24

Back at the boarding house, I went straight towards the narrow staircase that led up to our bedroom while Joan disappeared into the kitchen and shut the door behind her. I heard muffled voices as she filled whoever was in on everything that had happened.

Wearily I climbed the stairs and threw myself on the bed. I was bone tired, heartsick and at an utter loss about what to do. I was desperately keen for Audrey to return and tell me what she'd found out – and at the same time beside myself with dread about what she might tell me.

I simply couldn't believe that Donnie would leave for France without getting word to me somehow, or even turning up in the middle of the night to say goodbye. But I also couldn't believe that he would jilt me. I thought about him in Hyde Park yesterday, spinning round and telling the passing soldiers that we were getting married. Those didn't seem like the actions of a man who was about to run out on his fiancée.

And yet, I kept coming back to Audrey's words. That of course he'd be interested when I was young and pretty and slim and fun. But when life got too difficult – weddings, babies and the prospect of taking a strange British girl home to his perfect life in America – then he'd be off. Perhaps Donnie had just decided it was all too much. Maybe he would go home, marry a girl from Connecticut and forget all about me and our baby.

I lay on the bed for ages, going round in circles as I tried to make sense of my disastrous wedding day, but I couldn't. I simply couldn't understand what had happened.

After a while, I heard the sounds of people getting ready to go the theatre where we were performing that evening. Doors slamming, water running, music playing. I sat up just as Joan peeked her head round the door.

'How are you?' she said.

I threw my pillow at her.

'Don't,' I said. 'Don't do that sad voice.'

Joan came into the room properly, holding her hands up.

'I was just trying to be nice,' she said. 'It doesn't come naturally to me.'

'I know,' I said, almost managing to smile. 'Thank you.'

I watched her as she began brushing her beautiful hair.

'I'm going to come, too,' I said. 'I can't hide away in here.'

'Sure?' Joan asked.

'I'm sure,' I said. With a sigh, I pulled my dress over my head and threw it onto Joan's bed.

'Do you want it?' I said, trying to hide the catch in my voice. 'I don't need it any more.'

Joan paused in brushing her hair.

'Don't,' she said. 'Don't do this, Cora.'

I pulled on my uniform skirt.

'I have to,' I said. 'I have to be angry and I have to be uncaring because if I let myself show what I'm really feeling I'm scared that I'll start crying and never stop.'

Joan put her hairbrush down and made a move to come towards me. For a frightening moment I thought she was going to gather me up in her arms, so I turned away from her and took a shirt out of the wardrobe instead.

As I was doing up my buttons, Audrey came in. Her hair was

127

falling out of its roll and she had a streak of dust on one cheek. I stopped, stock still, and waited for her to speak, but she didn't say a word. Instead, she shut the bedroom door and leaned against it, looking at me with tears in her eyes.

'What?' I said. 'What is it? Is it Donnie? Where is he? Did you see him? Has he gone to France?'

Audrey shook her head.

'Sit down,' she said.

Numb with grief, I sat, my shirt still gaping open. Audrey came and sat next to me and took my hands in hers.

'I went to Waterloo,' she began. 'It took forever to get there, and I was worried I'd be too late, but I wasn't. They were just about to start getting on the train and I saw Paul, remember? That friend of Donnie's?'

I nodded, not understanding.

'So they'd not gone to France early?' I said. 'They were still in London.'

'They were,' Audrey said. 'But we're not sure about Donnie.'

I stared at her. It was as though I could hear the words but my brain couldn't put them into the right order to make sense of them.

Audrey carried on.

'As soon as Paul saw me, he grabbed me,' she said. 'He was shouting something and he kind of dragged me over to their lieutenant. It was packed on the platform and I wasn't sure what was happening.'

Joan sat down on the other side of me and began rolling on her stockings.

'Go on,' she said.

Audrey took a breath.

'It was so confusing at first, lots of people were shouting at me, and it was noisy and dirty, and it took me a while to understand.'

I stared at her.

128

'Where is Donnie?' I said, through gritted teeth. 'Where is he?'

Audrey shrugged.

'No one knows.'

'What?'

'No one knows.'

I tried to ask more questions, but I couldn't make a sound.

'They thought he'd run off with you,' Audrey said. 'That was why they all reacted so strangely when I arrived at the station. They were all asking where you were and what you were playing at.'

'But he hasn't run off,' I said, still trying to make sense of it all. 'He hasn't run off with me, because I'm here and he's not.'

Audrey squeezed my hand.

'I know, darling,' she said.

'So where is he?' I said, my voice shrill.

'Well,' said Audrey. 'It looks very much like he's gone AWOL.'

I stood up.

'No,' I said, feeling hysteria bubbling up in my throat. 'No. No No.'

'It's the only explanation for it,' said Audrey. 'He must have sneaked away when his day leave began, pretending he was going to come and meet you, but instead he went somewhere else. Got on a train, perhaps. Went to Southampton and got on a boat? Who knows?'

'No,' I said. 'You're wrong. Perhaps he's been in an accident. We need to phone the hospitals. We need to find him. Maybe he's hurt and needs our help.'

But Audrey was shaking her head.

'Dog tags,' she said. 'If something had happened to him, we'd know. Or at least his lieutenant would know.'

'Donnie wouldn't desert,' I said. 'He'll be shot. They'll find him and they'll shoot him.'

'Maybe they'll never find him,' Joan said. Audrey shot her a filthy glance.

129

'I'm sorry, Cora,' she said. 'He's gone and it looks like he's not coming back.

My head was pounding and my breath was coming in short bursts.

'What am I going to do?' I said, tears starting to come now. 'Oh Audrey, what am I going to do without him?'

Chapter 25

Patrick was right. Matty was a douchebag. The douchiest of douchebags, I thought to myself, even if I wasn't completely sure what a douchebag actually was.

The next day, the pictures taken by Matty's entourage were all over the *PostOnline* with the headline 'He's just not that into you'. It was horrible. I'd planned to look stoic as I came face to face with Matty, not humiliated. Again. As I was faced with him kissing another woman. Again. Still, at least I hadn't punched this one. In fact, I thought as I looked at the photos online, I actually wasn't that bothered. I tested my feelings the way you test a twisted ankle and discovered that while I was embarrassed – and, yes, jealous – about being replaced so publicly, I definitely wasn't pining for Matty. I was still in mourning for my old life where I had the routine of work every day, and parties every evening, and freebies being thrown at me everywhere I went, but when it came to my cheating ratbag of an ex – I was totally over him. Or at least, I was beginning to think there would be a day when I was actually totally over him – which I considered real progress. And I kind of hoped Babs would see the photos of my shame and decide my getting back with Matty was a terrible idea.

I'd just got out of the shower and I perched on the edge of my bed, wrapped in a towel, and scrolled through the pics once more. My hair looked a bit scruffy again, I thought. I'd have to sort out my extensions before the first *Strictly Stars Dancing* live show, which was just – I shuddered with nerves – two weeks away now.

My phone beeped with a message from Phil.

'Darling, just seen the pics. You okay?' it said.

'Fine,' I typed back. 'Just one of Babs's crazy plans that went a bit wrong. Drinks later?'

'No can do, sweetie,' Phil replied. 'Work thing.'

'No worries,' I wrote. 'Would be fab to catch up soon.'

I scowled as I threw my phone on the bed. I missed Phil and wanted a night out with him to share my woes and tell him about Cora. He and I had been best friends since we met at Rising Stars when I was fourteen. I'd nagged and nagged and nagged my mum to send me there, and when I'd finally got an audition, and then a place starting in year ten, I was thrilled.

I'd been a bit of a troublemaker at my old school but, as soon as I got there, I thrived. Blossomed. Bloomed. Whatever. I loved it so much, I worked really hard and I got really good grades – and some of the other kids didn't like that very much. But Phil did. He became my wingman and my protector, and I was his. He was still working out his sexuality back then and dabbling in set design, costume design and fashion, and I adored him from the very first time we met.

A year or so after I started at the school, when I was deep into studying for my GCSEs, loving every minute of my new life and planning to stay on at Rising Stars for A-levels, Mum met a new bloke. She'd had a few boyfriends over the years, but this one was different. Serious. And before too long they were making plans to move to Spain and run a bar. I was, obviously, devastated. I didn't want to move abroad when I was finally getting to do what I wanted to do, but I couldn't stay at home by myself, either.

If I stayed on my own I'd have to get a job – and that meant leaving school instead of doing A-levels like I'd planned.

Phil came to the rescue – at least his parents did. Mum moved to Spain with Graeme and I went to live with Phil. Mum gave them a bit of money towards my keep, and I worked at the local theatre – selling ice creams and programmes – at weekends and in the evenings to support myself. I loved living there, and I loved Phil's family. My own childhood had been a bit suffocating with it just being Mum and me. She'd wanted to be a West End star but getting pregnant with me when she was sixteen had stuffed up her plans – so she lived her ambitions through me instead. I didn't mind because I loved acting, but there was a lot of pressure on me and I felt like sometimes I was all Mum lived for. So I was pleased when she met Graeme and then had my baby brother and sister. It diluted the intensity of her ambition a bit and took the spotlight off me. But that didn't mean I hadn't missed her when she moved to Spain, no matter how fractious our relationship. It's hard enough being a teenage girl, without being one whose mum chose her new family over you.

Phil had stuck by me all these years but Bertie had come between us and I missed him now. I made up my mind to make more of an effort with boring Bert and get to know him. Perhaps if I could win him over, I could spend more time with Phil. I decided I'd invite them to my first live show. I could do with all the support I could get.

I looked at the photos again. God, I looked like such an idiot. This embarrassment had to make Babs think twice about me and Matty getting back together.

As though she could read my thoughts, Babs rang.

'Isn't it great?' she said before I even said hello. I winced. Clearly she wasn't about to abandon her plan.

'That's easy for you to say,' I said. 'You're not the one facing public humiliation.'

'Public adoration,' Babs said. 'The nation's going to take you

133

to their hearts. They're all rooting for you – have you read the comments?'

'I never read the comments,' I said, having learned my lesson about that a long time ago. 'If they're rooting for me, I'm pretty sure they won't want me to get back with Matty.'

'Rubbish,' Babs said. 'Balls.'

'Well, you know how it feels when you support a friend through a break-up and then they get back with the git who dumped them in the first place?' I said, glancing at the clock. Shit, it was late; I had to get ready for dance rehearsal. I put Babs on loud-speaker, and started to pull on leggings and a baggy T-shirt.

'You feel a bit put out, don't you?' I carried on. 'That all your advice and support was for nothing? What if the public think that way?'

There was a pause on the other end of the phone. I paused in pulling on my trainers and grinned. Perhaps Babs was going to listen to my opinion for once.

'Nah,' she said. 'You're more valuable together. Big *Yay!* spread on your rekindled love. Bob's your uncle. Money in the bank.'

I decided to change the subject. Maybe now she was pleased with me, I could tell her I wanted to be a serious actress without risking her wrath.

'Babs?' I said. 'I wanted to talk about some auditions for me?'

'Now is not the time to be worrying about auditions,' she said sternly. 'Concentrate on the bloody Rambo or whatever those dances are called, let me deal with your profile, and you'll have your pick of auditions by the time you're finished with *Strictly Stars Dancing*.'

'Sure?' I said. I felt uneasy about her advice, but, like I said, I was nervous about contradicting her at a time when I felt like I was on very thin ice, career-wise, and I thought – hoped – she knew what she was doing. My acting career may have taken a nosedive, but without Babs it would be over completely.

'Trust me.'

I ended the call, grabbed a bottle of water from the fridge and headed out of the door. I was actually looking forward to rehearsing today because Cora had got involved. She'd offered Patrick a studio in the school where she'd told me she used to teach and where she seemed to be well respected. It was just round the corner from the house so she had promised to look in on our practice session later that day.

I bounced down the road, eager to get started, and found Patrick sitting on the wall outside a huge double-fronted Victorian villa, with a modern extension to the side and the back.

'Is this it?' I blinked. The sign said London Academy of Theatre and Dancing so I knew it was.

'It is,' Patrick said. 'Pretty impressive, huh? There are more buildings, too – next door and on the other side of the road.'

'Wow,' I said, as we went inside the cool, tiled entrance hall and tried to locate the room we'd been given. 'What a great place.'

It was actually the perfect place to practise. The new term hadn't yet started so the building was quiet and still. The dance studio was at the back, in the new part of the school. It was well equipped and airy, with huge windows overlooking the common on one side, and three mirrored walls. It had great acoustics so our music sounded amazing, and best of all, I thought, the press had no idea we were here so I'd be left in peace. At least for a while.

We danced all morning and, apart from the odd grumble from Patrick, and the occasional – very small – tantrum from me when I got things wrong or didn't understand what he was asking me to do, things went very well.

Cora called in after lunch. She sat on a chair and watched us dance the whole routine all the way through twice before she said anything at all. Then she told us we were on the right track, offered Patrick some advice on choreography, which he accepted graciously, corrected my arms, sorted out our hold, and generally improved our dance. I felt so comfortable with her there, as though she was on my side. She wanted me to succeed because she loved dancing and she wanted everyone else to love it, too. It wasn't about the fame, or the applause, and it wasn't about her – which made her very different from my fame-hungry mother, and – though I hated to admit it – from media-savvy Babs.

'It really helps to have someone else involved,' said Patrick. 'I hope this doesn't count as cheating.'

'Course not,' I said, guzzling water in a most unladylike way. 'It's just making the most of our assets.'

Chapter 26

Cora was definitely an asset. We got into a routine of dancing on our own each morning, then going back to my flat for lunch, collecting Cora and going back to the studio with her in the afternoon for some of her advice and instruction. It worked brilliantly. I was learning what to do with my arms and legs, while Patrick, who'd never been on *Strictly Stars Dancing* before, was being taught how to teach. And Cora seemed to be getting younger by the day. She was full of energy – providing we didn't let her demonstrate the steps too often.

Patrick adored her. So did I, of course, but Patrick really adored her.

'She's done so much,' he said one morning as I put on my shoes before practice. 'I'd love to hear all her stories.'

'Well, from what she's said, I guess she started teaching in the late fifties or early sixties,' I said. 'God, it must have been brilliant to have been in London then. She'd have only been a bit older then than I am now. I bet she was gorgeous and always ready for a party.'

Patrick frowned.

'I wonder why she didn't perform,' he said. 'She's a wonderful dancer, even now. Why waste that talent on teaching?'

137

'Like you're wasting yours?' I teased. 'Maybe she didn't like performing. Not everyone does.'

'Weirdos,' Patrick said with a grin.

I chuckled. We were definitely on the same page when it came to that.

'My friend Phil hated it,' I said. 'He was a great actor, actually. But only when no one was watching. Put him on a stage and he dried. Mind blank. Hands sweaty. The works.'

Patrick shuddered.

'Think of all the things he's missing,' he said. 'The applause, the adoration …'

It was my time to shudder.

'Don't,' I said. 'I like TV when I get to do things over again if I make a mistake. The idea of dancing in front of real people is giving me goosebumps.'

Patrick pulled me to my feet and put his hands on my shoulders.

'Amy,' he said. 'You are a great dancer. You know the cha-cha backwards and forwards. You're picking up the American smooth like a pro. Your waltz is beautiful. Your samba is, well, not as disastrous as it once was …'

I punched him affectionately on his rock-hard bicep.

'You are going to love every minute of the live show. I promise you.'

And you know what? He was right. Eventually.

The day before the first show we spent rehearsing in the TV studio. At last I felt like I was on familiar territory. Back in my comfort zone, as it were. We were just round the corner from where *Turpin Road* was filmed and I thought about popping in, then changed my mind. It was all about *Strictly Stars Dancing* now.

I confess, I perhaps showed off a bit. Chatting with some of the crew that I recognized, showing Patrick round the studio and explaining how it all worked. I felt full of confidence and that only increased when I got into the costume department and tried on my dress. It was a super-short fringed bright-blue number, with a keyhole back to show off my tattoo of a shooting star in between my shoulder blades. When I put it on, the wardrobe assistants all applauded. What can I say – that's good for a girl's ego. They explained what they'd do with my hair, gave me a spray tan, and flattered me some more by telling me how beautiful I was and how amazing I'd look on screen. It was a pretty fun morning. But pride always comes before a fall and today was no exception.

Eventually, glowing with fake-sun-kissed health, and feeling ever-so-slightly smug, I pulled my jogging bottoms and vest back on and went to find Patrick, who was rehearsing with the other professionals for their group dance.

I sat at the edge of the dance floor in utter, absolute dumb-struck awe. They were incredible. Even just marking out the steps in between run-throughs they were better dancers than I ever hoped I could be.

One of the other competitors – Martin, the rugby player – came and sat down next to me and glanced at my stricken face.

'I know, right?' he said. 'Bloody brilliant.'

'It is their job,' I pointed out, trying to make myself feel better. 'I bet they wouldn't be so good at filming a scene, or swimming eight hundred metres.'

'That's true,' he admitted. We watched in silence as the pros finished their dance and then drifted away from the dance floor. One of them, a beautiful, willowy Aussie blonde beckoned to Martin.

'Time to practise with the band,' she said.

He gave me a look of pure terror.

'I'm up,' he said.

'Enjoy,' I called, as Patrick threw himself down next to me and I offered him a bottle of water.

'That was great,' I whispered. 'Really amazing.'

He gave me a killer smile.

'Nothing like it,' he said. 'It's just the best feeling. Now, shush and watch Martin and his partner Jessie. This is our chance to see where everyone else is at.'

Where everyone else was at was streets ahead of us. Martin was dancing the most beautiful waltz I'd ever seen. Even with him wearing tatty shorts and his beautiful partner in leggings that looked at odds with her ballroom shoes, it was beautiful.

'She's the world ballroom champion,' Patrick whispered.

I blinked in astonishment.

'She is?' I said. 'Wow. Are you a champion?'

Patrick made a modest face, then reeled off a list of achievements that made my head spin.

'Blimey,' I said. I was beginning to feel very out of my depth again.

'Patrick,' I said. 'I'm scared.'

He took my hand and I gripped it tightly.

'You'll be fine,' he said.

But actually I wasn't.

Our rehearsal with the band was a mess. I forgot the steps first time round. The next time I went back to turning left instead of right, and starting on the wrong foot, too. I almost fell over when Patrick spun me round. You name it, I did it. But it was our last rehearsal and we had no time to put it right.

When I got home that evening, I threw all my stuff into the flat, then went straight upstairs to see Cora. Her back door was open so I let myself in and found her drinking tea in the lounge, with some classical music playing.

She smiled at me when I came in.

'Darling Amy,' she said. 'How was the rehearsal?'

I sighed.

'Terrible,' I said. 'Dreadful. Awful. Embarrassing. A disaster. Do you want me to go on?'

Cora laughed.

140

'I think you've made your point,' she said. 'Don't worry, sweet-heart. You know the dance inside out. You'll be fine tomorrow.'

'Oh, no,' I said, knowing I was overreacting but not caring. 'Oh, no. I have been humiliated in public too many times recently. I can't do it again.'

Cora gave me a knowing look.

'Amy,' she said. 'Stop being dramatic.'

'I'm not being dramatic,' I wailed. Dramatically. 'This is how I feel. This is crazy. I'm hurt and tired and battered after breaking up with Matty and being sacked from my dream job. I need to go away somewhere – Spain, probably – to lick my wounds and stay with my mum. I don't want to go on national television and make a fool of myself.'

'Will visiting your mum help?' said Cora, who'd seen me cancel enough calls from my mother to realize we weren't exactly best friends.

'Yes,' I said. 'No. Probably not. But it'll help more than massive humiliation.'

Cora smiled in her calm way. She patted the sofa cushion next to her and I sat down. She took my hand and I looked at the difference between her lined pale skin with her perfect, shell-pink manicure, and my smooth brown hand with its raggedy nails and chipped polish.

'I know you probably can't imagine it but I was young once,' Cora said. 'Younger than you are now.'

I could imagine it, actually. Every time Cora danced the few steps she could manage now, I got a glimpse of the young woman she'd once been, but I didn't want to put her off, so I said nothing.

'When I was nineteen, just before the war ended, I was humil-iated by someone I thought was very close. Someone very special to me. Someone I thought I could trust.'

'Like Matty,' I said.

'Just like that,' Cora said. 'Of course that was long before celebrity magazines, or gossip columnists, but lots of people knew about it. And I was ashamed and embarrassed.'

'What happened?' I asked. But Cora shook her head.

'Oh, that's not important,' she said. 'What is important is how I got through it.'

'How did you get through it?' I said.

Cora patted my leg.

'I danced,' she said.

Chapter 27

Cora was right, of course. I was beginning to realize she was always bloody right. I wondered if all old people were as wise as she was. I didn't think so. Cora was one of a kind.

After I'd wailed all over her she gave me a stern look.

'So go on then,' she said.

'Go on then, what?'

'Dance.'

'I don't have the music,' I said.

Cora gave me a shove and I almost fell off the sofa.

'Not here,' she said. 'Go out. Go dancing. Phone Patrick. Phone that Phil. London is waiting for you.'

I sat up. Apart from the premiere, I'd not had a proper night out for ages. Suddenly it seemed very appealing. And, I thought, it might give me a chance to woo Bertie.

Grabbing my phone, I kissed Cora on her cheek and legged it out of the house and back to my flat, dialling Phil's number as I ran.

'Phil,' I said, when he answered, 'can I speak to Bertie?'

'Really?' he said, immediately suspicious. 'Why? Please don't tell him about those guys in Magaluf in 2006.'

'What guys in Magaluf?' I asked, momentarily distracted. 'I wasn't in Magaluf with you.'

'Never mind,' said Phil. 'Bertie! Bertie! Amy wants a word.'

'Hello, Amy.' Bertie came on the line, sounding distant and cool. 'You don't want to move back in, do you?'

'No,' I scoffed. 'I want you to take me dancing. All of us. Me, you, Phil and my partner, Patrick.'

There was a silence on the other end of the line.

'Dancing?' Bertie said eventually. 'What kind of dancing?'

'Your kind,' I said.

Bertie paused again.

'My way?' he asked.

'Absolutely.'

'Right. Meet us at Leicester Square tube in an hour,' he said briskly. 'Wear shoes you can walk in and don't wear too many clothes. It gets very hot in there.'

'An hour?' I said in alarm. 'But …'

'An hour,' Bertie said firmly.

He hung up. I rang Patrick and explained what was happening, expecting him to be a bit stuffy about going out the night before the live show. But he wasn't.

'Awesome,' he said. 'I'm leaving now. Meet you there.'

I dived into the shower and out again in record time, pulled my hair up into a topknot, threw on a little black playsuit and flat sparkly sandals – now it was September, the weather was turning and there was a whiff of autumn in the air so I thought it might be the last time I got to wear my summer clothes this year – then ran out of the door.

Bertie's kind of dancing was salsa. He was half Spanish and I knew there was a salsa club somewhere off Charing Cross Road that he went to sometimes. He led me, Phil and Patrick through the little side streets, down some iron steps and into a sweaty, heaving pounding mass of people. I stopped dead at the door and Phil and Patrick cannoned into me.

'Come on,' Bertie tugged my hand. 'Let's go.'

'I'm nervous,' I said, looking around. There didn't appear to be a dance floor. People were just dancing everywhere. 'Can't we just sit and watch for a while?'

Bertie gave me a prod.

'My way,' he said.

I shrugged.

'Go on then.'

Patrick was already twitching, his feet moving in time to the music.

'Have you been somewhere like this before?' I shouted in his ear.

He shook his head.

'Not really,' he said. 'I've done some flamenco, but this is different. It's brilliant, though. We can practise our cha-cha, too.'

He was right. It was brilliant. No one recognized me – or if they did, they didn't care. I danced with Patrick, I danced with Phil, I even danced with Bertie, who I realized was actually very nice, if a bit sarcastic. I wiggled my hips – something Patrick had been trying to teach me how to do for weeks – I shook my shoulders and I had a bloody ball.

When we finally emerged into the London streets, much later than I'd ever intended to stay out, I was giddy with fun and desperate – honestly, desperate – to get to the studio the next day for the live show. All nerves forgotten, I just wanted to dance. Cora was a clever old stick, I had to admit.

Of course, as I was getting dressed the next day I was trembling and terrified about all the things that could go wrong. I sat in the chair in make-up shaking so violently the make-up artist had to stop and get me a cup of tea. But at the same time I was keen to get out there.

And my goodness, was it fun? I'd never, ever imagined how much fun it could be. The other competitors were all so lovely and supportive. Some of them were amazing dancers, and others not so much. But we all whooped and cheered them on. The presenters were hilarious and the judges actually really kind. I felt like I was in a family where everyone just wanted me to do really well for myself, which was kind of odd because I'd never had much of a family growing up. Unless you counted Phil's parents – which I did, but it wasn't the same as having your own.

We were dancing fourth, which suited me. We didn't have to wait too long, but we weren't first. We stood nervously at the side of the dance floor while we were announced.

'Dancing the cha-cha, would Amy Lavender and her partner, Patrick Walker, please take to the floor …'

We got into position, I spotted Phil and Bertie in the front row of the audience, clapping furiously, the music started, and we were off.

At first it was hard not to be distracted. We'd practised on the dance floor with the band and the lights, but nothing could have prepared me for the noise of the crowd or the adrenaline that pulsed through my veins. And, inevitably, I messed up a few steps right at the start. But as the chorus began, Patrick pulled me close and whispered into my ear.

'Relax,' he said. 'Breathe. Clear your mind.'

And suddenly everything clicked and all I could hear was the music, all I could feel was Patrick's breath on my neck and the swish of the fronds on my dress, and all I could think about was what step came next.

As the music came to an end, I burst into tears.

'Don't cry,' Patrick said, putting his arm round me and taking me over to the judges. 'The audience hate whiners.'

But I wasn't whining. I was actually happy.

'Oh, I loved it, I loved it,' I told the judges who all laughed.

They all pointed out the mistakes I'd made but the head judge, whose name was Frank, lowered his glasses and gave me a grin.

'You messed it up a bit at the beginning,' he said. 'But you got it back and you delivered. Amy Lavender, I smell something very sweet with you.'

Overwhelmed with joy, Patrick and I rushed through the doors from the studio and jumped in delight.

'Well done,' he said, swinging me round. 'She's worked so hard,' he told the cameras that followed us everywhere. 'She really deserves this.' As we bounced up the stairs to join the rest of the competitors, Patrick squeezed my hand.

'You're a dancer now, Amy Lavender,' he said. 'You're always going to be a dancer.'

We got through to the next week of the competition, and I was thrilled. Even Babs sent me a message saying congratulations and that my tears as I finished were bound to help the public want my broken heart to heal. She'd started a rumour online that I'd cried because Matty wasn't there to see me dance, and though I wasn't happy about it, I was too excited about our next dance to care too much.

We were dancing an American smooth. It was based on a foxtrot, had three lifts in it, and we were dancing separately for a lot of it – which made me nervous – but it was the most beautiful dance I'd ever seen. Patrick had shown me clips on YouTube of it being danced and it reminded me of old-school Hollywood movies with Fred Astaire and Ginger Rogers. I'd even ordered some of the films from the internet, though I'd not had time to watch the DVDs yet – they were all stacked on top of my television, waiting for me to have some downtime.

And that gave me an idea.

It was the day after the live show and Patrick had given me some time off to recover before we started rehearsing again in earnest. I'd not seen Cora since yesterday morning when she'd wished me luck in the live show. I'd woken up still buzzing to find a note pushed through my letter box telling me how proud she was and saying she was out for the morning but we'd catch up this afternoon. So I hatched a plan. I dashed to the shops and bought some popcorn, and Coke in glass bottles. I wrote Cora a note asking her to join me for a special afternoon at two o'clock and stuck it to her front door. Then I spent the rest of the morning watching YouTube tutorials and trying to do my hair 1950s-style. I got there in the end; thanks to my trusty hair straighteners and a lot of hairspray, it was teased into loose waves and pulled away from my face. I added smoky eye make-up, red lips and wiggled into a pencil skirt. I felt amazing, actually – if a little overdressed for an afternoon watching films with my almost-ninety-year-old neighbour.

When Cora finally knocked at my door – at about one minute past two – I was super-excited.

'Hi, hello, hi!' I gabbled, showing her inside. She glanced at me, giving me a strange look as she took in my hair and make-up. I dragged her down the hall and into my living room.

'Ta-dah!' I said, throwing my arms out. 'Welcome to Amy's vintage cinema! I have popcorn, cola, and lots of Fred Astaire movies for us to watch.'

I grabbed the pile of DVDs.

'I've got *Swing Time*, and *Top Hat*, and *Shall We Dance?*' I showed her.

Cora looked … well, the only word for it was stricken. I was still holding out the DVDs but she didn't take them.

'Cora?' I said. 'What's the matter?'

'Oh, Amy,' she said, pushing my hand away. The DVDs fell to the floor with a clatter. 'I can't do this. I'm sorry.'

She spun round on her heel, remarkable quickly for a woman of her age, and left – letting the front door bang behind her.

I stood, shocked, in the middle of the room.

'What just happened?' I said out loud. Was Cora ill? Did she hate Fred Astaire? Did she not want to watch films all afternoon?

I had no idea. But what I did know was that Natasha had asked me to look out for her gran and so I had to find out.

Hoping she was okay, I went out the back door, up the steps into her garden and into Cora's kitchen, where I found her sitting at the table, looking very old for the first time since I'd met her.

'Oh, Cora,' I said, rushing over. 'Cora. What happened?'

She looked up and shook her head.

'I'm sorry, Amy,' she said, taking my hand and gripping it tightly. 'Sorry for worrying you. I'm fine.'

I dropped a kiss onto the top of her fine white hair.

'You don't look fine,' I pointed out. 'Let me make some tea and you can tell me all about it.'

Cora made to stand up but I pushed her down again.

'Don't even think about it,' I said. 'Have you any idea what you've done for me? I felt like an Olympic champion yesterday. I felt like I'd won at the competition that is my life – and that was because of you.'

Cora gave me a faint smile.

'It was all down to you and Patrick,' she said.

I waved away her protests.

'We danced it,' I said. 'But I did it because you told me how. You helped me so much, Cora. Let me help you.'

She looked at me and for a minute I thought she was going to send me away, then she sighed.

'Fine,' she said. 'Make the tea. There's some cake in the tin, too.'

I bustled round the kitchen. It felt good to be looking after someone else for a change. I made the tea in a pot, poured milk into a jug and arranged some slices of cake on a plate. I put it all on the table with some cups and saucers – Cora was very particular about her tea, which I liked – and looked at her expectantly.

'Go on then,' I said. 'Spill.'

'What a horrible expression,' Cora said, shuddering.

I gave her a sassy sideways glance.

'Don't change the subject, sister,' I said. 'Spill. What was that all about?'

Cora took a breath.

'When I was nineteen,' she said, 'all I wanted to do was be a film star like Ginger Rogers. The war was just coming to an end and I danced every night for the troops. I was part of the ENSA – do you know what that was?'

I shook my head as I poured the tea.

'We were in uniform,' Cora explained, a faraway expression on her face. 'We used to sing and dance and do comedy sketches all over the world – though I was too young to sign up until the war was almost at an end, so I mostly stayed in England. Dancing was my life. And I loved going to the pictures and watching my idols dance in the films. I planned to go to Hollywood, when the fighting was over. I wanted to be discovered. I wanted to be England's answer to Ginger Rogers.'

I frowned.

'But you didn't go?' I said. 'What happened?'

Cora lifted her chin.

'Donnie happened.'

'Oh, there's always a man involved,' I said, helping myself to cake. 'Did he break your heart?'

'He broke my heart and my spirit,' Cora said, looking so desolate that I felt tears pricking my own eyelids. 'He took my trust and he let me down and left me with nothing.'

I didn't speak. I couldn't speak.

'So I didn't go to Hollywood,' she said. 'Because I was broken-hearted when the war ended. Broken-hearted and alone.'

I got up and put my arm round Cora's shoulders.

'What did he do, this Donnie?' I asked.

'He left me at the altar,' Cora said. 'Wearing a dress just like the one Ginger Rogers wears in *Swing Time*.'

I gasped in horror.

'No way,' I said. 'That's so cruel. Did he ever give you an explanation?'

'Nothing,' she said. 'He went AWOL according to his commanding officer. I guessed he used the excuse of our wedding to disappear, but I never found out where he went.'

'Didn't you want to?' I said, aghast at the idea.

Cora shook her head.

'You have to understand what it was like at the end of the war,' she said. 'People were in the wrong places all over Europe. There were people looking for loved ones, parents searching for their children or children needing homes; there were soldiers returning as broken men – physically and mentally. It was chaos. And there were lots of women who'd been widowed, or abandoned. I wasn't so special.'

'So you gave up on your dreams?' I said, wiping away a tear.

Cora reached up and patted my arm.

'No,' she said. 'I didn't give up on my dreams. I just got some new ones.'

Chapter 29

Cora

1945

31 January, 1945
Dear Mum
I am writing to tell you some wonderful news. I am married! It all happened in a whirl because Jack – that's my husband's name – had to leave England in a hurry to go to France. I am sorry we didn't have time to tell you we were getting married. It was a lovely ceremony and I will tell you all about it when I next see you

I hope you are keeping well.
Your affectionate daughter,
Cora

***

10 April, 1945
Dear Mum
Sorry not to have told you my new name. I realized I'd not

told you Jack's surname as soon as I'd posted the letter, but
by then it was too late! It's Devonshire. I'm Mrs Cora
Devonshire – doesn't that sound grown-up?

I am very forgetful at the moment. Can you guess why?
It's because I am expecting a baby. I have told Jack and he is
delighted, as I'm hoping you will be, too. I hope to come down
to Worthing to see you soon

Yours,
Cora Devonshire

***

I chewed the end of my pen, going over what I was going to write
in my head. It was important to get it right and I only had one
chance.

It was the end of April – a month after my disastrous wedding
day – and I'd decided the time had come to tell my mother what
had happened. Or at least, tell her a whole pile of lies that I
thought would help her come to terms with having a daughter
who'd been left pregnant and alone.

I'd laid the groundwork carefully, writing a backdated letter
first (I hoped she'd assume it had been held up in the Post Office
– after all, things like that happened in wartime) to tell her I'd
got married to a fictional man named Jack – I took inspiration
from Donnie's surname, which was Jackson. Fat Joan, who was
a skilled and brilliant liar, had told me to stick to the truth as
much as possible.

'Means there's less to remember,' she'd said, chewing slowly
on a piece of gum she'd found in my sock drawer. 'So it takes
the pressure off you. You're less likely to slip up.'

So I'd invented Jack, who was like Donnie in every way except
one very important one. He'd not jilted me and run away somewhere. Even then I'd almost made a mistake when I'd not told
Mum what Jack's made-up surname was. I'd picked Devonshire

at random from a poster on the wall of the cafe where I'd written the letter. I'd bought a ring from Woolworth's at first but it turned my finger green. Audrey had come to the rescue, giving me a narrow band of gold that was polished smooth thanks to years of wear.

'Have this,' she said. 'It was my Auntie Vi's.'

I'd shaken my head.

'It's like a family heirloom,' I said, pushing her hand away. 'I can't take that.'

'Course you can,' Audrey said. 'None of us much liked Vi anyway. And she certainly didn't like her lying pig of a husband. So it's not like we're all in a rush to borrow it.'

I'd slipped it onto my wedding finger.

'From one lying pig of a husband to another,' I'd said, hugging Audrey. 'Thanks, Aud.'

So now I was Mrs Cora Devonshire, newly wed, mother-to-be, and – as Mum was about to discover – widow.

'NEXT,' the woman at the counter shouted. I jumped, startled out of my memories, and went to speak to her.

'I need to send a telegram,' I said.

'Fill this in,' she said, pushing some paper towards me. I picked up the pen and wrote 'Jack killed in action. Coming home. Cora'.

Then I pushed it back to her.

She glanced at it, then at me – her eyes dropping to my swelling stomach – and her face softened.

'Sixpence,' she said.

I paid her and turned to go.

'I'm sorry,' she said. I looked back. 'I'm sorry about your husband. Will you be all right?'

I shrugged, feeling guilty and angry that Donnie had put me in a position where I had to lie to nice people like her.

'I'll be fine,' I said.

I couldn't face going back to the boarding house. I knew I had to start packing – everyone was moving on and for the first time

I wasn't going with them. They were all heading to North Africa and Audrey was beside herself with excitement – mind you, it looked like the war would be over soon and I wasn't convinced their trip would happen. But nevertheless, I knew I couldn't go. My pregnancy was becoming much more pronounced and it was time for me to accept my lot and go back to Worthing. I had no money. No support. I wouldn't even have any friends in London once Audrey and Joan had gone. I had to swallow my pride and go back to Sussex.

I wandered along St Martin's Lane, taking in the bomb damage that made London look like a mouth full of missing teeth. I wondered what would happen to the city when the war was over and how it would be rebuilt and I felt sad that I wouldn't be here to see it.

'I'll come back,' I said aloud. 'One day. I'll come back.'

By the time I reached the boarding house, Mum had already replied to my telegram.

'Always welcome,' she had written. 'Send word which train you are on.'

I stood in the hall, staring at the telegram. This was not how I'd planned my life to be. I wanted to be a dancer. To dazzle audiences with my talent and to spread my love of movement. I wanted to dance on the stages of the gilded London theatres. I wanted to go to Hollywood and audition for producers – to give it my best effort, even if that effort came to nothing. I wanted Donnie. I did not want to go running home to my suffocating mother, and be tied down to a baby by the time I turned twenty.

'Come and have a cup of tea.' Audrey had found me. She tugged my sleeve gently. 'Come and sit down. I've got a plan.'

I gave her a small smile. Audrey always had a plan, but they didn't often come to much.

Audrey's plan was – as far as I could tell – to give her time to come up with a plan.

'Trust me,' she said. 'I've got a few irons in the fire.'

'I don't know what that means,' I said, sipping my tea.

Audrey shrugged.

'It means, trust me,' she said. 'I'm sorting it.'

'It's lovely of you,' I said. 'Really it is. But I just can't see what else to do.'

Audrey leaned across the kitchen table and lowered her voice. 'The war's nearly over,' she said.

'So they say,' I pointed out. 'But it's not up to us, is it? We're at the mercy of bloody Hitler and Churchill and whoever else wants to make decisions on our behalf.'

Audrey ignored me.

'It's over, Cora,' she said. 'And I reckon there's going to be a whole new world opening up for people like you and me.'

All I could imagine was hoards of damaged soldiers – like my poor dad – coming back to Britain and needing help. I couldn't see what Audrey saw.

'Give me a month,' she said. 'Go back to Worthing in a month.'

'Oh Audrey, I don't know …' I said. 'I can't wait that long.'

'Please, Cora,' she said.

I wavered.

'A week,' I said.

Audrey grinned.

'Two?'

'Fine. But then I have to go back to Worthing.'

I held up my left hand and showed her my wedding band.

'Or all Auntie Vi's troubles will have been in vain.'

Chapter 30

I barely saw Audrey for the next few days. She was up and out early, she was performing in the evening, and I saw her sneak out a few times clutching music and her dancing shoes and bits of paper that I thought might have been scripts. I had absolutely no idea what she was up to.

She was right about one thing, though. The war was over. Shortly after she'd got me to promise to stay in London for a while longer, Joan had burst into the kitchen.

'Mussolini's dead,' she'd announced with an air of satisfaction that suggested she was personally responsible. Then, just a couple of days later, Germany admitted that Hitler was dead, too, and suddenly things looked a lot brighter.

So, it was with a buzz of excitement that we'd gathered round the wireless to hear Mr Churchill announce that Germany had surrendered.

'Advance Britannia,' he said. 'Long live the cause of freedom.'

Joan reached over and switched the wireless off and we all sat for a moment in stunned silence.

'It's over,' Audrey whispered. 'It's bloody over.'

Joan let out a sort of strangled yelp of joy. Audrey glanced at her.

'Let it out, Joan,' she said. 'Go on, girl.'

Joan grinned, then she ran to the window and threw it open.

'It's over!' she screamed to the street. Below her, people cheered.

'Everyone's outside,' she said in excitement. 'There are folks standing on cars. Shall we go?'

Audrey nodded but I couldn't face crowds.

'You go,' I said. 'I'm tired.'

Outside the cheers and the shouts were growing louder.

'No,' Audrey said. She pointed out of the window. 'That there, that's history happening. Right in our faces. And we're going to go and be a part of it. Baby or no bleeding baby.'

'Audrey,' I protested weakly, but she wasn't listening.

'Mr Churchill said we were allowed a brief period of rejoicing,' she said, mimicking the prime minister's voice in a very funny way. She was always performing, Audrey. 'We can't argue with Mr Churchill.'

She handed me my shoes and obediently I put them on. Then we headed out into the streets of London to celebrate.

That first day, the parties were a bit haphazard, but by the following day people were starting to organize themselves. If there was anything we'd learned during the years of war it was how to make do with what we had. Everywhere we looked there were little children in fancy dress, people hanging bunting and throwing streamers. Folk singing and dancing, cheering, some crying. Someone dragged a piano out of a music shop in Charing Cross Road, and Audrey climbed on top and sang her heart out as Joan and I danced and the crowd around us cheered. It was bonkers and fun and I was so glad Audrey had encouraged me to be a part of it.

We wandered through the packed streets to Buckingham Palace and saw the King and Queen on the balcony with the princesses. I was the same age as Princess Elizabeth and I found myself wondering what she'd do in my position. She'd go home, I thought. If she was abandoned by a ruthless prince and left pregnant and penniless. But she'd be going home to a palace – not to a terraced house in Worthing with a mother who clung to her like a drowning man clings to a lifebelt.

Audrey looped her arm through mine.

'Bet you're glad you stayed, now, ain't you?' she said, beaming at me.

I nodded.

'Audrey,' I said. 'You're the best friend I've ever had.'

She nudged me.

'Oh, don't go all soppy on me now,' she said. 'I can't be bothered with it.'

But I knew she felt the same.

In the end I never got the train to Worthing. I sent Mum word that I was staying in London after all, and Audrey put her plan into action.

What she'd been doing these past weeks was visiting theatre people. Theatrical agents. Producers. Writers. Casting directors. Showing them what she could do and making sure they all knew her name.

I was astonished by her tenacity but I knew that, without my growing baby bump, I'd have been the same. Audrey wanted to act and that's what she was going to do.

Within about three days of Germany's surrender she'd had a meeting with one of London's best theatrical agents – a man called Harry Warner. She persuaded me to go with her, just so he'd know my name, too, and I grudgingly agreed.

Mr Warner's office was in a Soho side street, close to several theatres, and it was a mess.

'My secretary left me to go and work in the War Office,' he told us, apologizing for the chaos.

An idea struck me.

'I can't dance at the moment, but I could sort this out,' I said suddenly, looking at the piles of paper balancing on the dusty typewriter in the corner. 'Let me come and work for you.'

Mr Warner looked dubious, but Audrey, who'd been perching on the side of his desk, leapt to her feet.

'Cora's very organized,' she said. 'She's clever and she loves theatre.'

She lowered her voice and leaned towards Mr Warner.

'War widow,' she whispered as I pretended not to hear. 'It's very sad. She needs the money. You'd be doing a good thing.'

'What about that?' Mr Warner said, nodding at my stomach.

Audrey waved her hand as though my baby was a teeny tiny inconvenience that we could deal with much later.

'It's fine,' she said.

'All right,' Mr Warner said. 'Start tomorrow. And Audrey? You need to be at the Vaudeville at five o'clock for your audition. Do not be late.'

And that was it. The war was over and our new lives began.

Chapter 31

'So Cora never even tried to find him?' Patrick said, his brow furrowed. 'That's too sad.'

'Her friend tried.' I opened a can of Diet Coke and slurped gratefully – autumn was just around the corner now but the rehearsal studio was still too warm. 'But when she found out he'd gone AWOL, she just gave up.'

Patrick stretched out his legs. We were sitting on the floor in the studio, with our backs against the wall, eating lunch. It wasn't the most comfortable of spots, I had to admit, though I was sitting on a yoga mat I'd found in a cupboard, which took the edge off the hard floor.

'Here, sit on some of this,' I said, shuffling along to give Patrick some room. He shimmied onto the mat gratefully.

'Oh, that's better,' he said. We were very close together now. I could feel the blond hairs on his bare brown legs tickling my skin and the firmness of his muscled thigh against mine. His arm was pressed against my shoulder and I could smell his shampoo. It wasn't at all unpleasant. In fact, it was a very nice feeling. A very, very nice feeling …

'I could find out,' Patrick said.

I blinked at him, feeling myself blush at the thoughts I'd been having two seconds before.

'Find out what?' I said, confused. I stood up so I wasn't touching him any more and gathered up our rubbish.

Patrick grinned at me.

'Your head's in the clouds today,' he said. 'I could find out if this Donnie went AWOL.'

'Could you really?' I said. 'How on earth would you do that?'

Patrick held his hand out to me and I helped him up, enjoying the grip of his fingers on mine ... stop it, Amy, I told myself.

'I told you I'm a history nerd, right,' he said. 'I've done quite a lot of research into the war and I know where to look. He was a GI, right?'

'That's what Cora says,' I said. I danced a few steps of our American smooth just to check I was remembering them right.

'That's better,' Patrick said, watching in approval. 'So if he was a GI and he went AWOL it'll be recorded somewhere. Right, let's start from the beginning.'

He went over to the iPod and pressed play. We were dancing to 'Fly Me to the Moon' this time and I was loving every minute of the American smooth. I felt like a classical Hollywood star. Cora may not have wanted to watch the DVDs I'd bought, but I'd watched every single one, gobbling them up one after the other. I watched Fred Astaire, Ginger Rogers, Doris Day, then I watched Marilyn Monroe and Audrey Hepburn, Katharine Hepburn, Cary Grant – I watched them all. Sometimes I watched them on my own and sometimes Patrick joined me, pointing out moves in the dances that we could use and admiring their technique. I watched the acting, realizing again how much I loved it and how much I still had to learn.

I didn't ask Cora to join me, though. Her story had been so upsetting that I didn't want to rake it all up again. She was obviously still hurt by Donnie's betrayal, even though seventy years had passed.

'She said it was the not knowing that hurt her so much,' I told Patrick later as we walked home. 'That she had trusted him completely and believed in everything he'd said. She said even if he'd left her a note saying he was leaving she would have felt better.'

'Closure,' Patrick said. 'That would have given her closure.'

'Whatever,' I said. 'I'm not so sure. I knew exactly what Matty meant when he kissed that girl in front of me. And throwing all my clothes out of the window is about as closed as closure can get. Didn't make it any easier, though.'

'It would have,' Patrick pointed out. 'If this Babs hadn't stuck her nose in and forced you to open the closure.'

I giggled.

'Now you're not making any sense at all,' I said. But he was right. Matty's betrayal had been so huge, so absolute, that a definite line had been drawn under our relationship. In real life, I'd have grieved, and then I'd have moved on. But in my crazy, public, dictated-by-Babs life, I'd grieved and then, just when I was starting to feel better, gone back for more humiliation.

Somehow I didn't want to discuss Matty with Patrick, though.

'So do you think you can find out if Donnie went AWOL?' I said. 'And give Cora some closure?'

'I can definitely find him,' Patrick said. 'I've got a feeling the US Army shot deserters, though. So it might not be a happy ending.'

'I think at this stage it doesn't matter,' I said. 'As long as there's an ending.'

We'd arranged to spend the evening together watching *Gentlemen Prefer Blondes*, so Patrick came into the flat with me. While I had a shower, he made dinner. Then he had a shower and we took our plates of Caesar salad, sat on the sofa and ate in companionable silence.

While I put the DVD on, Patrick pulled his laptop out of his bag.

'I reckon I can make a start on finding him now,' he said. He connected to my Wi-Fi, jotted down the name Donald Jackson on the back of his hand, and began poring over various websites while I watched the film.

It had been a long day and I was tired. I'd thought I was fit before I started dancing, but training for hours every day was really taking it out of me. On the plus side, though, I'd never looked so toned and lithe. My fellow competitors all said the same – they'd all shed pounds, toned up, and our regular fake-tan sessions made us glow. It was like dancing was the magic ingredient we'd all been looking for to change our lives for the better.

I shifted on the sofa to get more comfortable, my eyes growing heavy. Patrick glanced at me.

'Come here,' he said, 'You look worn out.'

I rested my head on his shoulder and he put his arm around me, arranging himself so he could keep typing. I was warm and safe and – I suddenly realized – happier than I'd been for weeks. Months perhaps. I closed my eyes as Marilyn sang about diamonds being a girl's best friend.

'She's wrong,' I muttered. 'Diamonds mean nothing.'

Patrick chuckled.

'I thought every girl wanted diamonds,' he said.

'Not me,' I said. 'And not Cora, either. She just wanted Donnie. She didn't care about being rich or having a fancy wedding. She said all her friends collected their clothing coupons so she could have a dress.'

'That's sweet,' Patrick said.

'Matty bought me all sorts,' I said, opening my eyes. 'Shoes, mostly. But also dresses, jewellery, holidays. Some of it he got for free but it came with conditions. I had this ridiculous watch that he insisted I wore whenever we were likely to be photographed.'

'Which was every time you went out,' Patrick said. He'd stopped looking at the laptop and was looking at me instead.

'Oh, not every time,' I said, even though it pretty much was.

165

I knew Patrick would think the reality of my life with Matty was shallow and meaningless, and I didn't want him to know all the details.

'But he gave me all that stuff and it didn't mean anything because he was sleeping with other women,' I carried on. 'It was like he was decorating a Christmas tree with glittery baubles, but the Christmas tree itself was all dead and dried up.'

'Whoa, all righty there, Socrates,' said Patrick, giving me a cheeky grin. 'That's a bit deep.'

I laughed.

'I mean we were playing a part,' I said. 'It was just like I was being Betsy at work and Amy Lavender at home, but I never got to be me.'

'Do you miss her,' Patrick asked, his blue eyes studying my face so intently, I felt uncomfortable.

'Betsy?' I said. 'I do, actually. I miss her a lot. I liked her, even if she was always in trouble.'

'Not Betsy,' Patrick said. 'Amy Lavender. The old Amy Lavender. The fake Amy Lavender.'

'Oh, her?' I said, dismissively. 'I don't miss her one tiny bit.'

'Really?'

'Really.' I was firm. 'This is me, the real me. And frightening as it is to put myself out there, I think people like me.'

'I definitely like this one better than the other one,' Patrick said. He gave me a slow smile that made my stomach flip over. Oh, dear, I thought. Oh, dear.

'What about the douchebag, though?' Patrick said, oblivious to all the feelings I was feeling. 'Aren't you supposed to be getting back with him?'

I blinked at him.

'The douchebag,' he repeated. 'Matty. Aren't you supposed to be rekindling that flame?'

'Ah, I'll speak to Babs,' I said, deciding in that second to be more assertive with my agent. 'We'll come up with a new plan.'

166

Chapter 32

Babs, however, had plans of her own.

'Just phoning to wish you good luck for tonight,' she trilled down the phone as I sat in the make-up chair at *Strictly Stars Dancing* that Saturday night. 'You'll be brilliant.'

'I hope so,' I said. 'I really don't want to let Patrick down. He's worked really hard, and so has Cora.'

Cora had shown real determination as regards making me a dancer. She was in the audience tonight with Natasha. I wanted to make her proud of me and I was determined to dance as well as I could.

I had the most beautiful dress to wear – it was long and backless with a beaded bodice and a super-swishy skirt. I was discovering there were many good things about taking part in *Strictly Stars Dancing*, and the costumes were definitely up there among the best.

'So it should all work out beautifully,' Babs was saying. I'd completely missed what it was she was saying.

'Beautifully,' I agreed, watching the make-up artist spray-fix glitter to my cheekbones.

Babs laughed.

'I must say I thought you'd argue,' she said. 'But I'm glad you've come round to my way of thinking.'

Hold on, what had I just agreed to?

'Must dash, darling,' Babs said. 'Mwah!'

She hung up and I stared at the phone, wondering what she was planning. But then the make-up artist asked me to shut my eyes so she could put my false eyelashes on, and Marianne, the newsreader, started asking me about our dance, and I was caught up in the whirl that was show night on *Strictly Stars Dancing*.

The evening went by so fast, I felt dizzy. Just like last week it was a mixture of adrenaline, nerves, joy – every emotion. This time we were dancing last which was not fun as we had to stand and watch every other competitor doing their thing, feeling our nerves building until they were almost unbearable. But finally it was our turn.

'Ready?' Patrick whispered, as the band struck up 'Fly Me to the Moon.' 'Let's go.'

The dance went perfectly. I loved every second of it. I was Ginger Rogers, Doris Day and Marilyn Monroe all rolled into one. My heart was pounding and my cheeks were glowing. I was breathless and excited and just having so much fun.

As the dance ended, the audience exploded into applause and lots of them stood up. I was so thrilled I bounced up and down on my toes and Patrick gave me a huge bear hug.

'Come here,' said Melissa leading me over to the judges. 'What a way to finish the show. That was wonderful.'

'Oh, I loved it, I loved it,' I said.

'And you've got a special person in the audience tonight, haven't you, Amy,' Melissa said.

I beamed at her.

'I have,' I said, I turned round, searching for Cora, who I knew was sitting close to the band – I'd seen her when I'd come onto the dance floor and she'd given me a wink. But the presenter took my arm and turned me the other way.

'He's over there,' she said, conspiratorially. 'And doesn't he look proud?'

168

Confused, I looked over to where she pointed. Matty was sitting in the front row of the audience, clapping wildly. As I caught his eye, he blew me a kiss and the audience went crazy, whooping and shouting.

I froze, clutching Patrick's arm. So that's what Babs had told me. Why hadn't I listened?

'Keep smiling,' Patrick said into my ear. 'Keep smiling and it'll all be over soon.'

So I brought out fake Amy Lavender. Smiling like a loon as the judges said nice things, none of which I listened to, and grinning as we got our (brilliant, actually) scores. And then I sneaked backstage and phoned Babs to shout at her, while she gushed at how fabulous it all was.

'I don't want to see him,' I said. 'I'm not speaking to him. Not now.'

'You don't have to, doll,' she said. 'Your face when you saw him says enough. It'll be in all the papers tomorrow. And it's online already. Everyone wants you back together. You're going to be even bigger than you were before.'

'Baaaaaabs,' I wailed. 'I don't want him back. He's a douchebag.'

'He's a what?' Babs said.

'That's what Patrick calls him,' I said. 'He's right. He is a douchebag. He cheated on me, Babs.'

'He may have cheated on you,' she said. 'But he also helped create the Amy Lavender brand and you nearly destroyed that when you punched that little slut he was kissing. Matty is useful to us. Do you think you'd have got on *Strictly Stars Dancing* without being Matty's ex?'

'Maybe not,' I said.

'Definitely not,' Babs snapped. 'Listen, you guys are great together. You're super-cute, super-photogenic, and he's promised to give up all the other women. I'll get you a holiday for after this dancing is over and you can go away, get some sun, have a

169

bit of time together. You'll soon see that you're made for each other.'

'I don't want a holiday,' I hissed down the phone, the anger I felt at being caught out making me bold. 'And I don't want Matty. I want an audition.'

'Yeah, yeah,' Babs said. 'I know.'

Her voice softened.

'Listen, Amy. Don't you think you'll be better sticking to what you know? You can make a lot of money this way – endorsements and clothing lines and all that.'

'Babs,' I began. 'I'm an actress …'

'I've had a call from *Rosamund Street*,' she said. 'They're interested …'

'Stop,' I said. 'I loved *Turpin Road* but I don't want to do another soap. I want to do something different. A new challenge. I want to make the most of everything I learned on *Turpin Road* and take on something new.'

I took a deep breath. If I didn't tell her now, I'd never do it.

'I want to do *Downton*,' I said.

There was a pause.

'Okaaaaay.' Babs sounded doubtful. 'Well, I'll see what I can do. But I'm sure they'll be more interested if you're more high-profile.'

'It doesn't have to be *Downton*,' I said, starting to backtrack. 'Anything Sunday night drama-y. That army thing, maybe? Or a crime thing? What about that forensics one? That's good.'

'I'll sort it,' Babs said, in a tone that made me think she wouldn't. 'But you need to keep up your side of the bargain. I've spoken to Matty's agent and he agrees you're better together. You can do this, Amy. You know it makes sense.'

'So what about Matty and me – do we get a say in this?'

The silence at the end of the phone told me we probably didn't. I sighed.

'I was doing okay, you know?' I said. 'I like dancing, I've made new friends. Tonight was amazing. And I've learned that I'm fine on my own, Babs. I'm even finally getting over my bloody mother sodding off to Spain, finally. I'm okay.'

'I know, darling,' Babs said. 'I know.'

'Matty broke my heart,' I said. 'And it was horrible and awful, but I'm doing fine now. I don't want to go back there, Babs.'

'You're so much stronger than you think you are, doll,' Babs said softly. 'Own this. Make it yours. Go into it with your eyes open and make it work the way you want it to work.'

I leaned against the wall, suddenly exhausted. I could hear the cheers of the audience in the studio and more than anything I wanted to be in there with Patrick, watching the dancing.

'And you think it'll help my career?' I said.

'I know it'll help,' Babs said. 'If you do it on your own terms.'

'What do you mean?' I said.

'Use him,' she said bluntly. 'Use Matty to keep your face in the magazines, then dump him when we don't need him any more and make the most of that, too. This is just another step on your road to success, Amy.'

I shuddered.

'That's a terrible, terrible thing to do,' I said.

'It's what Matty's done up until now.'

She was right, even if it was hard to hear.

I took a breath.

'Fine,' I said. 'If you honestly think this is the right thing to do then I'll think about it.' I was annoyed that she'd taken the shine off the perfect evening but, as ever, I didn't tell her what I was honestly thinking. 'Just get me a bloody audition.'

I jabbed my phone crossly and went to get changed. I hung up my dress sadly, hoping I'd get to wear it again one day. Then I headed off to find Cora. She and Natasha had press tickets so we were meeting them in the bar, which was in a huge marquee at the side of the studio. I spotted them at once. Cora was regaling half the room with a story about something or other, and illus-

171

trating it with dance steps every so often. Around her, the professional dancers and contestants alike were rapt.

I hung back and watched her for a while. She really was wonderful.

'She's great, huh?' Patrick came up behind me.

'Oh, she's amazing,' I said.

He threw his arm casually round my shoulder and I felt my heart begin to beat a bit faster. What was going on here?

'So what about Matty turning up?' he said, nudging me.

I made a face. I couldn't bear to talk about it.

'Babs says it's all part of her plan,' I said. 'It's a nightmare.'

Patrick turned his head and kissed my temple. Immediately my legs went to jelly. I was relieved he still had his arm round me because, if he hadn't, I was sure I'd have fallen over. Oh, Amy, I thought. You really are in trouble.

'It'll all work out,' he said. 'You'll see.'

I gave him a weak smile.

'I bloody hope so,' I said.

Chapter 33

I was up and at Cora's kitchen door bright and early the next morning. So early, she was still in her dressing gown, pottering around the room, with her white hair in a cloud around her head.

'Amy, dear God,' she said, as I rattled the handle impatiently, waiting for her to let me in. 'What on earth are you doing here so early on a Sunday morning?'

'I need to speak to you,' I said. 'I need advice.'

Cora gave me a sharp look.

'Is it romantic advice?' she said.

'Yes,' I wailed. 'Please help me.'

'I'm not the romantic type,' she said. 'And I'm not dressed.'

'I'll buy you breakfast,' I said. 'I'll go now, and you can get dressed, and when I'm back with the food, we can eat and I'll talk.'

Cora rolled her eyes.

'Fine,' she said. 'But I'm not promising that I'll be any use.'

Thrilled and relieved in equal measure, I dashed off to the nearby cafe to buy two bacon sandwiches on their amazing freshly baked bread, plus some pastries, and fruit, and everything I could think of that would make a tasty breakfast.

I arranged it all on Cora's kitchen table, made some coffee and a pot of tea, then I sat and waited for her to appear.

She came down eventually, dressed in a white blouse and wide-legged black trousers. She'd done her hair and it was twisted into a knot on the back of her head, and she'd even put on some lipstick.

'You're so elegant,' I sighed, looking at her with undisguised envy.

'So are you,' she said, pulling out a chair and sitting down. 'When you want to be.'

I glanced down at my jeans and slouchy T-shirt and grinned.

'This is my Sunday outfit,' I said.

Cora raised an eyebrow, but her smile told me she wasn't really disappointed in me.

We sat and ate for a while, savouring the salty bacon and soft white bread, then she wiped her mouth carefully.

'So, tell me,' she said. 'What's bothering you?'

I sighed dramatically.

'Matty,' I said. 'He was there, you know, last night?'

'I saw. And I saw how you reacted when you spotted him. You weren't pleased to see him?'

I shook my head.

'He's a douchebag,' I said. 'If he wants me back then it's going to take more than Babs nagging me and him dragging his sorry arse to a television studio.'

'Do you want him back? Cora asked.

I paused, with my mug of coffee halfway to my mouth.

'No,' I said. 'I don't. But now Babs is saying we need him.'

Cora frowned.

'And you listen to Babs because …?'

'She's my agent,' I said. 'She's been really good to me over the years and I don't want to lose her. She knows what she's doing, Cora, and she's really the only person I've got left.'

Cora looked disbelieving.

174

'Well, that's not true,' she said. 'I worked for an agent for several years, you know?'

'I didn't know that,' I said, interested.

'He was a theatrical agent at first – television wasn't the big deal it is now, back then. He was brilliant at his job. He got my friend Audrey parts in all sorts of things – plays on the stage and on radio, a few films in the sixties, and when she'd all but given up acting, he was still trying to persuade her to go to auditions.'

I couldn't imagine giving up acting. I said so and Cora smiled.

'Life sometimes takes us down unexpected paths,' she said. 'Audrey discovered she loved teaching. So did I, in fact.'

'You never missed performing?' I asked.

Cora's eyes misted over for a second.

'At first,' she admitted. 'But I had a baby to look after, and that kept me very busy. It wasn't easy doing everything on my own.'

Of course. I'd not put two and two together when she'd spoken about Donnie before but suddenly I realized she must have been pregnant with Natasha's mum at the end of the war.

'Donnie left you when you were pregnant?' I said, aghast at the thought.

Cora nodded briskly.

'He did,' she said, pouring herself more coffee. 'But we got along without him.'

She looked at me over the top of her mug.

'So I know about agents,' she said. 'Even the very best ones – the brilliant ones, even, like my Mr Warner – are out for whatever they can get. This Babs might know what's best for her coffers, but does she know what's best for you?'

She had a point.

'I keep thinking maybe I could just give it a go,' I said. 'Go along with Babs's plans, get back with Matty. I miss acting, Cora. I'm an actress – even if I've not been doing much acting recently – and Babs seems to think if I can stay in the public eye, then

I'll get more auditions for serious acting jobs. So I can do all that, and if it doesn't work out with Matty, then so what? By then I'll be in *Downton* or *Mr Selfridge* or a pilot for a US drama. I'll have got what I needed and no harm done.'

Cora nodded.

'That's good; you're thinking practically,' she said. 'I've found it's better to be ruled by your head and not your heart. There's less chance of being caught out that way.'

I smiled at her, relieved she understood the way my mind was working on this issue.

'That's it exactly,' I said. 'Except there's a tiny problem.'

Cora looked questioning.

I took a breath.

'Patrick,' I muttered.

'What about him?'

'Well,' I said. 'We've been spending a lot of time together. Rehearsing and watching old movies. He's really funny, you know. And clever – he's so clever. And I just like hanging out with him. Being with him …'

Cora tutted.

'Oh, for God's sake,' she said. 'You've bloody well fallen for him.'

'Cora,' I wailed. 'I didn't mean to. What am I going to do?'

'Does he feel the same way?'

'No,' I said glumly. 'I think he could have done, right at the beginning, but I was very adamant I didn't want him to think of me like that.'

Cora tutted again.

'He treats me like his sister,' I explained. 'He's always wrestling me and getting me in a headlock. One day he's going to scrub his knuckles on my head and call me buddy, I swear.'

'Then you need to get over him,' Cora said. 'If it's not happening, so be it. Move on. Move back to Matty, if you want. Find someone new. Don't put your life on hold for a man.'

'Is that what you did?' I said softly. 'Put your life on hold for Donnie?'

Cora looked cross and for a second I thought she wouldn't answer. Then she looked past my shoulder, into the garden and I could see she was thinking about the question.

'In a way,' she said, 'I suppose I did. But I wasn't waiting for him to come back – I knew he wouldn't do that. It was more that I'd been burned. I'd not had any doubts about him. Not one single misgiving. Audrey was sceptical at first, because she'd seen how badly her mum was treated by her dad, but Donnie had even won her over by the day we were supposed to get married.'

'So you didn't trust yourself?' I said.

Cora nodded.

'If I'd misjudged him so badly, then maybe I'd do it again,' she said. 'And of course I had Ginny to think about. I couldn't get mixed up with the wrong man again. So it was easier to stay away.'

I reached across the table and took her hand.

'We can find out what happened to him,' I said. 'Patrick's a massive history geek. He's desperate to find Donnie for you and he's already started looking at some US Army records. Maybe we can track him down – he could even still be alive – and you can confront him. You could get some closure.'

'That's a horrible American word,' Cora grumbled.

'Do you want us to find him, Cora?'

She gripped my fingers tightly but she didn't answer.

'Cora,' I said again. 'Do you want us to look for Donnie?'

When she finally spoke, it was so quiet I had to strain to hear her.

'Yes, please,' she whispered. 'Find Donnie.'

177

Chapter 34

'So now we know his name, and his rank and everything, it should be a piece of cake to track him down,' Patrick said.

I handed him the piece of paper on which Cora had written Private Donald Jackson, 22nd Armored Division and he nodded.

'They were a liberating division,' he said.

I stared at him blankly.

'They were some of the troops that served in northern Europe right at the end of the war,' Patrick explained patiently. 'They liberated the concentration camps, some of them. They must have seen some dreadful things.'

I peered over his shoulder at the screen, but there were just rows and rows of names and I couldn't make head nor tail of it.

'Urgh, it'll take ages to go through all this,' I said. 'We'll never find him.'

Patrick grinned at me.

'I love this stuff,' he said. 'If he's there, I'll find him.'

He shut the laptop with a snap.

'But for now, we have to learn how to Charleston.'

I bounced up and down in excitement.

'This is the dance I've been waiting for,' I told him. 'I can't wait.'

We were dancing to a song from *Bugsy Malone*, which I was thrilled about.

'This was the first play I ever did,' I told Patrick, as he played the music. 'It was the one that gave me the acting bug.'

'And now you've got the dancing bug, too,' he said.

I certainly had. I'd never imagined enjoying *Strictly Stars Dancing* as much as I did, but I loved everything about it and I was so excited about dancing the Charleston, which struck me as a very actor-y sort of a dance.

'You should be good at this one,' Patrick said. 'It's very showy.'

I gave him a whack on his arm.

'What are you saying about me?' I laughed. I was trying very hard to keep things normal between us, despite the fact that every time he touched me – which was quite a lot considering we were dancing together all day every day – it was like little electric shocks fizzed their way all over my whole body. Matty had never given me electric shocks – unless you counted the time he tried to get his toast out of the toaster with a fork and blew it up. I was pretty shocked that day and electricity was involved …

'Concentrate, Amy,' Patrick said.

I giggled.

'Sorry, boss,' I said. 'Let's start at the beginning.'

All week our rehearsals went brilliantly. I picked up the steps so easily it was like I was a different person from the clumsy, clumpy girl who'd started the cha-cha on the wrong foot all those weeks ago. We were in the zone, in tune with each other, in harmony with the music and generally having a ball.

A couple of days before the live show, I was lying on the studio floor, exhausted, after another lively practice session when I had an idea.

'I'm going to get my hair cut,' I said, sitting up.

'Good story, bro,' Patrick said. 'Tell me another just like it.'

I stuck my tongue out at him.

'Oh, ha bloody ha,' I said. I pulled my long locks up off my neck and held them out. 'I need to get my extensions taken out anyway, and all this hair belongs to the old Amy. I need a new style.'

'Right,' Patrick said, without much interest.

'I'm going to go now,' I said, pulling my phone out. 'Francesca will fit me in, no problem. Meet me after and we can do some more Donnie stuff, right?'

'Okay, bossy,' Patrick said. 'Where do you want to meet?'

'Horse and Hounds?' I said, naming a local pub that did great food and was always friendly.

I kissed him goodbye, carefully making sure my lips didn't actually make contact with his skin, and raced off to find Francesca.

'Oh. My. God,' I said, staring at my reflection in the mirror.

Francesca looked horrified.

'You don't like it?'

I turned my head left and right, checking out my new look. I'd sat down in the chair with long dark hair, in tumbling waves. It was partly my own and partly my very expensive extensions. Francesca had taken out the extensions, lopped off the rest, and I now had a choppy, chin-length bob with blonde highlights. I was fairly petite with a small face and delicate features and I suddenly realized my old hair had dwarfed me. Now my eyes looked huge, and everything seemed more in proportion.

'I bloody love it,' I said. She looked relieved.

'Well, thank God for that,' she said.

I paid her the eye-watering amount she charged – worth every penny in my opinion – and went to meet Patrick. I spotted him outside the pub on his phone, and darted across the road to catch him.

He ended his call when he saw me and grabbed both my hands.

'Wow!' he said. 'You look so different.'

He spread my arms wide and leaned back, studying me. I

beamed at him, trying not to think about how pleased I was that he liked my new look.

'Gorgeous,' he said, nodding. 'And so right for the Charleston.'

'I know,' I said. 'Let's hope it's lucky.'

Over tapas, Patrick filled me in on what he'd found out about Donnie so far.

'I've found his war record,' he said. 'So we know he existed.'

'Of course he existed,' I said.

Patrick grinned.

'He could have told Cora a fake name,' he pointed out. 'If he was that much of a rat.'

''Spose,' I said. 'But at least we know he was who he said he was.'

He pulled up the page on his phone and zoomed in to show me. It was just a list of names, but about halfway down was the name Donald Jackson.

'I've submitted a request to get his record,' Patrick went on. 'It doesn't normally take very long – a week at the most, I reckon.'

'A week?' I was disappointed. 'Oh, I thought we'd be able to find it straightaway.'

'Might be faster,' Patrick said. 'Sometimes it comes back within a few hours, but sometimes it's days. Depends how many requests they've got at the time, I expect.'

'Fair enough,' I said. 'I just really want Cora to know what happened to him. Maybe he's still alive and she can find out why he left the way he did.'

I popped a garlic prawn into my mouth.

'It's really affected her,' I said. 'Being abandoned the way she was – left pregnant and heartbroken. She's very cynical about romance.'

'Not surprised,' Patrick said.

'She thinks I should get back with Matty,' I admitted. 'She says it's the practical thing to do.'

Patrick looked horrified.

'Really?'

'She's got a point,' I said. 'Babs reckons being with Matty will keep my profile high, so I can get some auditions for things I want to do.'

'You're a really good actress, Amy,' Patrick said. 'Surely any agent worth her salt can get you auditions without you having to saddle yourself with that loser?'

I shrugged.

'Apparently not,' I said. 'Babs knows about this stuff, Patrick.'

'You should be a bit firmer with her,' he said. 'Tell her to get you auditions or you'll get a new agent.'

'Yeah,' I said, but I knew I would never be that forceful with Babs. I was firmly of the opinion that I needed her way more than she needed me.

Chapter 35

I was having the best time. The lights were dazzling, the music loud, the audience cheering and I was enjoying every single second of dancing the Charleston in the live show. I was smiling so broadly, my cheeks ached and Patrick looked the same.

It was fun and cheeky and slick and I was so proud. I hoped Cora was watching on TV at home – she'd promised she would.

As the song came to an end, Patrick lifted me up above his head and I flung my arms out wide. And the audience erupted. Whooping, cheering, standing up. It was incredible. The judges were on their feet, too, I realized.

Patrick lowered me carefully to my feet and I threw my arms round him and hugged him tightly.

'Fabulous,' he said. 'Well done. Well done. Well done.'

I looked up at him. His face was flushed, his blond hair slightly scruffy, and his eyes shining. He stared at me and for a moment I couldn't hear the crowd any more – all I could hear was my heart pounding and a sort of rushing in my ears. Patrick bent his head and I thought he was going to kiss me. I tilted my head upwards, my lips parted and …

'Come on you two,' said Melissa. 'Let's hear what the judges have to say.'

Abruptly the spell was broken. Dazed, I looked round at the cheering crowd and grinned as I saw how wildly they were still clapping.

'I want to do it again,' I told the presenter.

She laughed.

'Well, let's hope you don't have to,' she said, taking my arm and leading me over to the judges.

They were gushing in their praise.

'You're an actress,' said Frank, the head judge. 'And tonight you also became a dancer.'

I gasped and Patrick gripped my hand tightly.

It was Justin the mean judge's turn. He fixed me with a stern glare.

'It was ah-may-zing,' he said. 'Amy, you could win this competition.'

I was flying high for the whole night. Buzzing on adrenaline and praise, I loved every second of the live show.

But in the back of my head was that moment with Patrick. That near kiss, in the middle of the dance floor. I wasn't sure what would have happened if we hadn't been interrupted and I wasn't sure who'd moved closer first – had I initiated it? Or had he? I couldn't remember. I had a horrible feeling, though, that it was all me. That I'd misinterpreted his pride at our dance for affection for me.

Later, as we all filed out of the artists' exit at the studio and waited for our cars home, I took Patrick's hand.

'Patrick,' I said. 'Sorry about – you know – what happened earlier.'

He looked at me, his tanned face unreadable.

'What do you mean?' he said.

'I didn't mean to make you uncomfortable,' I said, feeling stupid.

'Uncomfortable?'

I looked away.

'Sorry I nearly kissed you,' I muttered.

Patrick stopped walking and stared at me.

184

'*You* nearly kissed *me*?' he said.

I thought I had. Was I wrong?

'I'm just sorry,' I said again.

'Amy,' Patrick said, sounding exasperated. 'You're ...'

'I'm what?'

He shrugged. 'Never mind,' he said. 'Forget about it.'

'Can we meet tomorrow?' I asked him, wanting the awkwardness to be over. 'Maybe you'll have some news about Donnie?'

He opened his mouth to respond just as someone called his name – it was Sarah-Lou, the children's TV presenter. She came bounding over, her bunches bouncing.

'Share a car, Pat?' she squeaked. 'As we're going the same way.'

Pat? Seriously? And how did she know which way he was going.

'Actually, we were just ...' I began. But Patrick was already hoisting his bag up his shoulder and moving away.

'Sure,' he said to Sarah-Lou. He followed her to the waiting car and glanced at me over his shoulder.

'I can't tomorrow,' he said. 'I've already got plans.'

He slammed the car door shut and I was left staring after its red tail lights.

Oh, well, I thought as I got into my car. I could have a quiet day tomorrow, catch up on some TV, perhaps clean the flat. Potter around and do my own thing. It would be lovely and I'd try very hard not to think about Patrick. Or the kiss that might not have been a kiss after all. And I definitely wouldn't think about the fact that perky Miss Presenter obviously wanted to get her mitts on him.

To begin with, my Sunday went to plan. I slept in late, I had a shower and put on some more fake tan – I was growing quite fond of my ballroom-dancer-orange skin. Then just as I was wondering what to do next, Phil rang and invited me to meet him and Bertie for brunch and I accepted eagerly.

We met in the restaurant at the Covent Garden Hotel. It was quiet and there were often a few recognisable people in there, so I knew, even if anyone spotted me, that they wouldn't care.

'Shall we have bucks fizz?' Phil said. 'I think we should celebrate Amy's triumph last night.'

'And her gorgeous new hair,' said Bertie unexpectedly. I grinned at him. Perhaps we could be friends, after all.

'I'm always up for celebrating,' I said. 'Let's order, shall we? I'm starving all the time now I'm dancing so much.'

We chatted while we waited for our food, then Phil nipped off to the toilet as Bertie and I discussed dancing.

'It's the waltz next; then, if we stay in another week, we'll do the tango after that. It sounds terrifying.'

'Oh, no, it's wonderful,' he said. 'The passion is incredible. It's like making love through dance.'

I grimaced.

'I just find that idea really embarrassing,' I said, shuddering. 'And I'm not sure there's any passion between me and Patrick. We're more like brother and sister.'

'Oh, really?' said Phil, appearing next to me and waving a newspaper at me. 'Because I have never looked at my sister like this ...'

He unfolded the *Post on Sunday* and brandished it in my face. There on the front page – just to the side of a story about immigration lowering house prices – was a photo of Patrick and me on the dance floor last night. We had been captured right at the moment of our non-kiss. Our lips were inches apart, our eyes locked on each other and my hands wrapped around his neck. It was a lovely picture, actually, but it really, really looked like Patrick and I were a steamy hot couple. Lower down the page was a smaller shot of Patrick and me outside the pub just after my hair cut. He was holding my hands and looking at me with admiration. Sodding citizen journalists – there was no privacy anywhere any more.

'Shall I read it out?' Phil said with undisguised glee as he sat down at the table.

'No,' I said. But Phil was undeterred.

'Moving on?' he read. 'Shamed soapstar Amy Lavender looks

like she's put her turbulent love life behind her as she puckers up for a kiss with *Strictly Stars Dancing* partner Patrick Walker.'

'Shamed bloody soapstar,' I muttered. 'Cheek. Carry on.'

'Amy, twenty-six …' Phil started.

'I'm twenty-five,' I said, outraged.

'Amy, twenty-six, was publicly dumped by former fiancé Matty Hall and spent a night in the cells after punching her love rival, reality TV star Kayleigh Rogers.'

'I did not,' I spluttered. 'They let me go after they'd cautioned me.'

I downed my glass of bucks fizz and motioned to Phil to keep going.

'Amy is currently riding high in *Strictly Stars Dancing* and it's rumoured that Matty's regretting cheating now his ex is proving to be such hot property. Perhaps he's going to have to Battle for her affections now Patrick's on the scene.'

Phil looked up.

'Why have they written battle like that?' he said.

'It's one of Matty's tracks,' Bertie said, looking disgusted that Phil didn't know the name of Matty's biggest hit. Phil, who was more of an Elton John man, shrugged.

'Is this true?' he said. 'Are you and Patrick doing it?'

'Urgh,' I said. 'And no.'

Phil and Bertie both looked down at the photo in the paper, then up at me.

'Really?' Phil said, his eyes narrowed with suspicion

'No,' I repeated. 'But I kind of wish we were.'

'I knew it!' Phil said triumphantly.

'No, don't be all full of yourself,' I said. 'There's nothing going on. We're just mates, that's all. And Patrick's being chased by that kids' TV presenter anyway. And …'

I trailed off, wondering whether to tell Phil I was thinking about getting back with Matty.

'And?' Phil said.

'I might do what Babs wants,' I said quietly.

'Which is?'

'ImightgetbackwithMatty,' I gabbled.

'Oh, Amy,' Phil said, despairingly. 'Really? Why? Why now when things are going so well for you?'

'Just for a bit,' I assured him. 'Babs reckons I can have my pick of auditions once I'm back on top. And she says getting back with Matty is the way to do it.'

'He might not want to get back with you now you're snogging Patrick on the front page of the *Post*,' Bertie pointed out.

'Yes, thank you, Bertie. I had thought of that,' I said. 'I'll ring Babs later, I suppose.'

Phil frowned.

'Amy,' he said. 'Matty broke your heart. He treated you horribly badly and he is never going to change. This is a crazy idea.'

'But Babs says …' I began.

'Bollocks,' Phil said, staring at me intently. He reached out and put his hand over mine.

'Are you sure about this, Amy?' he said.

I thought about being with Matty, who I had loved once upon a time. We'd had a laugh together; I'd enjoyed our life. It wasn't all bad. And being in it with my eyes open – fully aware that Matty wasn't to be trusted – was surely a better way to be than risking being humiliated again. If I was with someone else, someone I could really fall for, like Patrick – the very thought gave me delicious shivers that I tried to ignore – then, like Cora had said, I'd always be worried. I'd always be fearful that my judgement was off and that he wasn't the man I thought he was. Cora had chosen to live her life alone. If she could do that, then choosing Matty seemed a much easier decision.

'Amy,' Phil said again. 'Are you sure?'

'Yes, I'm sure,' I said.

But I wasn't.

Chapter 36

Strangely enough, Babs wasn't nearly as cross as I thought she'd be about the photos of Patrick and me in the paper.

'You've made the front bloody page,' she hooted down the phone at me. 'Clever minx.'

'I didn't mean to,' I said. 'It wasn't planned.'

I stretched out on the sofa, relieved she wasn't angry.

'You're not annoyed?' I said.

There was a brief silence.

'I was a bit,' she admitted. 'But then I realized how huge this is. Two men fighting over you. It's brilliant. Have you wondered why I've not phoned you before now?'

'I had, actually.'

'Damage control,' Babs said in triumph. 'And, boy, have I earned my commission this morning.'

'Really?' I said drily. 'What have you done?'

Babs took a breath.

'I've spoken to Matty's agent,' she said. 'He's planning something big for this week. A public declaration.'

'A public what now?'

'Declaration, Amy. Don't interrupt.'

I made a face, glad Babs was on the end of a telephone and not in the same room as me.

'And I've made some other calls, too. If this all comes off you're going to want to up my commission, doll.'

'I doubt that very much,' I said. Despite my clear-headed thinking about Babs's plan, I still wasn't completely convinced getting back with Matty was the right thing to do. I decided to have one last go at changing her mind.

'Babs, surely I've done enough. With the dancing and these pics, I'm back to how I was before. Isn't that good enough? Can't we abandon this crazy plan to get back with Matty?'

'Absolutely not,' said Babs. 'You're riding high now, Doll, but it could all be over in a heartbeat. It just takes one dodgy disco move and you'll be out of *Strictly* and back on the scrap heap.'

I had nothing to say, but it didn't matter. Babs carried on regardless.

'Being back with Matty is the best way to make the most of all this,' she said. 'It makes total sense.'

'I know it does. But, at the same time, it makes no sense whatsoever,' I muttered. But either she didn't hear me, or she chose to ignore it.

'Have you got me any auditions?' I said, not wanting to discuss it any more. 'That dragons thing has got a new season. Should I be going to America?'

'Of course you should,' she said. 'But not yet. Let's do one step at a time, shall we?'

'Fine,' I said. 'But I want an audition, Babs.'

She tutted.

'I'm sorting it. Just keep an eye out for Matty's next move – and call me when you see it.'

She hung up and I stared at the phone for a second, wondering what on earth she was talking about. Then I realized there was no point in ever trying to second-guess Babs – or Matty – so I may as well not bother. And I went upstairs to see Cora instead.

Patrick and I were dancing a waltz next and I wanted to see what insights she could give me.

The public declaration, when it came, was enormous. More enormous than I could ever have imagined.

It was Tuesday morning and I was on the tube heading north. Patrick had arranged for us to go to a lunch club for senior citizens in East London. I had not been keen, but the film crew was following us today so it would make for a good VT before our dance on Saturday, and Patrick had promised we'd get some good tips about waltzing. He was meeting me there. He'd been a bit odd since the live show and the story in the *Post*. He'd laughed it all off and said something like 'don't believe everything you read', but I definitely sensed a slight air of discomfort between us. I had a horrible feeling I'd offended him somehow but I wasn't sure what I'd done.

So, I was a bit nervous as I sat on the train that morning. It was raining at ground level, so I was wearing my baseball cap – obviously – into which I'd tucked my new hair, and a storm jacket I'd found in the airing cupboard at my flat, which had clearly belonged to the last tenant. It was ugly, but very waterproof. And I was quite confident no one would recognize me in this get-up.

It was quite early and I was tired, so I sat with my eyes closed, dozing gently, until someone trod on my foot and woke me up.

I blinked in surprise and my eye was caught by the magazine that the woman sitting opposite me was reading. It was the new issue of *Hot* magazine and on the front cover was a huge picture of Matty. He was wearing a white T-shirt, his head resting on his hand, and he looked sad. Underneath the enormous close-up of his – I had to admit – very handsome face, it said: 'I love Amy and I want her back.'

My jaw dropped. I squinted to read what else it said.

'Exclusive!' I read. 'Matty reveals why he's made a BIG mistake!'

I needed that magazine. I had to find out what was in it. The train started to slow down as it approached a station and I made a split-second decision. I stood up, swaying with the movement of the tube, and hung on to the strap next to the woman reading *Hot*. She paid me absolutely no attention whatsoever. Good. As the train pulled into the station, and the doors opened, I pointed to the other end of the carriage, and I shrieked: 'Ohmygod! What on earth is that?'

As she – and the rest of the passengers – turned to look, I snatched the magazine from her hands, dived out of the door and legged it off up the platform before she had time to work out what had happened.

Up at street level, I ignored my thirty-five missed calls from Babs, and slumped into a taxi. Then, as we drove through the busy streets towards the lunch club, I read the interview over and over, wondering what the blinking bloody flip Matty was playing at.

I won't bore you with all the details, but let me give you a few choice extracts. And you have to imagine this across five pages of *Hot*, illustrated with pictures of Matty looking tortured, yet extremely well groomed. Showing off just enough of his buff biceps and – I'm not making this up – his new tattoo, which spelled out 'Amy' in curly black script on the inside of his arm.

'"I was an idiot," says Matty, curling up on the sofa of the flat he shared with Amy until a couple of months ago. "I didn't know how lucky I was until I lost her. But now the flat seems so empty and I've lost the only thing that made me want to come home …"'

'Oh, give me strength,' I muttered.

'As Matty talks about what love really is, his eyes fill with tears. "My parents have a very strong marriage," he reveals. "They've always worked things out in the end and I admire them so much for that. Because love is all that matters." Unconsciously he strokes the "Amy" tattoo on his arm. "Love is all you need."'

Matty's parents had been married for a thousand years, that was true. But they hated one another and would get divorced in a heartbeat if they thought it would do them any good. His dad, though, was terrified his mum would take him to the cleaner's – he had a point, she totally would – and his mum didn't want to give her husband the satisfaction of being single again. Hardly the best role models for a happy relationship, though perhaps it explained why Matty was the way he was.

"'I know Amy's career is important to her and her talent needs to be nurtured," he says as he gazes at a vast blown-up picture of Amy that hangs above his fireplace. "I'm prepared to put my DJ career on the backburner for a while, and support her as she becomes a star."'

I laughed out loud. Matty was a DJ, that was true, but if it hadn't been for his reality TV show, he'd still be spinning the wheels of steel at eighties night at the club his best friend owned in Ilford. He was hardly Mark Ronson.

But right at the end of the article was something that made me stop and think.

"'Amy's the best thing that ever happened to me," I read. "'I took her for granted and I trampled all over her heart, and I hate myself for it. I'm a nicer person because she was once my girlfriend and all I can do is hope that she gives me another chance to be even better."'

That sounded genuine, I thought, feeling tears prickle my eyelids. Whatever Matty had done, we had a lot of fun together and I had really loved him once upon a time. Maybe he was sorry, after all?

As we pulled up outside the day-care centre, my phone rang again and this time I answered it.

'Well,' said Babs. I could actually hear her smiling. 'Have you read it?'

'I've read it,' I said, handing the taxi driver some money.

'And?'

'And nothing,' I said.

Babs snorted.

'That last bit's good, eh?' she said. 'That's from the heart, that is.'

'Don't,' I said.

'Don't throw this away, doll,' Babs said. 'This is your big chance to get back on top. Make the right decision.'

'Oh, sod off,' I said, but she'd already ended the call.

I shoved the magazine into my bag and went inside to find Patrick.

Chapter 37

Patrick was inside the centre, surrounded by adoring elderly ladies. He was dancing with one of them, who was wearing skinny jeans and ballet pumps and looked about twenty-five from the back. It was only when she turned round that I realized she had to be at least seventy, possibly even older.

'I'm hoping you guys can teach us a thing or two today,' he was saying.

I smiled to myself. He was such a nice man. He wasn't putting this on for the cameras – though he was being filmed. He was genuinely interested in all these people and I didn't doubt for one minute that, even though he was a professional dancer, a world champion even, and we'd topped the leader board in last week's show, he honestly believed we could learn a thing or two from these Hackney pensioners who'd been waltzing for years.

My heart swelled with affection for him and – as he came over to say hello and kiss me on the cheek – my tummy flipped with what I was pretty sure was lust.

'Hi,' I said weakly. 'Let me just dump my bag.'

I stuck my bag, and the offending *Hot* magazine, into a cupboard, pulled on my dancing shoes, and headed back to the dance floor.

'Ready to work hard?' Matty said.

I glanced round at the elderly people who were all taking their partners, ready to begin.

'I think I can handle it,' I joked.

But, oh, my God, could those people dance! We waltzed for hours – with just a brief break for tea and cake and, I had to admit, I learned a lot. I danced with all the elderly men, who were all so smartly dressed that I beamed with pride. I compared shoes with some of the women, and listened to their tips on using sandpaper on my soles to stop slipping, and putting soap on my tights if I got a run in them.

In exchange I told them all about Cora and what a wonderful dancer she still was, and gave them some – pretty indiscreet – gossip about some of their favourite soap stars.

Eventually, Patrick and I took to the floor and showed off our waltz. We were dancing to a song by Adele and we'd not practised much yet, but we got a standing ovation from all our new friends. It was lovely.

'They're all so nice,' I said as we changed our shoes and got ready to leave. 'It was a really good idea you had to come here.'

Patrick grinned at me, and I felt my heart flip over once more.

'That couple over there …' he began, nodding to a smartly dressed pair by the door. The man was helping the woman on with her raincoat. 'They've been married for almost sixty years.'

'Blimey,' I said. 'I can't imagine that.'

I gazed at them for a while, trying to picture a grey-haired Matty helping me on with my coat. But I couldn't.

Patrick was looking at them, too, a soppy expression on his face.

'You're such a softie,' I teased.

'I know,' he said. 'I just like seeing people in love, that's all. I hope I have that some day. That partnership, where you're better together than apart.'

I thought about Matty saying I made him a better person and winced. Patrick looked at me.

'Did I say something wrong?' he said.

I opened my bag, pulled out the magazine and held it up for him to see.

'Woah,' he said, as he took in the cover. Silently, I turned to the page where Matty's interview began, then I handed it to him to read.

I couldn't bear to watch him as he read it, so I went to the loo, deliberately taking my time, and when I came back he'd finished.

The day-care centre was empty now – there was just us in the corner and the film crew who were packing up.

'What are you going to do?' Patrick said as I sat down next to him again.

I shrugged.

'Dunno,' I said. 'It's weird but I think he means it. Some of it, anyway.'

Patrick looked doubtful.

'Really?' he said.

'Maybe not,' I said. 'But maybe it doesn't matter.'

'How so?'

'Cora really loved Donnie, right?' I said. 'She really loved him and she thought he'd stand by her, and they'd be together for ever – like that old couple.'

'I have no idea where you're going with this,' Patrick said.

I was getting into my stride.

'And I loved Matty. I trusted him, and he stamped all over my heart.'

'Okay …'

'What I mean is, you can't ever be sure, can you? That someone's the right one? Because what if you're wrong. It's just too painful to imagine. Cora hasn't been with anyone else, Patrick. She's been alone for years because she couldn't ever trust herself

197

to feel that way again. So obviously the best thing to do is expect the worst. Go into a relationship with your eyes wide open. And then you can't get hurt again.'

'Sounds pretty miserable to me,' Patrick said.

'It's not,' I said, sounding more sure than I was. 'It's grown-up. It's sensible. If I get back with Matty he can help me with my career, Babs can get me the auditions I want, and he can't hurt me again because this time I won't let him.'

I sat back in my plastic chair triumphantly.

'It's perfect.'

'Is it?' Patrick said.

For a moment I stared at him, taking in his wide cheekbones, clear blue eyes, messy blond hair and beautiful lips. I wondered what he would do if I kissed him right there and then. But no! That's what I meant. If I kissed him, or told him I thought I was falling for him, then he could turn me down, or push me away, or – I shuddered – laugh at me. It would be awful. I'd be opening myself up for more heartache. Whereas I knew Matty wanted me, even if it was more about our profiles than passion. We could do each other good, and if it didn't work out, then so what? I wouldn't be too invested, anyway.

'It's perfect,' I said again.

Patrick stood up.

'So I guess you'd better go tell the douchebag the good news,' he said. He sounded a bit pissed off but I didn't really know why.

'Want to share a cab?' I asked.

Patrick pulled his phone out of his pocket.

'Oh, thanks, but no thanks,' he said. 'I have plans. A date, actually.'

'A date?'

'With Sarah-Lou.'

'Oh,' I said. 'That sounds nice.'

'Yeah, it will be,' Patrick said. 'I just need to make the final arrangements. If you'll excuse me …'

He turned his back on me and wandered over to the other side of the hall as he phoned.

I watched him, wondering if he really had a date all along, or if he was just phoning her now to suggest it. Could he be using her to make me jealous? Or was that just wishful thinking.

'Bye then,' I called across the room, picking up my bag. Patrick gave me a half-hearted wave then went back to his call, laughing at something Sarah-Lou had said.

As I left the day-care centre, I took my own phone out and scrolled through my contacts list until I found Matty's number. I looked at it for a moment, then I took a deep breath and pressed call.

'Matty?' I said when he answered. 'It's me. I think we need to talk ...'

Chapter 38

Matty didn't sound too surprised to hear from me. In fact, if I'd had to put a name to the way he sounded, I'd say it was resigned. Which wasn't exactly romantic, but hey ho. I'd decided to turn my back on romance, remember? To follow my head instead of my heart. Perhaps he'd done the same.

'Can you come to the flat?' he said. 'Now?'

'I'm in Hackney,' I said. 'Be there in about half an hour?'

'Fine,' he said. Again, not exactly romantic. 'Oh, and Amy, do you have the magazine?'

'Yes,' I said. 'Why?'

'Can you carry it when you arrive – in your hand?'

'What?' I said, wondering what he meant then realizing he'd probably have tipped off some photographers that I'd be on my way. 'No, Matty.'

'Just do it,' he said, hanging up.

So I did. I felt a bit silly as I got out of my cab, clutching *Hot* magazine, but I could see that it would make a good picture. I put my head down, folded the magazine in half, with the cover outwards, and headed into the flat, deliberately ignoring the throngs of photographers who blinded me with their flashes as I walked.

Matty buzzed me in and I climbed the stairs to his flat. My heart was thumping and I was pretty sure it wasn't just the effort of going upwards. I was really nervous about what was going to happen and still not completely convinced it was the right thing to do. And I'd not been here since Matty threw all my clothes out so it was kind of strange to be back.

As I reached the top floor, the door opened and there was Matty, wearing a similar outfit to the one in the *Hot* photo shoot.

I pulled the magazine out from under my arm and whacked him with it.

'You bloody idiot,' I said. 'Why are there photographers here?'

Matty gave me his dazzling smile. The one that used to make me go weak at the knees. So I whacked him again.

'Stop it,' I said.

I walked past him into the flat. It was clean and tidy – of course, Matty had cleaners – and very little had changed except for a huge canvas of me hanging over the mantelpiece. It was from a shoot I'd done for *Cosmopolitan* – Amy stripped bare – and it showed me sitting hugging my knees in front of an open window. I was naked but there was nothing to see. It was just my back view, my hair tumbling down my spine, and I was silhouetted in the light from the window. I'd turned my head slightly to the side, so my profile was visible, but that was all. It was a lovely picture and one I'd been quite proud of. In fact, I'd loved the whole interview, which had been honest and funny and – you know – in flipping *Cosmo*. But I absolutely did not want it hanging up in my living room.

'I love what you've done with the place,' I said, gesturing to the photo.

Matty came over to me and ran his finger down my arm.

'I adore that shot,' he said. I felt his breath on my neck and smelled his sharp aftershave. 'I look at it every day and it reminds me what I'm missing.'

He caressed my neck gently and despite myself I shivered with pleasure.

'I like your hair,' he said. 'You look hot.'

He bent his head and kissed my neck.

'Matty,' I said, in a warning tone but not moving away. 'I thought I'd come here so we could talk?'

'What is there to talk about?' he said, kissing me again.

This time I did pull away.

'Erm, the cheating, the taking me for granted, the fact you humiliated me,' I said.

'And the fact that you broke someone's nose?' Matty said. He sat down on the white sofa and pulled me down next to him. 'And your dancer geezer,' he said. 'You've been sleeping with him, right?'

'No,' I said, wishing he'd not mentioned Patrick.

Matty raised his eyebrows in disbelief.

'We're quits,' he said. 'Even stevens. It's done. Let's move on.'

He gave me his best puppy dog look. He was pretty perfect, physically. His hair, his tan, his teeth, his muscles – he had it all.

'I missed you, babe,' he said. 'I even got a new tattoo.'

He thrust his arm in my face and I slowly ran my fingers over the Amy that was written there.

'That's permanent, you know,' I said with a small smile.

'I know,' Matty said. 'And so are you. Us. I don't want to lose you again, Amy.'

It was actually quite hard to concentrate with him so close to me. My trouble was I fancied Matty like mad. Always had done. Now I knew his flaws, of course, and I took everything he was saying with a pinch of salt. But that didn't change the fact that he was here, in front of me, looking gorgeous and offering me the world.

'Did you mean what you said in the interview?' I said, feeling my breath begin to quicken. I was still stroking his arm, which was probably a mistake but somehow I couldn't stop.

202

'I meant all of it,' Matty said, staring at me intently.

'The thing at the end about you being a better person because you had me as your girlfriend?' I said. 'Did you mean that?'

'Every word,' Matty said. He kissed me on the lips and I kissed him back. He was a really good kisser. I'd forgotten that.

Inevitably I ended up staying the night. I'd known it would happen from the moment I walked into the flat but I felt a bit ashamed of myself when I woke up in my old bed the next morning. Perhaps I should have made him work a bit harder to win me over. But then again, I thought as I looked at Matty asleep next to me, we'd had fun and everyone got what they wanted. There were no losers in this situation. Except perhaps Cupid. But what did he know, anyway? He'd only ever got me into trouble.

Quietly I slid out of bed and started putting my clothes on. Matty stirred and opened his eyes.

'Where are you going, Amy?' he said. 'Come back to bed. Let's start the day properly.'

He grabbed my hand and pulled me on top of him, which wasn't entirely unpleasant.

'I have to go and dance,' I said, giggling. 'And I've got to go home first.'

Dramatically, Matty threw himself back against the pillows.

'I'll misssssss you,' he wailed. 'When are you going to move back in? Later?'

I paused in pulling my jeans on.

'I'm not moving back in,' I said. 'Not yet. I made a commitment to Cora and I need to see it through.'

'Who's Cora?' Matty said.

I sighed. I'd told him all about her last night.

'She's my landlady,' I said. 'The one who lives upstairs.'

'Oh, her,' Matty said without interest. 'I'll pay your rent, babe. Just move back in as soon as you can.'

I had no intention of doing that but I didn't have time to argue – I had to get back to Clapham, get showered, changed –

for some reason I didn't want Patrick to know I'd been out all night – and out to the rehearsal studio.

'I'll move in when I can,' I said. I crawled across the bed and kissed Matty. 'See you later?'

'Great,' he said. 'There's some fashion show thing. I'll get us on the guest list.'

'Sounds good,' I lied. I picked up my bag, but left *Hot* magazine lying on the bedside table. 'Bye then.'

There was one photographer still outside. I wondered if he'd been there all night just on the off-chance of getting the money shot and felt a slight flash of admiration for him. I gave him a beaming smile as I walked past. That would make his night on the street worthwhile.

Then, feeling weirdly uncomfortable and a tiny bit embarrassed, though I wasn't sure why, I headed for the tube back south – and home.

Chapter 39

Cora

1953

'Mummy, come on.' Ginny tugged my hand impatiently and I smiled down at her.

'Is everyone ready?' I asked her.

'They're all waiting for you,' she said, furrowing her little brow. 'Come ON. You have to introduce us.'

I couldn't help smiling at my daughter's eagerness to take to the stage. I knew where she got that from. I'd been teaching her and some of her friends dancing for a while – nothing serious, just at weekends or when we had time – and they wanted to put on a show for their mums and dads. We'd commandeered the church hall and I'd roped Audrey in to play piano.

I pushed my way through the curtain and waited for the mumble of voices to die down. Reenie, Audrey's mum, who looked after Ginny for me when I was at work, and who I'd come to consider as my own family, was in the front row, looking proud as punch.

'Hello, everyone,' I said. 'We've put together some dances for you. Hope you enjoy them.'

I stepped aside and let the little girls take to the stage – led by my Ginny, of course. She really was a chip off the old block.

Audrey played a jaunty tune on the piano, the girls held out their little skirts and off they went, polkaing round the stage.

I watched them proudly. I'd loved teaching them and it had surprised me really how much I loved passing on my passion for dancing. Some of the girls' mums had asked if I charged for lessons, and I'd started wondering if I could make a living from it.

I still worked for Mr Warner, and I enjoyed it a lot. I loved him – in all his grumpy, disorganized glory – and I loved being a part of the theatre world. But I missed dancing more than I could imagine. Teaching had helped me find myself again and I was eager to do more of it.

Audrey finished the tune with a flourish, hammering the piano keys so hard the vicar, who was watching from the back, winced. The little girls all curtseyed, beautifully, and the mums all clapped.

I wiped away a tear. I was so proud of my Ginny. She'd not had the best start in life, but she'd grown into the funniest, boldest, kindest little girl I'd ever had the good fortune to meet. I'd struggled when she was born, I couldn't lie. It had all been such a shock – being jilted by Donnie, then having to get ready for her arrival. Audrey, though, had been brilliant. She'd found us a little two-up, two-down house round the corner from Reenie in Camberwell. She'd begged, borrowed and – I suspected – stolen all the bits and pieces I needed for my baby, and she'd been on hand when Ginny arrived and I cried and cried because she looked so much like Donnie.

Reenie, who spent her whole time surrounded by kids, had kept a watchful eye on me. She took Ginny when I couldn't cope, and eventually shoved me out of the door one day and told me to tell Mr Warner I was coming back to work.

Audrey, meanwhile, had become something of a sensation. She performed in concerts, acted in the West End, was in every radio play I seemed to hear, and was very excited about television.

'I've got an idea,' she said into my ear as I watched the girls soak up the applause.

I turned round and looked at her with interest. Audrey's ideas tended to be rather good.

'Why don't we start a school?' she said.

I frowned.

'Because we're not teachers?'

'We'd employ teachers,' she said. 'For things like arithmetic, at least.'

'And?' I said, not understanding what she meant.

'And we'd teach the other stuff,' she said, gripping my arm. 'Dancing, acting, singing, music – we know lots of people who'd be great teachers.'

I looked at the little girls and then back at Audrey.

'So we'd be a stage school?' I said.

'Exactly.'

'What about money?' I said. 'I've got some savings but not enough.'

Audrey waved her arm.

'It's fine,' she said. 'We split what we can. But I need somewhere to put all my cash. I thought I could provide the money, and you can be the headteacher.'

'Got it all worked out, haven't you?' I said.

'You've been thinking about teaching for ages,' Audrey said. 'That's what gave me the idea.'

She paused.

'What do you think?'

'I think it's the best idea you've ever had,' I said.

It took us five years, in the end. Five years of hard work, building up from evening classes and weekend lessons, finding the right building – a run-down Victorian villa in Clapham – and getting it rebuilt the way we needed it to be, finding teachers for the boring stuff like arithmetic and geography, as well as for acting, singing, dancing, stage fighting – everything you could think of. Audrey proved herself to be an excellent businesswoman, and I recruited Mr Warner to help with the promise of a never-ending stream of new talent directed to his doorstep when the first pupils arrived.

And eventually the London Academy of Theatre and Dancing opened its doors in September 1958. We threw a huge party to celebrate in the garden of the school, with Audrey inviting all her friends from the world of television – where she was working more and more by then. I went through Mr Warner's client list and invited everyone he represented. All our pupils, and their parents, turned up. Ginny, who was almost thirteen and who'd grown into a beautiful, willowy, red-haired girl, handed out drinks, and Audrey and I stood on the terrace and watched in satisfaction.

'We've done well,' she said, looping her arm through mine.

'We have,' I said.

Ginny walked by, flashing us a grin over her shoulder as she went. I caught my breath. Most of the time I didn't think about Donnie. I'd put him out of my mind and gone on with my life. But every now and then, it would catch me unawares. I'd see one of the films we'd watched together was on at the pictures, or I'd hear an American accent when I wasn't expecting it, or Ginny would give me a particular look – like she had just then – and she'd look so much like her dad that I'd feel dizzy all over again with the hurt and the pain that was more than a decade old.

'She looks like him, doesn't she?' Audrey said, reading my thoughts. 'More so, now, than ever.'

I nodded, my lips pressed together tightly.

'Are you ever going to tell her the truth?'

'What, that her father was a cowardly rat who got me pregnant then ran away?' I said. 'Absolutely not. Let her believe in Jack

Devonshire, the brave GI who loved me very much and who was killed honourably in action, right at the end of the war.'

'She might try to find her family, you know,' Audrey said. 'When she's older.'

'Well, she won't find them, will she?' I snapped.

I tossed my hair over my shoulder and gazed out over the garden. On the lawn a smartly dressed, handsome man raised his glass to me and smiled. I raised mine back.

'Niiiice,' said Audrey. 'Is it going well with you two?'

I shrugged. Francis was a dancer I'd met through work. He was very good looking, a wonderful dancer, and he was lovely, that was true. He treated me like a lady and made me feel like I was really special. And he had a cheeky side that I adored. And yet ...

'He's perfect,' I told Audrey. 'But so was Donnie. And look what happened there.'

'Oh, but ...' Audrey began.

'No,' I said. 'I truly believed that everything I felt for Donnie, and what he felt for me, was real. I trusted him, Audrey, and he broke my heart.'

'But Francis wouldn't be like that,' Audrey said.

'He might,' I said. 'How would I know? I can't trust my own judgement any more. I can't risk that happening again. Not now I've got Ginny to look after.'

'Well, I think that's sad,' Audrey said. 'You're only young. You can't be on your own for ever.'

'I won't be on my own,' I said. 'I like men. I like spending time with men. I like Francis. But I'm never going to marry.'

Audrey looked surprised but I didn't care

'I just don't want to give myself up for a man,' I said. 'Not again. I'm in control now, and that's the way I like it.'

Chapter 40

'Amy, Amy, over here, love!'

I spun round and gave the bank of photographers a dazzling smile.

'And one with Matty?'

Matty slid his arm round my waist and we posed together, blinking in the flashes.

'Feels good to be back, huh? he whispered in my ear as we walked up the red carpet into the event. What the event was I didn't know. Since Matty and I had got back together – and since I'd made it to the quarter-final of *SSD* – we'd been out every night. Life the last couple of weeks had been glittering and show-bizzy and fabulous. An endless round of parties, launches, photo shoots, interviews – and rehearsing, of course, though I felt like I'd barely seen Patrick or Cora for days and days.

Matty had stayed over at mine a few times. It was strange seeing him in a place that had been just for me. One day I came home and discovered he'd replaced my flamenco dancer print with another of his blown-up canvases. This one was a photo of the two of us from a *Yay!* magazine shoot we'd done when we got engaged. It was hideous and I definitely did not want it in my lounge. So, as soon as he'd gone, I took it down – he'd managed to hang it properly – and propped my flamenco dancer back up again. Now I was in the ridiculous situation of having to change the pictures over every time he came round.

I was pleased to be back with him, though – I thought. It was nice being back in demand again, and having offers of work left, right and centre. But I'd got into a sort of quiet rhythm of dance lessons with Cora, and hanging out with Patrick, and Matty suddenly seemed too loud, too brash, too 'on it', for my liking.

Patrick was keeping his distance. He seemed to be spending a lot of time with Sarah-Lou, even though she'd been knocked out of *Strictly Stars Dancing* thanks to a particularly twee tango. He didn't seem very happy about it, though. In fact, he didn't seem very happy about anything. He was short with me and snappy and the only time we really got on was when we were dancing.

This week it was our turn to dance a tango. I was nervous about it because it seemed a bit grown-up and sexy for me, but I was keen to give it a try. So far – mostly thanks to Cora's help – it was going well. Cora had told me to make up a story about our dance, and to play the part – like I'd done in the Charleston – and it definitely helped. Except sometimes I caught a glimpse of my fierce tango face in the mirror while we were dancing and it made me laugh. I just hoped it wouldn't have the same effect on the judges.

'We need to split, baby,' Matty whispered in my ear. I looked round in surprise, lost in my own thoughts. The event – it seemed to be some sort of exhibition – was in full swing and there was lunch being served, but I had a meeting with Babs and Matty had to be somewhere else. We did this a lot – being photographed on the way in to a do and then virtually walking straight through and out the back door. It was good for our profiles, Babs said.

Feeling a bit dizzy from all the rushing about, I kissed Matty goodbye then raced round to Babs's Soho office, where I sat on the sofa and slurped coffee like my life depended on it.

'So these are all the job offers I've got for you,' she said, brandishing a bundle of papers.

'You shouldn't waste so much paper,' I said. 'I can't do them all.'

She ignored me, as ever.

'Right,' she said. 'Here's what we've got.'

I listened as she went through sponsorship ideas, beauty products and food brands that wanted me to endorse them in exchange for staggering amounts of money, a celeb magazine that wanted me to write a weekly column for them …

'I can't write,' I said.

Babs scanned the email.

'Doesn't matter,' she said. 'They'll write it for you.'

'Then what … oh, never mind,' I said. 'Put it in the maybe pile.'

Babs put it on the coffee table. So far there was a growing pile of 'no's, a smaller pile of 'maybe's and nothing in the 'yes' pile at all.

'Sexy calendar?'

'No.'

'Toothpaste.'

'No.'

'Autobiography.'

'I'm twenty-five.'

'Hair dye.'

'No.'

'*Doctor Who*?'

I sat up straighter.

'Maybe,' I said. 'Companion?'

Babs checked.

'Alien,' she said.

'No.'

Babs fixed me with a stern glare. She was tiny, with short cropped bleach-blonde hair. Soaking wet she probably weighed about seven stone, but she scared the bejeezus out of me.

'Amy,' she said. 'I've never had so many offers in on one day. Would you please consider some of them?'

'I'll consider them,' I said, scared she was going to poke me with her highlighter pen. 'But I want to act, Babs. You said getting back with Matty would give me the pick of acting jobs.'

'I know,' Babs said. 'I just don't think you should have to audition – not an actress of your calibre. I'm playing hardball.'

I was horrified.

'Of course I have to audition,' I said. 'I want to audition. I love auditioning.'

Babs looked unconvinced.

'Look,' I said. 'I want to wear a corset, or solve a murder, or both. And if that means I have to audition then so be it.'

'Fine,' said Babs, sounding annoyed that I was being so forceful. 'I'll make some calls.'

'Good,' I said. I was proud of myself for not backing down for once. 'Now, if you'll excuse me, I have to go and learn how to tango.'

As soon as I got to rehearsal I found myself relaxing. It was just so easy to be with Patrick, even if he was being a bit grumpy. Cora was busy today, so it was just the two of us in the studio, stomping around to the Amy Winehouse song we were dancing to.

'You look exhausted,' Patrick said as we took a break for a drink a bit later.

I grimaced.

'I really am,' I said. 'It's so full on at the moment, but Babs says it's all going to help me in my quest to become a "serious actress".'

I made what I considered to be a "serious actress" face and Patrick chuckled.

'Cora's worried about you overdoing it,' he said.

'Oh, bless her.' I opened my water bottle and drank some. 'She's such a sweetheart. I've hardly seen her this week, actually. I must pop up and say hello later.'

'I was hoping we'd have some news about Donnie,' Patrick said, pulling his phone out of his pocket. 'Actually, let me just check if it's arrived …' I went to the loo, and when I came back Patrick was staring at his phone, an odd expression on his face.

'What is it?' I said. 'Has your login arrived? Can you get on to the archive site?'

'Yes and yes,' Patrick said.

'So what's wrong? Have you found Donnie?'

Silently Patrick handed me the phone. On the screen was the service record of Donald Jackson. And across the top was stamped 'killed in service'.

'Oh, no,' I said, covering my mouth with my hand. 'Oh, no. He died? Donnie died?'

Patrick nodded.

'He died,' he said. 'Right before the end of the war, I guess. Which seems kind of cruel.'

I started to cry.

'Oh, Patrick,' I said. 'What are we going to tell Cora?'

Chapter 41

We didn't feel much like dancing after that. Instead, we went back to my flat and settled down with my laptop to see if we could find out more.

Donnie pulled up the military records website again, entered the login he'd been sent and we stared once more at Donnie's details.

'So he didn't go AWOL, after all?' I said, confused. 'That's strange. Cora said her friend went to find him after their wedding, and no one knew where he was. But according to this he died in action …'

Patrick frowned.

'Yes, that is kinda odd. I wonder if we can find the date he died and the location? That might help us figure it out.'

He clicked on Donnie's name, typed in a few more details, and a new page of information came up.

'What does it say?' I said. We were sitting on the sofa and I was cross that I couldn't see the screen properly. I wriggled in behind Patrick and leant on his back so I could see everything that was written down.

'Curiouser and curiouser,' Patrick said. I gave him a quizzical look and he nudged me. 'That's what Alice says when she gets to Wonderland,' he said. 'You heathen.'

I giggled.

'Never read it,' I said, unashamed. 'What does it say about Donnie?'

'It says he died in London,' Patrick said.

I stared at him.

'But there wasn't fighting in London,' I said.

'There were bombs,' Patrick pointed out. 'But not right at the end of the war, surely?'

'Maybe this isn't our Donnie,' I said. 'Find out when he died – if he died before Cora met him, then we'll know. She said they didn't get together until 1944. Have you got that paper?'

Patrick nodded. He bent down and pulled a sheet of paper out of the side pocket of his bag. Cora had written down all the information we needed to know about Donnie – his name, his rank, the dates he was stationed in England – and the date of their wedding that never was.'

I peered at Cora's neat writing.

'Yes, they definitely didn't know each other until 1944,' I said. 'When did this Donald Jackson die?'

'Oh,' Patrick said. 'Oh, shit. Let me see those dates.'

I gave him the paper, my heart beginning to pound. How silly to be so invested in the life of someone I'd never met. But it was someone who was important to someone I cared about, I supposed, which made it worthwhile.

'Shit,' Patrick said again. I poked him.

'What?' I said. 'What?'

'Cora and Donnie were meant to get married on 26 March 1945, according to her,' Patrick said.

'Right …'

'But Donnie died on 25 March.'

I felt sick.

'He died right before the wedding?' I said.

'Seems so.'

'That's why he didn't turn up. But why didn't anyone tell her he'd died?' I said, bewildered. 'Why did they just leave her standing at the church, waiting?'

Donnie shrugged.

'No idea,' he said. 'But we can find out.'

We spent the rest of the afternoon researching Donnie's death. Patrick tracked down more military records that confirmed he definitely had been killed in London on that date – for a while we thought we were wrong – and I found my iPad and set about finding out what could have happened.

'Listen to this,' I said to Patrick as I found out something interesting. 'I thought the Blitz was it when it came to bombs, but there were things called V1 and V2 bombs that the Germans used right at the end of the war. South London was very badly hit, and there were some in central London, too.'

'See if you can find one that fell on the right date,' Patrick said.

I put the date and V2 into Google and there it was. A direct hit on Tottenham Court Road that killed ten people.

'Look,' I said, turning the screen to show Patrick. 'A bomb blast in London, on the right day, that killed lots of people.'

'That could be it,' he said. 'Let's see if we can find out more about it.'

It took us ages but we eventually found out the details thanks to a report of the last months of the war we found on the Imperial War Museum website. The bomb had fallen in the evening, destroying a church and some of the surrounding shops. It had taken days to clear the site – and this was presumably why no one knew Donnie had been involved at first.

'He'd have been wearing his dog tags,' Patrick said. 'He'd have been easy to identify.'

'But I still don't understand why no one told Cora,' I said.

Patrick took my hand.

'His unit went to Europe, right?' he said.

I nodded.

'So think about it. Like I said, they were a liberating division.

217

They were going through France, pushing the Germans back. They'd have seen whole towns devastated by the war. It was a tough gig, Amy. And it was chaotic. I imagine Donnie's commanding officers only found out what had happened to him weeks afterwards. Then they'd have had to write to his family. And then they would have had to tell Cora – if they knew about her, of course.'

'She changed her name,' I said, remembering what Cora had told me about the dark days after Donnie abandoned her. 'She pretended to be a war widow. I guess it was just easier back then. She even lied to her mum.'

Patrick made a face.

'Jeez,' he said. 'She had it pretty tough, didn't she?'

'She wanted to go to Hollywood,' I told him. 'She and Donnie had it all planned. She wanted to dance in films like Ginger Rogers.'

'Oh,' said Patrick. 'That's why she doesn't like watching those movies?'

I nodded.

'It's so sad,' I said. 'She called her daughter Virginia, you know? After Ginger Rogers. That was the closest she got.'

A thought struck me.

'I suppose if she'd known he was dead, she could have gone,' I said. 'She could have gone to America like she'd planned. She wouldn't have felt she had to hide away and teach little kids ballet for the rest of her life.'

'She's had a good life, Amy,' Patrick said. 'She's got a family, she's been successful, she's got good friends ...'

'But she never found anyone else,' I said. 'And she stopped performing. She lost Donnie and she lost dancing. That's awful.' A tear slid down my cheek. 'It's just so sad,' I said again. 'And the worst thing is, I don't know if knowing he died is going to make it better for Cora. How can we tell her, Patrick?'

I was crying properly now. Patrick put his arm round me and I sobbed into his neck.

218

'Oh, this is nice,' Matty said. I'd not heard him come in but he was suddenly standing in the lounge, looking cross. 'Am I interrupting?'

I wiped my tears away with the heel of my hand.

'Oh, Matty,' I said. 'Sorry, sweetheart, we just had some bad news.'

Matty looked concerned. He held out his arms to me and I left Patrick's side and went to him.

'What happened, baby,' he said in a cutesie voice. 'Did your dancing go wrong? Did you step on someone's toes?'

Patrick shut the laptop with a snap, and stood up.

'I'd better go,' he said.

'Bye then,' said Matty. I elbowed him in the ribs.

'We've just found out someone died,' I said. 'A bit of empathy would go a long way, you know.'

'Shit,' said Matty looking genuinely ashamed of himself. 'Sorry. Who died?'

'Donnie,' I said. 'He was meant to marry Cora but he died the day before the wedding.'

Matty looked blank. 'Cora …?'

I sighed.

'Cora who lives upstairs,' I said for the four hundredth time. 'She was engaged to a GI and he died.'

I felt my tears starting again. Patrick pulled a pack of tissues from his pocket and handed them to me and I gave him a grateful smile.

Matty stared at me.

'A GI?' he said. 'When exactly did this tragic death take place?'

'1945,' I wailed. I buried my head in Matty's chest and he squeezed me tight and stroked my hair, his chin resting on my head.

'Amy,' he said after a minute. 'What have you done with my picture?'

Chapter 42

Matty and I had a furious row. We were right back to how we'd been before the whole Kayleigh punching incident. I may have broken a glass. And perhaps I told him exactly what I thought of his stupid blown-up photo of me. And there is a teeny, tiny chance that I opened the patio doors and threw that canvas outside into the rain.

'I can't believe you'd be so heartless,' I yelled at him. 'How can you not care about Cora?'

'About some old woman I've never met?' he shouted back. 'You're the heartless one, getting rid of that picture. I made that for you, Amy. To show you how much I love you.'

'Oh, really? The only person you love is yourself.'

There was a pause and Matty and I stood in the middle of the room – Patrick had scarpered ages ago – facing each other and breathing heavily. Then Matty grinned.

'You're right there, baby,' he said. In one swift move he pulled his T-shirt over his head. 'Who wouldn't love this body?'

He posed like a body builder, flexing his muscles, and despite myself I laughed.

Matty winked.

'You like what you see, eh?' he said. 'You want some of this?'

I puckered my lips.

'Well,' I said. 'It's not bad.'

'Not bad?' Matty said. 'Not bloody bad? It's magnificent.'

I shrugged.

'Yeah, it's good,' I said.

'So do you want it?'

'Oh, go on then …'

'Well, you're going to have to catch me first.'

Matty spun round and ran into the bedroom. And, after a second's hesitation, I followed.

This was our thing, you see. It's what we did. Massive, screaming, hurtful rows and then amazing, hot make-up sex. And yes it was exhausting, and sometimes disconcerting, but it was also exciting and kept me on my toes. I just hoped Cora hadn't heard the rowing – or the sex. Somehow I wanted her to think I had a bit more class.

The next morning I got up early and went to rehearsal without waking Matty. I wanted to apologize to Patrick for my charming boyfriend's antics the day before, and of course decide what we were going to do about telling Cora.

Patrick was waiting in the studio when I arrived, even though it was only eight o'clock. The kids were at school now, of course, well into the new term, but Cora had pulled some strings and made sure we still had a space to practise in. Patrick was dancing when I arrived and I stood by the door, watching him. He was going through our tango and it was amazing to watch him. He looked strong and powerful, and a bit vulnerable, too. I found I couldn't take my eyes off him, which was a worry.

When the music finished, he turned to me and I realized he'd known I was there all along.

'Pretty good,' I said as I handed him the coffee I'd bought en route. 'I think we'll make a dancer of you yet.'

He grinned at me.

'You're early,' he said. We both sat down on a bench at one end of the studio and I shrugged my bag off my back.

221

'Wanted to see you,' I said, sipping at my own latte. 'Sorry about Matty yesterday.'

Patrick looked down at his feet.

'I don't think Matty and I will ever be friends,' he said.

'Fair enough,' I said. 'He's a bit selfish.'

Patrick raised his eyebrows.

'A bit?' he said.

He ran his thumb over the top of his coffee cup.

'Are you happy, Amy?' he said. 'With him?'

I leaned back against the wall and looked at him.

'I think so,' I said. 'We're good together. We want the same things.'

'Money? Fame? Adoration?' said Patrick, his lip curling in disgust.

'Don't,' I said. 'Don't make it all sound so shitty.'

Patrick shrugged.

'You're better than that, Amy,' he said. 'What about your auditions?'

'Babs said once I was back on top I'd have the pick of auditions,' I said. 'Being with Matty is part of her plan.'

'But what about you?' Patrick said. He frowned at me. 'You're not some pawn in Babs and Matty's game. You need to do what's right for you – you don't have to play at being Amy Lavender if you don't want to be.'

I smiled at him.

'You're adorable,' I said. 'Worrying about me like that. But this is right for me. It's who I am, Patrick. It's what I do.'

Something that looked like disappointment flashed across Patrick's face. I changed the subject.

'What are we going to do about Donnie?'

He bit his lip.

'Is Cora coming in today?' he said.

I shook my head.

'She's got something on,' I said. 'She's going to come tomorrow.'

'Oh, that's a relief,' Patrick said. 'I'm not sure I could face her knowing what we know.'

'We have to tell her,' I said. 'We do. We can't let her think that Donnie abandoned her and her baby when he didn't.'

Patrick nodded.

'You're right,' he said. 'But it just seems so harsh.'

'I know,' I said. 'She basically changed the way she saw the world because Donnie jilted her. And we're going to tell her he didn't. It's like her whole life view is going to have to be rewritten.'

'I had an idea,' Patrick said. 'But tell me if you think it's dumb.'

'Go on,' I said, intrigued.

'I thought I might try to find Donnie's family,' he said. 'Maybe he had siblings? Perhaps he's got nieces and nephews? It might help her, you know?'

I looked at him.

'Do you think it's stupid?' he said.

'I think it's lovely,' I said. 'It's more than lovely. I think it's really thoughtful and caring and just generally wonderful.'

Patrick beamed at me and I smiled back.

'And I think you're wonderful,' I said.

We stared at each other for a second, then Patrick broke the eye contact.

'So let's tango,' he said.

It was easy to imagine myself as a woman in a relationship that was full of break-ups and make-ups – the back story for my dance that Cora had given me – because that was basically my life with Matty. But it was an odd sensation.

Like I'd told Patrick, I often felt like I was playing the role of Amy Lavender when I was being the celebrity version of myself. So now I was putting that into my dance, but dancing with Patrick, who I could be totally at ease with. It was a bit strange and it had quite an effect on me.

As we danced, I felt like all my nerve endings were tingling. It was a close dance, the tango – we were in contact all the time – and I had never been so aware of Patrick's sheer presence as I was that morning.

There was a tricky part in the dance that I'd been struggling with. A backwards bend that involved Patrick holding my waist and me curling backwards – almost folding in half. I had been nervous about doing it and hadn't managed to get it right yet. But today, the dance flowed beautifully and as Patrick gripped my waist I knew I trusted him completely. I bent back, my hair almost trailing on the floor, then snapped back up. Perfect.

'Yes!' Patrick said, abandoning the dance and lifting me up off my feet. 'I knew you could do it.'

'Nailed it,' I said. I wrapped my arms round his neck and then, without really knowing what I was doing, I kissed him. Just a small, gentle peck at first. I pulled away and Patrick put me back down on the floor, then he kissed me back more deeply.

I could feel my heart hammering against my ribs and I wondered if Patrick could feel it, too, as we stood in the middle of the dance floor, arms entwined, bodies pressed close together.

And then my phone rang, buzzing violently in my pocket, which was jammed up against Patrick's hip. So that broke the mood completely.

'Sorry,' I said, giggling and pulling it out so I could end the call. It was Matty. With a jolt of realization I suddenly came to my senses. I'd got back with Matty for a reason – lots of reasons – and here I was kissing my dance partner. Who, as far as I knew, was still romancing twee Sarah-Lou. I was no better than horrible Kayleigh, who I'd punched for kissing my boyfriend. And Babs would be furious. Matty would be heartbroken. Probably. What was I thinking?

'Shit,' I said to Patrick. 'I have to go.'

'No,' he said, grabbing my hand. 'NO. Amy, if you go now, you're making a choice and you're choosing to be Amy Lavender – the fake Amy Lavender. Is that how you want to live your life?'

I pulled my hand away.

'I'm sorry,' I said. 'It's who I am.'

Chapter 43

The ironic thing was, I didn't even ring Matty back and I certainly didn't go to him. Instead I went to Phil. He was just shutting the shop up – he closed early on Friday afternoons – but he took one look at my face and bustled me inside, locking the door behind me.

'What's happened?' he said. 'What's going on?'

He eyed me suspiciously.

'Is it Matty?'

With a lurch, I realized I'd not even bothered to tell him I'd got back with Matty. I'd not spoken to him for ages, actually. Some friend I was. Of course, he'd have seen our rekindled romance in the *PostOnline*, which was Phil's guilty pleasure, if nowhere else.

I threw myself onto the sofa.

'It's Matty,' I wailed. 'And it's Patrick.'

Phil sat down next to me.

'Ooh it's always the hot dance partner,' he said. 'Spill.'

As I poured out the whole sorry tale I started to realize how silly it all was. Matty had broken my heart and made me look like a fool. I'd even got a police caution because of him. It was crazy to go back to him. Even if I hadn't fallen for Patrick who was kind, loving and – Phil was right – totally hot.

'So why did you get back with Matty?' Phil said. 'I saw the thing he did in *Hot* magazine. It was a bit creepy.'

'You think?' I said, surprised. 'I thought it was romantic.'

Phil rolled his eyes.

'You would,' he said. 'Gestures like that aren't romantic. They're just for show. Real romance is tiny things. Everyday things. Like Bertie making me a cup of tea every morning before he leaves for work.'

'And Patrick looking for Donnie,' I muttered.

'Cora told me to follow my head and not my heart,' I said, louder. 'It makes complete sense for me and Matty to be together. We're good together. We're a brand. We make each other better. Babs even said it would improve my chances of getting on a drama.'

'Sounds like a business decision,' Phil pointed out. 'That's not very romantic.'

'Cora said romance just leads to trouble,' I said. 'It's not worth the heartache.'

I paused.

'But Cora was wrong,' I said slowly, realizing that all her advice had been based on Donnie jilting her. And Donnie hadn't jilted her after all. 'Cora was wrong.'

Phil looked at me, bewildered. I buried my face in my hands.

'What should I do, Phil?' I said. 'I've made so many wrong decisions and now I've made a huge mess of everything.'

Phil put his arm round me.

'I know exactly what you should do,' he said. I looked up at him hopefully.

'Get drunk,' he said.

Which was indeed a brilliant idea at four o'clock on a Friday evening when I was confused and heartsick and just wanted to get through the day. But seemed much less brilliant when I was on my way to the studio early the next morning for a dress rehearsal before the live show that evening.

I sat mutely in the car, hidden behind sunglasses. I didn't speak to the costume girls, really, as they flitted around me pinning me into the black dress I was wearing for the tango. I nodded when the hairdresser showed me her ideas to pull my hair back off my face and give me bright red lips, even though I knew red lipstick didn't suit me.

I was hungover, without a doubt, but I was mostly feeling really awful about running out on Patrick. I was horribly aware we'd not rehearsed our dance as much as we should have, and I had a nagging voice in my head telling me this was bound to be our last week on the show. We'd gone as far as we could, I thought. On Sunday I'd be back to business as usual. The very thought made me want to cry, so I pinched my lips together and said nothing at all.

When Patrick eventually showed up, five minutes before our dress rehearsal slot, he barely acknowledged me. He was busy messaging on his phone – Sarah-Lou, I thought. He gave me an abrupt nod and said 'ready?' and that was it.

But I wasn't ready. Not even a bit. As the band struck up the opening notes of 'Back to Black', my mind went blank. And not in a good way. I honestly didn't know what to do. I followed Patrick's lead, but I was a bit behind the whole time, and I didn't do the backwards bend properly at all.

The dress rehearsal wasn't great. But Patrick didn't hang about afterwards to give me notes like he'd done in the past. He disappeared off somewhere and only came back as the live show was starting. So by the time we took to the stage, I was almost throwing up because I was so nervous. I was glad that Cora hadn't made it tonight, and that Matty was doing some club night in Manchester. I didn't want anyone to witness my failure.

And, as if I'd willed it to happen, the dance was a disaster from start to finish. I trod on my dress. I went left instead of right. I stepped on Patrick's foot. And, worst of all, I tensed up when I went to bend backwards, meaning Patrick fumbled and almost dropped me on my head. It was embarrassing. The audience gave us good-natured applause but, by the time we went to hear what the judges had to say, I was almost in tears.

'It was a disaster, darling,' said one. Another told us, quite sternly, that we'd disappointed him. Then the twinkly-eyed head judge, Frank, took off his glasses and looked at us.

'Something's happened with you two,' he said in his rough cockney tones. 'I don't know what it is, but I suggest you sort it out quick bloody smart.'

'Tensions do run high at this stage in the competition,' said Melissa, the presenter. I glared at her. What did she know?

'It's all good,' Patrick said, taking my hand. I clung on to it. 'We're good. This was a tricky dance.'

Frank looked disbelieving.

'I just hope the audience see enough in you to keep you here for another week,' he said. 'You deserve to be in the semi-final in my opinion, but it's not up to me.'

As we went through the double doors, out of sight of the cameras, Patrick dropped my hand and headed off down the corridor.

'Patrick,' I called.

He turned back and looked at me.

'Sorry,' I said.

But he didn't respond.

And that wasn't even the worst of it. Of course we were in the bottom two – alongside the Olympic swimmer who was dressed as Tarzan and dancing a jive. We had to dance again to stay in the competition and I was terrified.

I tried my best to dance the tango better this time and it was marginally improved. But we were under-rehearsed, awkward and unhappy and it showed.

'I never want to dance that tango ever again,' I told Melissa as she led us out to wait for the judges' verdict.

She laughed, but I hadn't been joking.

In the end, I think, it was purely due to the Tarzan costume that we stayed in. Frank was no fan of 'silly outfits' as he called them and, as he held the deciding vote, his decision to keep us in for another week won through. But it was close. Really close. And Patrick was furious.

'Let's take Monday off, too,' he said, marching out of the studio with me almost running to keep up with him. 'See if two days off can't improve our dancing a bit.'

'Do you think we should clear the air?' I said, breathlessly. 'Maybe we should talk about what happened?'

He stopped walking.

'There's nothing to talk about,' he said. 'I misread the signals, Amy. Just like I misread them when I nearly kissed you after our Charleston. I thought perhaps we had something, but I was wrong.'

'We do have something,' I said quietly, my head reeling in surprise that he thought he'd instigated our almost-kiss after our dance that time. I was under the impression it had all been me. 'Maybe in another time or place we could have been something special.'

Patrick gave me a furious look.

'Oh, that's bull,' he said. 'You're ruining your life by chasing Matty and going after celebrity and if you can't see that, I can't help you.'

'Don't be so superior,' I said. 'You just hate that I'm ambitious for something other than bloody dancing.'

Patrick shook his head.

'I hate that you're not ambitious enough,' he said. 'You're amazing, Amy. You deserve so much more than this.'

He turned away from me and walked towards the door.

'See you on Tuesday,' he said.

Chapter 44

I barely slept that night. I kept going over our dance in my head, working out where it had gone wrong, and what had happened. And always coming to the same conclusion: it was my fault. If I'd not run out on Patrick, we'd have practised more, things wouldn't have been so awkward and perhaps we wouldn't have said those horrible things to one another. I cringed thinking about how he'd said I was shallow and how I'd proved him right. In fact, that was the most awful thing about it, that he was right.

But, said a little voice in my head at about four in the morning, he didn't have to be so smug and sanctimonious about it. He didn't have to be so downright nasty.

Suddenly angry I sat up in my tangled duvet and threw my pillow across the room.

'He's the douchebag,' I said to the empty room. 'Not Matty.'

Although, thinking about it, I'd not even heard from Matty. I'd messaged him on my way home from the studio asking him to call but he hadn't.

I threw my other pillow.

'They're all douchebags.'

Giving up on sleep, I got out of bed, wrapped a cardigan round myself and jammed my feet into slippers, and went into the living room where I watched Fred Astaire and Ginger Rogers films until the sun came up. And that's when exhaustion finally caught up with me and I slept. I woke up much later to the sound of Cora knocking on the patio doors.

Bleary-eyed, I let her in and staggered back to the sofa, making sure I turned the DVD off before she realized I was watching Ginger.

Cora handed me a plate loaded with slices of lemon drizzle cake and went off to the kitchen area to make tea.

'Do you want to tell me about it?' she said as the kettle boiled.

'No.'

'Fine.' She poured water into mugs and searched for a teaspoon.

'I'm very angry,' I said.

'Good,' Cora smiled. 'That will put some fire in your belly. What's your next dance?'

'Foxtrot,' I said sulkily. 'And rumba.'

Cora whistled.

'Tricky,' she said.

'I know.'

'Not talking to Patrick at all?' She handed me a mug and I shook my head.

'We kissed,' I admitted. 'Then I ran away and he was annoyed. He said I'm throwing my life away chasing fame.'

Cora looked thoughtful.

'Are you?'

I shrugged.

'Probably,' I said. 'I'm following my head and not my heart, like you said.'

'I said that?'

'Yes, you did.'

Cora sat down next to me and wrapped her fingers round her mug. I knew the warmth eased the pain of her arthritis and I wondered if she was doing okay. I generally forgot how old she was day to day, but every now and then I got a reminder.

'Talking about Donnie with you has stirred up emotions I thought I'd buried long ago,' she said. 'I've been remembering things, revisiting choices I made years ago. Thinking about old faces from the past.'

With a start I remembered that she didn't yet know Donnie had died.

'Cora,' I began. She held up her hand to stop me.

'I've had a happy life, Amy,' she said. 'I love my Ginny, and Natasha and her brood. I've been successful with the school.'

'It's a great school,' I said.

Cora smiled.

'It's ours, you know?' she said. 'My friend Audrey and I started it, back in the fifties.'

'No. Way,' I said, impressed. I'd assumed she'd just been one of several teachers.

Cora nodded.

'I'm very proud of what we did there,' she said. 'I've had a wonderful career. And I had Audrey, and other friends who became my family. But I can't deny that I sometimes felt lonely. I think I missed opportunities to build a life with someone because I was afraid to trust my instincts.'

I stared at her. What was she trying to say?

'I had a few men friends over the years,' she carried on. 'One in particular, I think, could have been rather good for me. But I turned him down and he married someone else.'

I felt awful. How could I tell her about Donnie now, knowing she was horribly aware that she'd avoided relationships because he'd jilted her?

She patted my knee.

'I think perhaps I gave you some misguided advice,' she said, oblivious that my stricken face was due to guilt and not dismay at her story.

'I don't know what to do,' I said, meaning Matty, Patrick, my career – and whether to tell her the truth about Donnie.

Cora stood up and held out her hand.

'Why don't you show me your foxtrot?' she said.

I looked down at myself.

'I'm wearing my pyjamas,' I said, with a small smile. 'And my slippers.'

'So?'

'We've barely started working on this one,' I warned her. 'We just did little pieces last week when Patrick wanted to give me a break from our tango.'

'So show me the bits you know.'

I started to mark out the steps and Cora watched silently. Then, as I grew more confident, she began giving me tips.

'Your shoulders are up round your ears,' she said. 'Relax.'

'I feel silly,' I said.

We were giggling over my slippered feet when Matty arrived home. He threw his bag on the sofa next to where Cora was perching and glared at her.

'Hi, babe,' he said, kissing my neck and wrapping his arms round my waist from behind. He smelled of stale beer and his eyes were wide and staring. I wondered if he'd taken something – he certainly wasn't a stranger to cocaine.

'Good time last night?'

'Say hello to Cora,' I said like a disapproving teacher. 'And no, not really.'

Matty mumbled hello to Cora.

'Get rid of her,' he hissed in my ear. 'I'm so hot for you. Let's go back to bed.'

He tugged at the waistband of my pyjama bottoms and I slapped his hand away.

'Matty,' I said, embarrassed at his antics. 'Behave.'

Cora looked awkward and I felt myself blushing as Matty's hand snaked up my pyjama top and I wriggled away.

'Don't,' I said. 'Sorry, Cora.'

'I'll be off,' she said.

'Yeah, off you go, Grandma,' said Matty. 'We've got things to do.'

That did it. I pulled his arms off me and turned round to face him.

'How dare you speak to Cora like that!' I said. I wasn't shouting but I was close. 'How dare you even look at Cora like that?'

'Oh, babe,' Matty whined. 'I just wanted some alone time with you.'

'Well, I'm busy,' I said. 'So alone time is going to have to wait.'

'You're only dancing,' he whined. 'Dancing isn't busy. You can make time for Matty.'

Cora was still standing behind me, like a sentry, at the patio doors. I thought of her, missing her chances at happiness and I realized I didn't want to look back on my life when I was her age and think that I'd made some huge mistakes – and I certainly didn't want to be shackled to a loser, drugged-up DJ who couldn't even be polite to an elderly lady who deserved his respect.

'I can't make time for Matty,' I said, picking up his bag and shoving it at him. 'Not now, not later, not ever.'

He gaped at me.

'We're over,' I hissed.

'Babe …'

'Get out.'

Matty reached for me and I batted his hand away.

'Get out.'

Realizing I wasn't joking, he hoisted his bag onto his shoulder and made for the front door.

'I'll call you later,' he said.

'I won't answer.'

'Then you'll be making a big mistake,' he said, his handsome face twisted with anger.

'Oh, I don't think so,' I said. I felt strangely calm and more in control than I'd felt for weeks. Months, even. 'I think I've just avoided making the biggest mistake of my life.'

Chapter 45

Cora, bless her heart, stayed with me as I cried for what seemed like the whole afternoon. But as the evening approached she told me she had tickets for the theatre with a friend.

'Go,' I said, sniffing loudly. 'I'll be fine, honestly.'

'I'm busy tomorrow morning,' she said. 'But I'll call in after lunch.'

'I'm fine,' I lied. 'I'll call Phil if I need a shoulder to cry on.'

But I didn't. I lay on the sofa sobbing, then I dragged myself to bed and sobbed some more.

On Monday morning I dragged myself back to the sofa and watched Jeremy Kyle shouting at people while I ignored the relentless ringing of my phone. I didn't want to switch it off in case Patrick phoned, so instead I cancelled two calls from Matty – he wasn't trying that hard to get hold of me – a handful of calls from showbiz journalists, and approximately four hundred from Babs, who'd clearly heard the news. From Matty's agent, I assumed.

At lunchtime, while I was watching *Neighbours* and playing with a bowl of cereal, she rang again.

'Amy Lavender,' she told my voicemail in her most strident tone. A tone that would – and had – made grown men weep.

'This is unacceptable. I deserve an explanation. And I'm coming to get one. I'll be there in ten minutes.'

There was a muffled conversation with someone in the background.

'Clapham?' she said, sounding alarmed. There was more muffled chat, then: 'An hour. I'll be there in an hour.'

I cancelled the call listlessly. She won't come, I thought in despair. She'll probably think better of it and instead she'll just fire me, and that will be that. No job, no agent, no boyfriend – back to square bloody one.

So I was fairly surprised when – almost exactly an hour later – my doorbell rang. Thankfully I had forced myself to have a shower and get dressed earlier, so I wasn't wearing the same pyjamas I'd been wearing for twenty-four hours any more, but I knew I looked far, far removed from the sparkling celeb Babs expected me to be.

I slouched through the hall to the front door and opened it.

'Babs,' I said gruffly.

'Guess again.'

It was Patrick. He was wrapped up in a winter jacket – the temperature had suddenly dropped – and had a black beanie hat on his head. His expression suggested he wasn't sure how I would react to seeing him.

Surprised that he wasn't Babs and caught unawares, I jumped sideways and stubbed my toe violently on the skirting board.

'Ow, ow, ow,' I said, hopping and trying to rub it better.

'You need some ice on that,' said Patrick. He stepped into the hall, took my arm and guided me towards the kitchen.

'Just so you know,' I said, through gritted teeth, 'I'm very angry with you, and if I could walk I wouldn't have let you in the flat. In my head, I'm slamming the door in your face.'

'That's fine,' said Patrick, the tiniest glimmer of a smile on his face. 'I'm angry with you, too.'

He helped me onto the sofa and went to the kitchen area.

'Do you have ice?' he said.

'No idea,' I admitted. 'I've never opened the freezer.'

Patrick rolled his eyes and wrenched it open.

'You do,' he said, pulling out a frosty ice cube tray. 'And a very old bag of peas.'

'Nice,' I said.

Patrick knocked the ice into a tea towel and wrapped it up, then he handed it to me and I held it on my toe.

'Why are you here?' I said rudely. I wasn't ready to see him yet – I wasn't prepared.

Patrick pulled off his hat, then he wandered over to the patio doors and looked out at the garden, which was looking a bit bleak now all the leaves had dropped off the trees.

'I came to apologize,' he said, not looking at me.

I wasn't expecting that.

'Pardon?' I said, wondering if I'd misheard.

This time Patrick looked at me.

'I came to say sorry,' he said. 'So, you know … sorry.'

I wasn't letting him off the hook that easily.

'For …'

'For questioning your life choices, and for saying you're shallow and throwing your life away.'

I winced inwardly at hearing the words again but I still wanted to make the apology count.

'For being smug and sanctimonious,' I said.

'That too,' Patrick said.

There was a pause.

'I'm sorry, too,' I said. 'I flew off the handle because you were right.'

'Really?' said Patrick. 'What do you mean, I was right?'

I nodded. The ice was beginning to melt and drip down my foot. I watched it for a second, then I looked up at Patrick again.

'I've been so messed up,' I said. 'Because it's turned out that what I thought I wanted wasn't what I wanted at all.'

Patrick shrugged his jacket off, then sat down on the floor and looked at me.

'Go on,' he said.

'When I got the part in *Turpin Road*, and then I met Matty, my life went down a certain path,' I said slowly. 'It was really fun, you know? The photo shoots, and the parties, and the money.'

Patrick nodded.

'But somewhere in among all of that, I forgot that the thing I loved most of all was acting.'

I took the tea towel off my foot and examined my toe so I didn't have to look at Patrick.

'I threw Matty out,' I said gruffly. 'He's not what I wanted, either.'

Patrick flushed and I gabbled on.

'Not for you,' I said. 'I didn't dump him for you. I'm not like Kayleigh – I don't go around kissing men with girlfriends. I'm sorry if I messed things up with you and Sarah-Lou.'

'I finished things with her, actually,' Patrick said, still looking a bit embarrassed.

'Really?' I was quite pleased, but I didn't want him to see it. 'Was she too twee?'

Patrick flushed again.

'The opposite,' he said. 'Did you read *50 Shades of Grey*?'

I made a face.

'Some of it.'

'Well, she's living it,' Patrick said. 'She's got a room in her flat, just for – you know – sex games.'

'What?' I was astonished. 'Sweet little Sarah-Lou?'

'She doesn't look so sweet when she's coming at you with a whip, let me tell you,' Patrick said.

I tried to smile, but I was uncomfortable talking about him playing sex games with some other woman.

'I have never made so many excuses, or left an apartment so fast,' Patrick said, watching me intently. 'I think she was a bit cross that we never sealed the deal.'

238

That was a relief.

'So we're both single,' Patrick said.

'We are,' I said, sadly. 'But I don't think this is the right time for us.'

Patrick nodded – I liked that I never had to explain myself to him.

'I mean, I like you, but this is bigger than all that. I think I just need some time by myself to get my head straight. To get Amy Lavender back on track.'

'Makes sense,' Patrick said.

'Those other things – the parties and the paparazzi and the launches – they're all fun but they're not important,' I said. 'What's important is doing something I love every day. And I had that at *Turpin Road* and I threw it away because of all the other stuff. And I'm not going to let that happen again.'

'You don't have to stop going to parties,' Patrick said. 'You love parties.'

'That's true,' I admitted. 'I do. But I want to be an actress, not a celebrity. And, yes, I want people to like me, and I want to look good, and I like photo shoots. But surely, if I put my mind to it, and I'm clever about it all, I can have those things and achieve my goals.'

'Which are?'

I shrugged.

'BAFTAs? Emmys? An Oscar? Who knows?'

Patrick gave me a broad smile.

'I have absolutely no doubt you'll do it,' he said. 'No doubt at all.'

'Well, first I need bloody Babs to get me some proper auditions,' I said. 'Instead of sponsorship deals for breakfast cereal and sexy calendars.'

'I bet Cora can help,' said Patrick. 'She used to work for an agent, right? And the kids at school must all have agents. I bet she's got loads of contacts.'

'Now that's an idea,' I said. A thought struck me.

'The school's hers, you know,' I said. 'She's the principal. She and her friend Audrey set it up.'

'I know,' Patrick said.

'You do?' I was surprised. 'How do you know?'

'Her name's on the sign outside,' he said, rolling his eyes.

I giggled.

'Oh,' I said. 'She's fabulous, isn't she? Maybe I will ask her for some help.'

'You should definitely ask her,' Patrick said. 'I know she thinks you're not fulfilling your potential.'

'She does?' I said, surprised. 'Have you been discussing me?'

'Nooooo,' said Patrick. 'Never. Well, a little bit. Just every now and then.'

'Babs has been my agent for ever,' I said. 'She's the only agent I've ever had. I'm frightened about what would happen to me if I didn't have her.'

'Maybe it's time for a change,' Patrick pointed out. 'Find someone who can get you the auditions you want.'

'You're right,' I said. 'I'll ask Cora what she thinks.'

'Speaking of Cora,' said Patrick, fidgeting in his seat and pulling some folded paper out of his jeans pocket. 'She's the other reason I came ...'

'Ohmygod,' I breathed. 'Have you found his family? Donnie's family. Do you know where they are?'

Patrick unfolded the paper, which was covered in his scribbled writing.

'I have,' he said. 'I've found them.'

Chapter 46

'Ohmygod,' I squealed again. 'Tell me everything. Who have you found?'

Patrick smoothed out the paper and squinted at it.

'My writing is terrible,' he said.

'Patrick,' I warned. 'Tell me.'

He threw me an exasperated glance.

'Right, so Donnie was the eldest of three kids,' he said. 'He had a sister who was in her late teens at the end of the war – Lois – and a younger brother who was twelve in 1945.'

'And?' I said.

'Lois died a few years ago,' Patrick said. 'But Walter's still alive. He's in his eighties now and he also had two kids – a son and a daughter, who are both sixty-something.'

'And?' I said again. 'Do you know where they are?'

'I do,' said Patrick, making his smug face. 'Well, I know where the son is. His name is Charlie and I emailed him as soon as I'd tracked him down.'

'Did he reply?' I was so impatient to know what was going on that Patrick's sloooooow telling of the story was driving me mad.

'I told him I'd stumbled upon some information about his Uncle Donald from the time he spent in London during the war and asked if I could ring him to chat about it,' Patrick said. 'And he emailed me his number.'

'Ohmygod,' I said. 'Where is he? America? What time is it there? Can we call him now?'

Patrick grinned at me and pulled out his phone.

'He's in New York,' he said. 'It's about ten in the morning there and, yes, we can call him now.'

I was shaking as he dialled the number and introduced himself when Charlie answered.

'Speakerphone,' I hissed at him. 'Put him on speakerphone.'

'Mr Jackson, my friend is here and she'd like to join in the conversation, would that be okay?' Patrick said. I was impressed by how polite he was. Cora would be, too, I thought.

With Charlie on loudspeaker, Patrick and I explained how we were friends with Cora and she'd known his uncle during the war.

'Oh, my,' Charlie said. 'That would be Uncle Donnie's mysterious wife.'

'You know about her?' I said, surprised.

'Sure I do,' said Charlie. 'She was something of a legend in our family. Uncle Donnie wrote to my grandma telling her all about this woman he'd met, and how he was going to marry her. And he even wrote to my dad – he was just a kid during the war – but he wrote to him telling him how wonderful this woman was. He sent photos, I think.'

'They never got married,' I said, my voice catching in my throat. 'Donnie was killed the day before their wedding.'

'Well, now isn't that just too sad,' Charlie said. 'I'll bet she was devastated.'

'She didn't know,' Patrick said. 'She didn't know he'd died. She thought he'd gone AWOL – that he'd jilted her.'

There was silence on the other end of the line.

'Jeez,' said Charlie after a minute. 'That's rough. And it explains a lot. I know my grandma tried to find her. She was cut up when

242

Uncle Donnie died, obviously, and my dad said she wanted to find someone who'd loved him as much as she had.'

'Cora changed her name,' I said.

'To Jackson?' Charlie said in surprise. 'I believe Grandma looked for her under that name.'

Patrick and I exchanged a glance and he gave me a slight nod.

'No,' I said. 'Not Jackson. Cora changed her name to Devonshire. It was just a name she chose at random. She pretended to be a widow, you see, because …'

I took a breath.

'… she was pregnant. She was pregnant with Donnie's baby.'

Charlie was silent, this time for even longer.

'She had a baby?'

'She did,' I said. 'A girl. Ginny. And Ginny has a daughter, too – Natasha. And Natasha's got loads of kids. Three, I think.'

'Four,' said Patrick.

'Four,' I said.

'Well, I'll be damned,' said Charlie. 'Cousins.'

'Cousins,' I said.

'And Cora?' Charlie said. 'What about Cora? Is she still with us?'

Patrick and I laughed, both amazed that we'd not told him about the most important person in all of this.

'She's alive and kicking,' I said. 'She's almost ninety but she's fabulous. Suffers a bit with her arthritis but she's incredible.'

'I'd like to meet her,' Charlie said. 'And my kids would, too, I bet. My daughter even studied in England for a while – she could have walked right by one of her cousins and not known.'

'We've not told her,' I blurted out. 'Cora doesn't know what we've found out. She doesn't know Donnie died before the wedding and she doesn't know Patrick's tracked you guys down.'

'Ah,' said Charlie. 'You going to tell her?'

I glanced at Patrick again and he gave me a firm nod.

'Absolutely,' I said. 'Right now if we can. She'll be so sad about

Donnie, but knowing that Ginny and Natasha have a whole new family will help, I'm sure. I bet she'd love to chat with your dad, too, and share memories of Donnie.'

'Dad would love that,' said Charlie with a chuckle. 'We've all heard his stories a thousand times – Cora would be a new audience for him!'

He paused.

'Listen,' he said. 'I know my dad has a box of stuff from the war. Lots of memorabilia from when Donnie died – letters, photos, medals. My Aunt Lois kept it but, when she passed away, Dad took it. We thought someone should have it.'

'I'm pleased you did,' said Patrick.

'I used to look through it when I was a kid,' said Charlie. 'I've not so much as lifted the lid in years but I know where it is. How about I scooch over to my dad's now and dig it out. See if there's anything that might help you tell Cora. This is pretty big news for anyone to take in, especially a lady in her eighties.'

'You're right,' I said, touched by his compassion for someone he'd never even met. 'It's going to be a shock for her.'

'Let's see if we can soften the blow,' Charlie said. 'I'll go over to Dad's now, and email you whatever I can. Give me a couple of hours, yeah?'

We said our goodbyes and Patrick ended the call. Then we both stared at one another in astonishment.

'Have we done the right thing?' I said, as the enormity of our discovery began to sink in. 'Or have we just opened an enormous can of worms?'

Patrick looked exhausted.

'I have no idea,' he admitted. 'It's good, I think. Better that she knows, right? Donnie didn't jilt her and we can prove it. That's got to be an improvement on what she thought before.'

I nodded slowly.

'You're right,' I said. 'It's just she was talking about missed opportunities and letting life pass you by the other day.'

I caught Patrick's eye and felt myself blush as I realized it was pretty obvious why that subject had come up. I looked away and carried on.

'I just hope she doesn't start thinking of her whole life as one huge missed opportunity.'

'She's done good things, Amy,' Patrick said. 'She's loved, she's successful – she may have let some chances slip by but she definitely made the most of others.'

'You're right,' I said, feeling slightly more positive. 'I just want to tell her now and get it over with.'

I felt fizzy inside with nerves and excitement and very restless.

'How's your toe?' asked Patrick.

I'd actually forgotten all about it. Now I flexed it to see if it still hurt. It didn't.

'It's fine,' I said. 'Bit cold.'

'Great,' said Patrick. 'Because I know one sure-fire way to distract us while we're waiting for Charlie to email all that stuff.'

He did? Was he suggesting what I thought he was suggesting? Even though we'd only just agreed to keep our relationship firmly in the friends zone? I looked at him with a combination of surprise and desire.

'Really?' I said, lowering my gaze and looking up at him from under my eyelashes. 'And what would that be?'

Patrick held out his hand to me.

'Foxtrot,' he said.

245

Chapter 47

Cora

2015

I was enjoying a late-afternoon snooze in front of *Cash in the Attic* when Patrick and Amy arrived. I heard them knock on the back door, chatting in what they thought were quiet voices, and then Amy called out to see if I was home.

'In the lounge, darling,' I said. 'Bring tea.'

I didn't really want tea, but I definitely didn't want them to see me hunched in my chair, blanket over my knees. I was an old woman, yes, but I was a vain one and I liked to be looking elegant when I received guests.

I stood up, groaning a bit. That's a sign of being old, I thought, if you can't stand up without groaning or sit down without sighing in relief. I'd noticed Ginny doing that now, too. That was a real shock, when I realized my daughter was old now. Her seventieth birthday was approaching and, though she also liked to look after herself, I could see she was beginning to slow down a bit.

I tidied my hair in the mirror, reapplied my lipstick, and draped my blanket over the back of the sofa. Then I settled myself in

246

the chair again and turned off the TV just as Patrick and Amy shuffled in.

Amy put the tray of tea on the low table in front of me, and they both stood – looking nervous and awkward.

'Sit down,' I said, wondering what was going on. 'You both look like you've come to see your headmistress.'

They sat simultaneously and Amy chewed her lip. I studied her. She was astonishingly pretty. Even more so now she'd tamed her mop of hair. I'd never tell her so – she was pleased enough with herself – but I'd watched lots of clips of her show on Natasha's iPad and I thought she was a wonderful actress. She had a great future in front of her, I was sure. But now she looked like she was going to burst into tears.

'Do you want me to do it?' Patrick asked her.

Amy shook her head.

'It should come from me,' she said.

I felt the first stirrings of alarm. What was she going to say?

'Is everything all right?' I said.

Amy leaned forward.

'Cora,' she said. 'Do you remember you asked us to find Donnie?'

His name made my heart thump, just as it always had, and the shock of hearing Amy say it made me snappy.

'Of course I remember,' I said. 'I'm old, not insane.'

Amy frowned at me.

'Cora,' she said. 'It's not good news, I'm afraid.'

I looked down at my hands. They were shaking but when I spoke my voice was steady.

'Married?' I said. 'Or dead?'

Amy took a breath.

'He's dead, Cora,' she said. 'I'm sorry.'

I raised my chin.

'I'd expected as much,' I said. 'He'd have been ninety-one now – lots of my friends are gone. Poor Audrey didn't make it to seventy-five.'

I smiled as I thought of darling Audrey, cigarette in hand, telling me what to do.

'When did he go, Donnie?' I carried on. 'Did he keel over on the golf course? Or pass away surrounded by his loving family?'

Amy and Patrick looked grim-faced. Amy got up and came to me. She knelt on the floor at my feet and took both my hands in hers.

'Cora, he died in 1945,' she said carefully. 'He was killed in a bomb that fell in London on 25 March. He didn't jilt you – he was already dead.'

I felt like the whole room had tilted and I was sliding off. I put my hand to my head trying to steady myself.

'I don't understand,' I said.

'It was a V2 attack,' Patrick said. 'There were quite a few, right at the end of the war.'

'I remember,' I said. Now my voice was shaky. 'There were lots down in Camberwell and round here. But none where Donnie was stationed.'

Amy looked at Patrick for help and he continued.

'It hit Tottenham Court Road,' he said. 'Killed ten people. Donnie was one of them. But it took them days to clear the site and I guess by the time they'd worked out he was one of the victims, you'd moved on.'

I shook my head.

'I saw Donnie that day,' I said. I remembered meeting in Hyde Park in the spring sunshine and him dashing off to do something. 'I don't know where he went afterwards. Why would he go to Tottenham Court Road? What was he doing?' Amy was talking but she sounded like she was very far away.

'Cora,' she said. 'Do you want to lie down?'

I did. She helped me over to the sofa and put the blanket over me.

I closed my eyes, wondering if this was all a dream, but all I could see was Donnie up ahead of me on the path, shouting that we were getting married. The scene replayed itself over and over on my eyelids.

'Do you want me to phone Natasha?' Cora said. 'Or the doctor?'

'No,' I croaked. 'No. Just give me a minute to take this in.'

'I know it's a shock,' she said. She stroked my hair gently. 'But Cora, that's not all.'

I opened my eyes and stared at her. She was leaning over me, her pretty face etched with concern and her wide brown eyes worried.

'We've found Donnie's family,' she said. 'We spoke to his nephew, Charlie. He's the son of Donnie's brother, Walter.'

I nodded. I remembered Donnie's tales of Wally and the scrapes he got into.

'And Charlie's found some things,' Amy said. 'Photos, letters, other memories. He's emailed some of them.'

I struggled to sit up.

'Do you have them?' I said. I was shaking violently now. 'Can I see?'

Patrick helped me sit up properly – apparently nothing made one feel every moment of one's eighty-nine years more than finding out one's fiancé had died seventy years ago – and then he sat on one side of me and Amy on the other. To all intents and purposes they were all that was keeping me upright.

Patrick opened his computer and clicked a few buttons. Suddenly the screen was filled with a photograph of me in uniform.

'Ohhhhh,' I said. Grief hit me like a physical pain and for a moment I thought I was having a heart attack.

'Cora,' Amy said. 'Oh, God, Patrick, put it away.'

Patrick moved the computer but with a superhuman effort I gulped some air and managed to speak.

'No,' I said. 'I want to see.'

'Oh, Cora, are you sure?' Amy sounded close to tears – as I was myself – but I knew I had to find out more.

I pointed at the screen with my lumpy, shaky knuckle.

'That's me,' I said. 'Obviously. I gave Donnie that photograph. I wrote a message on the back.'

Patrick clicked again and this time the screen showed the back of the photo.

'Darling Donnie,' I'd written all those years before. 'Forever yours, Cora.'

I looked up at the ceiling, trying not to cry. Just like on my wedding day, I feared that if I started I'd never stop.

'Is there anything else?' I asked. Patrick nodded.

He showed me a photograph of Donnie in uniform, and some of his division – there were familiar faces among them but I didn't linger. There was the telegram announcing his death, and a letter from his commanding officer telling Donnie's mother what a good soldier he was.

And then Patrick paused.

'Charlie said there are lots of letters,' he told me. 'Donnie's mother kept them all. He's not sent them all but he's sent the one that matters. The one about you.'

I closed my eyes again, and again I saw Donnie up ahead, turning round, smiling at me over his shoulder.

'Can you read it to me?' I asked Amy. 'Will you do that for me?'

'Are you sure?'

I gripped her hand tightly.

'Please,' I said. 'Please.'

Chapter 48

Amy began to read, her voice clear and steady. I closed my eyes and listened – hearing Donnie's voice in every line.

'*London. March 25, 1945,*' Amy began.

'*Dear Mom and Dad. I have no way of telling if my letters are arriving in the right order, or if they are even arriving at all, so I feel I must start over telling my stories each time I write. This letter is more important than most because I am writing it on the eve of my wedding. Yes, you read that right. I'm getting married. I've told you about Cora. She is just wonderful and she and I have decided to tie the knot right here in London – tomorrow. As you know – I hope, if my letters have arrived – we are being sent to France once more and so Cora and I didn't want to wait a second longer than we had to. We have booked the ceremony for tomorrow afternoon and we are so excited to become Mr and Mrs Jackson.*'

Amy looked up at me.

'Do you want me to carry on?' she said. I couldn't speak but I managed to nod and so she continued.

'*Let me tell you a little about Cora,*' she said. '*She is beautiful, of course. I enclose a photograph that I tore from a newsletter. She has blonde hair, and clear, bright-blue eyes. She is a dancer and, as I told you before, I met her when her company – the Entertainment*

National Service Association – performed for we rowdy GIs last year. When you see her on stage, as I'm sure you will one day, you'll understand why she caught my eye. When she dances, you can't take your eyes off her. She wants to be in movies like Ginger Rogers and I know she'll be a big star someday. She's so funny – she makes me laugh like a drain most of the time – and she's really smart. She's a great singer, and a comedienne. She likes dogs, and she hates getting her face wet, and she makes me the happiest man alive'

Amy looked at me again. I was crying now, fat tears slipping down my cheeks, but I didn't care.

'Please keep going,' I whispered.

'Cora doesn't have any brothers or sisters so she's eager to meet Wally and Lois, though I have warned her that Lois never shuts up and that Wally will probably get her to play cowboys with him as soon as she arrives. Because that's our plan, Mom and Dad. We want to build a life together in America and as soon as the war is over we want to head to LA and Hollywood and see if we can't just get Cora discovered by some big-time movie producer. But if that doesn't happen, that's okay, too. We'll make a life in Connecticut instead. Cora's going to write you after the wedding as I'd really like her to make her way to the States as soon as possible. London's not the safest of places and I want my bride to be out of harm's way

'Mom, Dad, I'm sorry you won't be at the wedding. That's how it goes in wartime I guess. Maybe we can have a party to celebrate when all this is over? Invite all the family so they can meet Cora. Perhaps she'll dance for us all. I know Lois would love that. Cora loves putting on a show. In fact, I've got a surprise for her after the wedding. We'll have a few hours before I go to France, so I've arranged a room in a pub nearby – you know what a pub is, right? – where Cora and her friends can sing and dance to their heart's content and celebrate our marriage. I'm there now, in fact. I've just said goodbye to Cora in Hyde Park and come to the pub – it's called the Whitefield Tavern – isn't that just the most English name? I'm sitting here, chatting to the landlord – that's what they call

252

bartenders here – and drinking beer and arranging the party for tomorrow. When I've finished my drink, I'll mail this letter and then head back to meet the rest of my division

'There's always a strange atmosphere with the men the night before we go someplace, but I like the way we all pull together at these times. I'm scared of going back to Europe, but knowing Cora's waiting for me will make me even more determined to come home

'Tell Lois I miss her, and tell Wally to stay out of my room. And I miss him, too. I'll see you all soon.

'Your loving son, Donald'

Amy took a deep, juddering breath and looked at me.

'He really loved you, Cora,' she said. 'He didn't run out on you. He loved you and he wanted to marry you.'

I pulled my hanky out of my sleeve and wiped my eyes.

'I loved him, too,' I said. 'I loved him so much. We could have had a wonderful life together.'

Amy squeezed my hand gently.

'I know,' she said. 'I know.'

She put her arm round me and I cried and cried. She cried too. And Patrick made more tea and put his arms round us both and said soothing things as the room grew dark.

Eventually, when I had no more tears to cry, I started to think about the implications of all this.

'Ginny,' I said. 'Oh, my word. I have to tell Ginny.'

'Does she know who her dad was?' Amy said.

I shook my head.

'Bits and pieces,' I admitted. 'I once had a friend who told me that the best lies are full of truths. When Donnie left …' I caught myself. 'When Donnie died, I called myself Cora Devonshire, as you know. I told everyone – including my mother, and Ginny – that I'd married a GI who'd been killed in action.'

Amy was looking shocked.

'It wasn't easy being a single mother in those days,' I said. 'War or no war. It was much better to be a widow.'

She nodded.

'Did Ginny never ask?'

I shrugged.

'She knew his name – Jackson Devonshire – and I told her all the photos were lost,' I said. 'Lots of her friends had lost their fathers in the war. It wasn't so strange. A couple of times she tried to find his family, but that was before the internet, of course, and because Jackson Devonshire didn't exist, she didn't get very far.'

I could tell Amy thought I'd done a terrible thing. Maybe I had. I'd lied to Ginny for so long it almost didn't feel like a lie any more. But I'd done it to protect myself. It was part of a barrier I'd put up round myself and I'd done what I had to do to survive. People had done all sorts of things in the war – things they were proud of and things they weren't so proud of – and it was hard for Amy and Patrick and Natasha and everyone who was so far away from it to understand. I wondered if Ginny would realize that I'd done what I did simply for self-preservation. I hoped so.

'I'm very tired,' I said, feeling exhaustion hit me like a wave. 'Amy, darling, could you help me to bed?'

Fussing over me like a mother hen, Amy took me into the bedroom and helped me put on my nightdress. I remembered Audrey doing the same to me once upon a time. I'd been so lucky having Audrey as a friend, and now I had Amy, too. It was female friendships that had kept me on track all these years, I realized. Audrey would have loved Amy. And she'd definitely be pleased Donnie had turned out to be a 'good'un' after all, I thought. I wondered if they were together somewhere looking down – or up, more likely, given Audrey's antics over the years – at me and saying: 'Stop moping, you silly old cow.'

Gently, Amy lifted my feet up and tucked me into bed. Then she kissed me on the forehead.

'Night, Cora,' she said. 'I'm sorry this has all been such a shock.'

I caught her hand.

'It is a shock,' I said. 'It's been a terrible shock. But Amy, I'm so glad to finally know what happened. I've doubted myself all these years and you've changed my whole world.'

She gave my hand a gentle squeeze, mindful of my arthritis.

'You've changed mine,' she said. 'I've never had many friends. Just Phil, really. And now I have you. You're my best friend and my surrogate granny all rolled into one.'

I felt teary again so I pulled Amy close to me and hugged her tightly so she couldn't see I was about to cry.

'You're a special woman,' I said.

She returned my hug, then she stood up and treated me to one of her dazzling smiles.

'Nah,' she said. 'You're the special one.'

She blew me a kiss, and turned off the light.

Chapter 49

The dressing room at *Strictly Stars Dancing* was frighteningly empty. We'd gone from ten couples to four and suddenly I could see just how far we'd come in the competition.

Along with me and Patrick, there was Martin the rugby player, who was surprisingly agile for a man of his size. There was Leo, who'd been in a boy band fifteen years earlier. I'd fancied him rotten when I was twelve and I couldn't even speak to him properly now in case I told him I'd had his *Smash Hits* sticker on my pencil case in year seven. And there was Alice, a sporty, jolly-hockey-sticks kind of girl. She'd started out in kids' television but now did all sorts of stuff from consumer affairs to royal weddings. She was very pretty, very nice and a really, really good dancer.

I was in a frenzy of excitement and nerves rolled into one. I jiggled in the make-up chair and laughed when the stylist told me off.

'I can't help it,' I said. 'I'm so desperate to get going.'

I was wearing my rumba dress. It was a scrap of white material, with a flesh-coloured leotard thing underneath. It was beautiful and I felt a bit like a fairy from *A Midsummer's Night Dream* in it. I couldn't wait to dance in it – it was so perfect for Patrick's choreography, which was emotional and a bit flighty.

'You're done,' said the stylist and I slid off the chair and wafted about the room in my dress.

'You look gorgeous,' said Alice, who was having her hair teased into a nineteen-twenties-style bob for her Charleston. 'Wish I had your figure.'

'I basically don't eat,' I told her cheerfully. 'And I see my personal trainer more than I see my friends. It's no life for someone nice like you.'

She laughed and I carried on wafting, dancing a few steps of our rumba here and a bit of our foxtrot there. I was buzzing with nervous energy.

Patrick came into the room, looking – I had to admit – amazing in his rumba costume. He was wearing tight-fitting black trousers and a shirt open to his waist.

'Amy,' he babbled, grabbing my hand. 'Are you busy? Are you done? Can we talk?'

He was obviously just as nervously excited as I was. I grinned at him.

'What?' I said. 'What's up?'

'I've got an email from Charlie,' he said, bouncing up and down on his toes like a little kid. 'He wants to come over. With his wife, and his kids and their families. He wants to meet Cora.'

'No way,' I said. 'Do you think she'll be up for it?'

I thought about how Cora had dealt with the news that Donnie hadn't ditched her after all. She'd had an astonishing physical reaction – reading all the letters from the war had exhausted her completely and she'd gone to bed for a whole day. But now a few days had passed and she was beginning to seem more like her old self. Patrick had printed everything out for her and she could read it all when she wanted to. She hadn't told her daughter yet, though, despite me urging her to, and I thought that was the most important thing, really.

'I think she'll want to meet them,' Patrick said. 'But she's going to have to tell Ginny the truth if she does.'

257

'Exactly what I was thinking,' I said. 'So when are they going to come?'

'Charlie's not sure, but he asked if we could maybe have a little memorial service at the spot where the bomb fell,' Patrick said. 'I think that's kind of nice.'

'Oh, that's lovely,' I said. 'Cora would finally get a chance to say goodbye.'

Alice had been listening to our conversation.

'Is this your landlady?' she said. 'The one who dances?'

I nodded.

'She's just found out that the man she was supposed to marry died in the war,' I explained. 'She thought he'd jilted her at the altar but Patrick did some research and found out he'd been killed.'

'Oh, that's terribly sad,' said Alice.

'I know,' I said. 'So sad.'

A runner poked her head round the door and told us we had five minutes.

'Come on then,' Patrick said, taking my hand. 'Let's go and show them what we're made of.'

Because it was the semi-final, we had two dances each. Our rumba was first, obviously. I loved the dance but I found it made me very emotional. Because we'd been rehearsing it so much this week, while we were completely wrapped up in everything that had happened with Cora and Donnie, I associated it with their story. It was quite a sad dance in my opinion, and when I threw myself into it – like I did then – I felt all sorts of emotions bubbling up.

And that meant when we finished dancing, I burst into tears.

'Ooh, what's wrong?' said Melissa, putting her arms round me as we faced the judges. 'You didn't do anything wrong?'

'No,' I sniffed. 'I just find that dance so sad.'

Patrick took my hand.

'It's been quite an emotional week,' he said. 'It's bound to have an effect.'

Frank, the head judge, gave me a wink.

258

'You've got nothing to cry about, my love,' he said. 'That was your best dance yet. I loved it.'

By the time we got our scores I had composed myself a bit. But then we got full marks – the first time we'd achieved that – and that made me cry all over again.

Our foxtrot also went really well. That was a joyful dance, and I adored it, so luckily it didn't make me cry. But it still made me think of Cora. I wondered if she'd watch some Ginger Rogers films with me now.

This time we didn't get full marks but we were close. We were top of the leader board and I was desperate to get through to the final, but I was even more desperate to check on Cora.

I rang her in the break we had before the audience votes were counted.

'Darling,' she said. 'What a triumph.'

I was thrilled. Hearing the audience whoop and cheer for us was amazing, obviously, but gaining Cora's approval meant an awful lot to me.

'Your timing was a bit off in the middle of the foxtrot,' she carried on. 'But only someone with eagle eyes would have spotted that one.'

I giggled.

'How are you feeling?' I said.

'Oh, not too bad,' she huffed. 'Ginny's back in the country.'

'Oh,' I said. 'Have you seen her?'

'Not yet. She's coming over tomorrow.'

'Will you tell her?'

Cora paused. I heard her breathing down the line.

'I think so,' she said.

I played with the skirt on my dress.

'Want me to be there?'

'No,' said Cora. 'I'm an adult. I can handle this.'

'Really?'

'No,' she said. 'Would you mind? You can explain how you tracked him down.'

259

I didn't mind at all. I told her so, and then we were being called back to the studio so I hung up and raced back to Patrick's side.

It was poor Martin who went home. I was sad to see him go, but overwhelmed to be in the final. We'd dance our favourite dance from the competition, which I thought would be the Charleston, the judges would choose one – I had a horrible feeling they'd choose our tango – and then we'd do a fancy show dance. We'd been practising bits here and there over the weeks but we had a lot of work to do.

As we headed for home, Patrick threw his arm round my shoulder. He seemed to be having no trouble whatsoever keeping our relationship in the friend zone. I, however, was struggling a bit. I knew that being single while I sorted my life out was the right thing to do. But he was just so handsome. And so close to me the whole time. Now I looked down at his hand, which was casually resting on my shoulder, and felt dizzy. He had strong fingers, dusted with freckles and with a sprinkling of golden hairs. I remembered – which in itself was remarkable given how much I'd drunk the night we spent together – how it had felt to have those hands on my body.

'We did good,' he said. 'You can have tomorrow off but then we've got a lot of work to do.'

I looked away, hoping my flushed cheeks wouldn't give any clue what I'd been thinking about.'

'Great,' I said. 'I've got stuff to do tomorrow anyway. I'm going to be with Cora when she tells Ginny, and I'm going to meet Babs, too. I've got to put my "serious" actress plan into action.'

Patrick grinned.

'I've got something up my sleeve, too,' he said. 'Show you on Monday. Good luck with Cora. Let me know how you get on?'

'I will,' I said, getting into the car. 'See you on Monday.'

I wondered what he was up to for about thirty seconds and then I fell asleep. Being a finalist on *Strictly Stars Dancing* was an exhausting business.

260

Chapter 50

I was up and at it bright and early the next day. I was determined not to miss any opportunities and being in the final of *Strictly Stars Dancing* was the best one yet.

I sat at my laptop and made a list of all the shows I was interested in. *Downton* was top, of course, but I included some crime dramas, a spy thriller, and some adaptations of classic novels that I'd heard were in the pipeline. I thought I'd probably missed the *Poldark* boat, but anything like that would suit me. I googled casting directors, I researched what TV shows had been given the green light and which had already been cancelled. In short, I did what Babs should have done.

I spent about an hour choosing what to wear to meet Babs in town. Eventually I settled on skinny jeans, with flat over-the-knee boots and a slouchy jumper layered over a vest top. Smart but casual. Informal yet business-like. I pulled my hair off my face into a tiny bun, and put on an extra coat of lipstick for courage. Then, armed with my list of agents and info, I headed off to meet her for lunch.

I was very nervous. An actor lives and breathes according to their agent and I knew I'd really annoyed Babs by dumping Matty and ignoring her calls. But I also knew that she'd lost sight of my ambitions – just as I had – and I had to remind her of what I wanted or find someone new. Though the very idea of telling her I wanted a new agent gave me palpitations. I'd have to cross that bridge when I came to it.

I was slightly boosted when I arrived to see that Babs was already there – looking just as nervous as I felt. I took a deep breath, threw my shoulders back, and went to sit opposite her.

'Amy,' she said, kissing me hello. 'Glad you could make it.'

'I've got a lot to say,' I said, putting my hands flat on the table. 'So I think I might just start talking.'

Babs looked alarmed.

'Can we order a drink first?'

She signalled to the waiter and ordered a glass of wine. I asked for a Diet Coke – I needed a clear head for this.

'Right,' I said briskly. 'Here's the deal. I don't want to be a poster girl for toothpaste, or breakfast cereal, or hair dye. I don't want to do any more reality TV, I don't want to spend my life at photo shoots doing tell-all interviews, and I really, really don't want to get back with Matty.'

Babs looked like she was going to say something but I held my hand up.

'No,' I said. 'I know we were good together once, but he's not what I want any more. I don't want my old life back. I want to make new opportunities.' I dug into my bag and pulled out my list.

'Here are some of the shows I'm interested in. I've jotted down some casting directors, too. I also want a US agent, so if you can find someone you can work with that's great. And I'd like to have a go at theatre, too.'

The waiter brought our drinks and Babs swigged her wine like someone who'd been stuck in the desert.

I took a mouthful of my Coke.

'Real theatre,' I said. 'Not pantomime. And not Agatha Christie. I hate Agatha Christie.'

'Harsh,' said Babs. 'Considering you've got an audition for *Poirot*.'

My jaw dropped.

'Really?' I whispered.

She grinned.

'Not for a few weeks, but yes, really.'

I was speechless.

'When you threw Matty out, he came to see me with his agent,' Babs said. 'He was furious and shouting the odds. But suddenly I realized he had more to lose than you do. You don't need him, Amy.'

'Well, that's what I've been telling you for weeks,' I said.

Babs gave me a sheepish smile.

'I know,' she said. 'I'm sorry.'

She took another mouthful of wine.

'It wasn't just you who got seduced by that whole celebrity lifestyle thing,' she said. 'The commission was pretty good as well, you know?'

I smiled.

'I know.'

She pulled out a list of her own. Hers, though, was on her iPad and looked very business-like compared to my scribbled notes.

'I've put lots of feelers out, and there are a few interesting things in the pipeline,' she said. 'Couple of TV shows. A film. An adaptation of some Thomas Hardy thing. Some ads in Japan – you know, to keep the wolf from the door.'

She leafed through her papers.

'What about the *Strictly Stars Dancing* live tour?' she said.

'Ooh, yes,' I said eagerly. 'Is Patrick doing it?'

'No idea,' said Babs, making a note on her tablet. 'They swap all the partners round on the tour anyway.'

'Oh,' I said, disappointed.

'How do you feel about photo shoots and interviews?' she said, carrying on regardless.

I thought about it. Talking about myself for half an hour. Being styled and wearing interesting clothes. Having my hair and make-up done. Being photographed …

'I bloody love them,' I said.

Babs beamed.

'Great,' she said. 'How about now?'

'Now?' I said, surprised.

'I've got a journalist from *Yay!* magazine waiting in the foyer,' Babs admitted. 'They want it for this week's issue – perfect timing for the final, I thought. You can talk all about what you're planning for the future and how you're putting Matty behind you. Then if you've got time they've got a studio booked for an hour to do a few pics.'

'I've got a couple of hours,' I said, checking my watch. 'But I've got plans for later.' I wasn't going to let Cora down – not when she'd asked me to be there when she broke the news to Ginny.

'I can't believe you've organized all this so fast,' I said.

'It seems you're even more in demand now than you ever were,' Babs said. She looked proud, as though it was completely down to her. 'Everyone wants a piece of Amy the survivor.'

'No more Amy Lavender the brand,' I said, sensing she was on a roll again. 'Just me being myself.'

She looked cross for a minute, then smiled.

'Fine,' she said. She picked up her phone and typed a brief text message.

'She'll be here in five minutes,' she said. 'Shall we run through what you should talk about?'

I gave her a fierce look.

'I'll be fine,' I said. 'Anyway, what about *Downton*? I really want something in a period drama.'

Babs screwed her nose up.

'Nothing yet,' she said. 'But they've just been given the go-ahead for the next series so I'll keep at it.'

She waved across the room as the journalist appeared. I recognized her as one who'd interviewed me a few times before. I knew she was nice and unthreatening and I knew she'd make me sound very brave in the interview. Brave, bold and ready for a new challenge – exactly how I wanted to come across. I winked at Babs.

'All righty then,' I said, downing my Coke and standing up to greet the writer. 'Let's do this. Amy Lavender's back in business.'

Chapter 51

It was a whirlwind of a day, but I loved every minute. I realized I'd been a bit hasty in saying I wanted to ditch the celeb lifestyle altogether. I just had to make sure it didn't interfere with my acting ambitions, that was all. My interview had gone really well and the photos were great – not overly sexy or too posed, just me looking happy. Babs was fully on board now, and had even suggested speaking to Cora to see if she could recommend an acting coach – she thought I should sharpen up my skills before I started auditioning and I thought it was a good idea.

But first we had to tell Ginny – and Natasha – all about Donnie.

Natasha came to get me, knocking on the back door as I lay on the sofa reading *Glamour* magazine.

'Granny has asked me to invite you up for a drink,' she said. 'Are you busy?'

I threw *Glamour* down and stood up – I'd been ready for the last twenty minutes.

'Nope,' I said. 'I'm all yours.'

'She's being very mysterious,' Natasha said. 'And she doesn't look very well. She says she's got something to tell us. I'm terrified she's got some awful illness.'

266

We went out into the garden and I shut the patio doors behind us.

'She's fine,' I said. 'I'm sure she's fine.'

Natasha gave me an odd look.

'Do you know what this is about?' she said.

I assumed an innocent expression.

'Not sure,' I muttered. 'Shall we go in?'

Cora didn't look well, Natasha was right about that. She was sitting in her winged-back chair with a blanket over her knees. She looked pale and delicate and her lipstick was like a pink slash across her white face.

'Oh, Cora,' I said. I went to her and took her hand. She squeezed gently.

'Amy,' Natasha said as another woman came into the room. 'This is my mother, Virginia.'

Ginny was tall and willowy like Natasha but she had faded strawberry-blonde hair that tumbled down her back in curls. She was wearing pink patterned leggings, several layers of brightly coloured tops and an enormous necklace. On her wrist she wore lots of chunky bangles. She was very pretty and looked nothing like the classically elegant Cora, or chic Natasha. I wondered if she looked like Donnie.

'Nice to meet you, Amy,' said Ginny. 'I hear you've done a great job looking out for Mum.'

'I tried,' I mumbled, aware that Cora didn't look her usual sparky self at all.

'Amy's changed my life,' Cora said. Ginny and Natasha both looked at her and then me in surprise. 'Ginny, darling, you'd better sit down. I've got something to tell you that might come as a shock.'

'Oh God, Mum, you're not a lesbian, are you?' Ginny said. 'I did wonder about you and Audrey for a while back in the seventies.'

'Oh, Ginny, honestly,' Cora said, sounding cross but looking

267

amused, and I got a glimpse of what their relationship had been like over the years.

'Sit down and listen.'

Ginny sat obediently. I perched on the arm of Cora's chair, still holding her hand.

'What do you remember me telling you about your father?' Cora began.

Ginny's eyes widened and she exchanged a glance with Natasha.

'Not much,' she said. 'That he was a GI who you met when you were dancing for the troops. That you loved him very much but he died at the end of the war. That his name was Jackson Devonshire.'

She paused.

'What part of that wasn't true?' she said. 'I'm guessing most of it, right?'

It was Cora's turn to look surprised.

'What do you mean?' she said.

Ginny raised her chin just as Cora did when she was annoyed.

'Oh, I'm not stupid, Mum,' she said. 'I've googled him and not found any mention of Jackson Devonshire. So how much of it is made up? What was he? A one-night stand? A quick fumble round the back of the parade hall?'

Cora's mouth dropped open and her eyes filled with tears. I wondered if I should intervene but Ginny saw her mother's reaction and changed tack.

'Oh, Mum,' she said, putting her hand to her mouth. 'Were you raped?'

Cora tried to smile.

'No, darling,' she said. 'I wasn't raped. I did love your father very much, that bit is true. His name was Donald Jackson, but everyone called him Donnie. And he – I've just found out – loved me, too. We were supposed to be getting married, in 1945 when I was expecting you. But he didn't show up at the wedding and I thought he'd jilted me.'

'Shit,' said Ginny. 'Really?'

Cora nodded.

'I was heartbroken and so I lied. I invented Jackson Devonshire so you'd have a dad. So I could be a proud war widow rather than just another woman who'd got herself knocked up by a love-rat GI.'

Natasha was staring at Cora, open-mouthed. Ginny looked bemused.

'I've always wondered what happened to Donnie and so Amy tracked him down.'

Natasha and Ginny both shifted their gaze to me and I wriggled uncomfortably.

'My friend Patrick did it,' I said. 'He's interested in history and he's found old army friends of his granddad so he knew where to look.'

Ginny stood up.

'Is he still alive?' she said in a shaky voice. 'Is my father still alive?'

'Oh, darling, no, I'm so sorry,' Cora said. 'He's not.'

I jumped in.

'He died in 1945,' I said. 'The day before he was supposed to marry Cora. That's why he didn't turn up – he'd been killed when a bomb fell.'

'And no one told you?' Ginny said, turning to her mother. 'Oh, Mum, that's awful.'

Cora grimaced.

'I didn't find out until the other day,' she said.

'We've found his family,' I said. In for a penny, in for a pound, I thought. We may as well tell the whole lot now. 'They all live in America – Connecticut. His sister, Lois, passed away a while ago, but his younger brother, Walter, is still alive. And Walter's son, Charlie. And Charlie's kids, too.'

I looked at Cora.

'They want to come over to England,' I told her. 'They want

269

to meet you and Ginny, and they'd like to hold a memorial service where the bomb fell. Do something to remember Donnie.'

'I'd like that,' Cora said.

'Oh, my God,' Ginny said. 'This is astonishing. I've got an uncle? And cousins?'

Cora smiled at her.

'It's taken me days to really let it sink in,' she admitted. 'I've spent seventy years thinking Donnie betrayed me. That he'd run off from the army and probably married someone else and never given me – or you – a second thought.'

Ginny sat on the other arm of Cora's chair and hugged her mum tightly.

'I never minded not having a dad,' she said. 'Well, sometimes I minded. But there were lots of kids like me, weren't there? Who'd lost a dad in the war. And we always had people round us. Audrey, and Nanna Reenie …'

She trailed off.

'Mum,' she said. 'Did they know about my dad?'

Cora looked down at her knees.

'They did,' she said. 'But my mum, your Granny Cassidy, she didn't.'

Ginny looked shocked.

'So many lies,' she said. 'Your chakras must be all over the place.'

'Are you angry?' Cora said, her voice quavering. 'Are you angry with me for lying?'

Ginny looked thoughtful, as though she was trying to work it out.

'I don't think so,' she said. 'But I might be later.'

Natasha gave an exasperated sigh. She was obviously used to her mum's quirky ways.

'Granny did what she had to do,' she said. 'Didn't you, Granny?'

Cora nodded.

'But I shouldn't have lied,' she said. 'Not to you, Ginny.'

Ginny shrugged.

'Everyone lies,' she said. 'But the truth always comes out in the end.'

I was amazed at how well Ginny was taking the news and Cora looked terribly relieved. I suspected Ginny was unpredictable and she could just have easily reacted badly. But the fact was, she seemed fine right now.

'We've got photos,' I said. 'Do you want to see them?'

Chapter 52

Ginny may have been good-natured about Cora's lies, but there was no denying she pored over the photos of Donnie that Charlie had sent, desperate for every bit of information about her father.

'I look like him, don't you think?' she said, leafing through one of Cora's photo albums for a snap of her at a similar age. 'It's funny that we'll never know how he would have aged. I wonder if his hair would have faded like mine has?'

'His hair was blonder than yours,' Cora said, wrapping a strand of Ginny's reddish locks round her finger. 'I'm not sure where you got your carrot-top from.'

They carried on looking at the photos and pointing out resemblances between relations. I felt a bit awkward sitting on the edge of the family, so I got up to go.

'I'm going to leave you to it,' I said.

Natasha stopped me.

'Please stay,' she said. 'This is all down to you. Shall we get some drinks?'

Together we went into the kitchen and Natasha went in search of wine.

'You've done an amazing thing,' she said, opening the fridge and pulling out a bottle.

'We thought Donnie might still be alive,' I admitted. 'At least, that's what I hoped. I sort of thought we could bring them back together, they'd have a blazing row, and then they could get on with their lives.'

'Like you and Matty,' Natasha said, casually.

'Oh, I know that tone,' I said, giving her a grin. 'You may work for one of those posh mags, but you're still a hack at heart.'

Natasha laughed loudly.

'Busted,' she said. 'I pretend not to be interested but who doesn't bookmark the *PostOnline*?'

I opened the cupboard to get out some glasses.

'That's the trouble,' I said. 'Everyone reads it even if they pretend they don't – and that's why everyone knew everything about me and Matty.'

'Is it really over between you two?' Natasha said. 'This time I promise I'm asking as a friend and not a journalist.'

She pulled the cork out of the bottle with a pop, and began pouring wine into the glasses.

'It's really over,' I said, taking the glass she handed me. 'It was over the moment I punched that poor girl in the nose.'

Natasha made a face.

'That wasn't one of your best decisions,' she said.

'Do you know what, though?' I said, leaning against Cora's work surface. 'It's all worked out fine. If I'd not punched Kayleigh I wouldn't have been sacked, and if I'd not been sacked, I'd not have got on *Strictly Stars Dancing*. Or met your gran. Or …'

I paused, not wanting to mention Patrick. Of course it was too late. Natasha was there already.

'Or met your dance partner,' she said. 'What's his name?'

'Patrick,' I said, staring into my glass. 'His name's Patrick.'

Natasha squealed in a way that did not suit her elegant appearance.

'You fancy him,' she said.

'Do not.'

273

'Oh, you do. Look at that blush.'

'Stop it,' I said. 'It's not happening. Let's not talk about it.'

I picked up the bottle of wine and a glass for Cora, and took it into the front room. Natasha followed.

'Amy fancies her dance partner,' she announced. 'Patrick.'

'Natasha,' I protested.

Cora looked interested.

'Still?' she said. 'Lots of people fancy their partners to begin with but then they find the attraction wanes after a while.'

'It's not waning,' I said. 'It's the opposite, actually, whatever that is.'

'Waxing,' said Ginny helpfully.

I stared at her, not understanding.

'It's the opposite of waxing.'

'Oh,' I said, still a bit bemused by Ginny altogether. 'Yes, then in that case, my attraction to Patrick is waxing.'

'I knew it,' said Natasha.

'It was him, you know, who found Donnie and tracked down his family,' I said. 'He said he could understand why Cora needed to know what had happened, even after all this time.'

Ginny looked approving.

'Empathy,' she said, nodding. 'That's a good character trait to have. What does he look like, this Patrick?'

Natasha found a photo on her phone and showed her mum, who breathed in sharply through pursed lips.

'Wowsers,' she said. 'Look at that chest.'

I scowled at her.

'You're not helping,' I said.

Natasha laughed again.

'So, he's kind and ripped,' she said. 'What else?'

'He's funny,' I said. 'I'm not always very good at laughing at myself but he sort of makes the world funnier. And he believes in me. He's been encouraging me to be firmer with my agent and get her to find me some auditions and she has. I'd never have done that without him on my side. I feel stronger now because I've met him. And I think I'm a better person because he taught me how to dance …'

I trailed off, realizing I'd unconsciously echoed what Matty said about me in *Hot* magazine. Though Babs had told me his agent had told him to say it. Looking up, I realized Natasha, Ginny and Cora were all staring at me.

'Oh, dear,' Cora said, gleefully. 'You've got it bad.'

'Really bad,' said Ginny. 'I think this might be love.'

Natasha nudged me violently.

'Does he feel the same about you?'

'No,' I said. 'Maybe. I don't know. I feel like I've let him down too many times. We spent the night together before *Strictly Stars Dancing* began – we didn't know we'd be partners then, obviously. And I was horrible to him the next day.'

I winced, thinking about how cold I'd been.

'But he forgave me. Then we kissed and I ran away. And he forgave me again. I've just been a cow, but he's been great. And then I told him I just wanted to be friends and he seems fine with it. Really.' I put my head in my hands. 'Oh, man,' I said. 'Have I missed my chance?'

Cora, who'd necked half her glass of wine already, ditched the blanket she'd had over her knees and was looking more like her old self now, stood up.

'Amy,' she said, taking my hands so I stood up, too. 'I want you to listen to me – and listen carefully.'

'Crikey,' I said, but I listened.

'I gave you some advice before but I was wrong,' Cora said. 'So wrong. I can see that now. I want you to seize every chance of happiness you get and live every day as though it's your last.' She looked dreamy for a second.

'The last time I saw Donnie,' she said, 'was in Hyde Park. It was sunny and he was walking away from me, smiling. He spun round and shouted that we were getting married and two soldiers

275

who were walking nearby congratulated him. The very last words he said to me were "I love you, Cora Cassidy". I may not have Donnie, but I've got that memory.'

I breathed in, still floored by the sadness of all Cora's 'what ifs'.

'What would you tell Patrick if you thought you'd never see him again?' Cora said.

I chewed my lip.

'I'd tell him that he's one of the nicest, kindest people I've ever met,' I began.

'Well, that's not very hot,' Ginny grumbled. 'Makes him sound like a sob story on *Surprise Surprise*.'

I laughed.

'I'd tell him that when he touches me, my skin fizzes,' I said.

'Better,' Ginny said. Natasha frowned at her to be quiet.

'I'd tell him that sometimes when he looks at me, my stomach does this snakey thing and I feel sick and weak and,' I lowered my voice, 'really, really hot – you know?'

Ginny clapped her hands.

'That dancing with him is like the promise of the best sex I've ever had, and the best sex, and the afterwards of the best sex all rolled into one,' I said, feeling myself blushing again. 'And that I can't bear to think that on Saturday this will all be over and I might never even see him again.'

Cora squeezed my fingers tightly.

'You need to tell him,' she said. 'Tell him what you've told us.'

'What if he doesn't feel the same?' I said.

Cora shrugged.

'Tell him after the final,' she said. 'Then if it goes wrong, you never have to see him again.'

I looked at her and thought about how she'd had a whole life wishing things had turned out differently.

'Seize my chance of happiness?' I said.

'Seize it,' Cora said.

'Okay,' I said. I lifted my chin, Cora-style. 'I will.'

I gave her a hug.

'But you seize it, too,' I said. 'Maybe now you know the truth about Donnie you can find someone to love.'

Cora laughed.

'Oh, I think that boat has sailed,' she said. 'And that's just fine with me. But you, Amy, you're still young. Your boat's still in the harbour.'

I giggled, suddenly giddy with hope and excitement about what the future held.

'Right,' I said. 'I'm off to bed. I've got a whole lot of seizing to do tomorrow.'

Chapter 53

'Are you ready?' Patrick said. We were standing in the *Strictly Stars Dancing* costume department, very early on Monday morning. In front of us were two mannequins, both covered in sheets, and a very excited costume designer called Annie.

Patrick had forced me to go all the way to the studio at some ungodly hour, so he could show me what he had planned for our show dance in the final. I was bleary-eyed after being up late with Cora, and I hoped it was going to be worth it.

'Ready as I'll ever be,' I said, eyeing him over the top of my takeaway coffee cup. 'Show me.'

'Tah-dah!' said Annie, pulling off the sheet.

I gasped in delight. The mannequin was wearing a long, bright-pink strapless dress just like the one Marilyn Monroe wore in *Gentlemen Prefer Blondes*. After Patrick and I had watched the film together I'd watched it over and over again because I'd loved it so much. My favourite bit was when she sang 'Diamonds Are a Girl's Best Friend' – wearing a dress just like this one.

'It's like Marilyn's,' I said. Patrick was smiling so widely I thought his face must hurt.

'I know how much you love that film,' Patrick said. 'So I thought we'd have a kind of vintage feel to the start of the show dance. We've practised a few bits, right?'

I nodded. We had gone over some of the steps but not in the right order and not with music – Patrick had kept it all under his hat.

'So the first half of the dance is going to be very Marilyn. A quickstep with some American smooth thrown in for good measure. Couple of lifts. A few extra dancers like Marilyn has in the film – you know the kind of thing.'

'Gorgeous,' I said.

Annie took over.

'The dress has a fuller skirt and a split because you need to be able to move your legs,' she explained. And it's got a flesh-coloured top so it won't fall down. We've got long gloves, too, like she has in the film.'

I walked round the mannequin, admiring the dress. It really was pretty. Down the back was a row of fastenings, which looked slightly odd.

'What's this?' I asked.

'Ah,' Patrick said, looking even more proud of himself. 'That's for the second part of the dance.'

'There's more?' I said.

'Well, less really,' said Annie with a grin. Deftly, she unfastened the back of the dress and pulled it off the mannequin. Underneath was a dazzling sparkly leotard with a trailing sequined skirt to one side.

'Oh, my,' I said. 'It's like a very shiny snakeskin.'

'For the rumba part of the dance,' Patrick said. 'Well, it's based around a rumba more or less, with some other bits thrown in. We're dancing to 'Diamonds' by Rihanna.'

'That's my favourite song,' I said.

Patrick pretended to look surprised.

'It is?'

I gave him a punch on the arm.

'This is incredible, Patrick,' I said. Suddenly I felt like I wanted to cry, but not because I was sad. 'I honestly think it's the nicest thing anyone's ever done for me.'

Patrick looked at me for a second, and I thought he was going to say something. Then he grinned.

'Bet you're not saying that when I make you quickstep for four hours non-stop,' he said. 'And we've got to sort out that back bend in the tango. And you need to not cry during the rumba.'

I turned away slightly and sneakily wiped away a tear that was threatening to drip. 'Lots to do,' I said. 'Shall we get on with it?'

I had never worked as hard as I worked those last five days on *Strictly Stars Dancing*. Never. I'd put in long days and late nights on *Turpin Road*, of course – anyone who thinks being on a soap is an easy ride has clearly never been on a soap. I'd done night shoots, a few stunts, some emotional stories that took a lot of research and drained me so much I felt like it was all real. But I'd never been so full on. From that early morning on the Monday, we danced for twelve, sometimes fourteen hours each day. We paused for snacks and drinks. On Wednesday we cracked the back bend in the tango and celebrated with a cheeky Nando's. But even then we were hard at it again shortly afterwards. On the Thursday, we didn't go outside the studio for ten hours and, when we finally headed home, we were shocked to see it was snowing.

I was thrilled. I bounded down the steps from the school's front door and out onto the street. It was dark and the streetlights shone orange beams onto the snowy pavements. The road was quiet and still – there were no cars – and it was like we'd been transported from Clapham to Narnia.

'Ohmygod,' I said, standing with my arms outstretched. 'We've been working so hard I didn't even notice winter had arrived.'

Patrick was standing very still, on the bottom step. The stairs were undercover, so they weren't snowy, but his next footstep would take him onto the icy path.

'Come on,' I said, twirling round. 'Let's walk across the common. It'll be beautiful.'

'Can we take a cab?' Patrick said.

I laughed. Patrick didn't.

'Oh, you're serious,' I said. 'What's the matter?'

'It's snowing,' Patrick said. 'And I'm from California.'

'So?'

'So, we don't do snow in California,' he said through chattering teeth. 'It barely even rains in California.'

I was delighted.

'Ohmygod are you scared of the snow?' I said with glee. 'Are you scared of the ittybitty snowflakes?'

Patrick sighed.

'No, I'm not scared,' he said. 'Just wary.'

'Scared.'

He made a face.

'I'm terrified,' he wailed. 'Come help me, Amy.'

Giggling, I took his hand.

'You're wearing boots,' I said. 'You'll be fine. Just walk normally.'

Slowly, we made our way through the deserted streets. Patrick kept making little yelps and gasps whenever his foot slipped and I could not stop laughing. It was so funny to see him out of his comfort zone.

'I like that I'm in charge for once,' I teased.

'Well, don't get used to it,' Patrick said. 'I'm back being the boss of you tomorrow.'

He stumbled as his foot shot out in front of him.

'Catch me,' he squealed and I threw my arms round him, shaking with laughter.

'I've got you,' I said. 'You're safe.'

I looked up at him. He was wearing his black beanie hat, and his blond hair stuck out from underneath. His cheeks were rosy and his eyes sparkled like the diamonds in Rihanna's song. I wanted to touch his face and kiss him and tell him I loved him, but I also wanted to win *Strictly Stars Dancing* and with the final just two days away I couldn't risk ruining our relationship, which was going so well.

I'll tell him as soon as the show ends, I thought. I'll tell him the minute the cameras stop.

Patrick's feet slipped again and I caught him once more. He started to laugh, too.

'This is crazy,' he said. 'I'm never going to make it home.'

'You're just being a bit pathetic,' I said sternly. 'But you can stay at mine if you like?'

Patrick looked at me.

'On the sofa,' I babbled. 'It turns into a bed. It's fine. I didn't mean share with me. Don't worry.'

He nodded.

'On the sofa,' he said. 'Thanks. I'd like that.'

'We've got to get home first,' I said, beginning to giggle again. 'Can you walk?'

'Only if you hold my hand,' Patrick said. 'Don't let go.'

We made it back to the flat eventually, but it wasn't easy.

'God, I thought we'd be stuck out there for ever,' Patrick said as we stamped our feet on the doormat. I kind of wished we had been. It had been lovely, being needed by him, and helping him like he'd helped me. And of course being so close to him. I glanced out of the window, wondering whether to suggest a snowball fight in the garden. But Patrick was already stripping off his jacket and gloves and looked so relieved to be indoors that I knew my idea wouldn't go down well.

'Come on then, Mr California,' I said. 'Let's go and make up your bed.'

Chapter 54

'Would Amy Lavender and her partner, Patrick Walker, please take to the dance floor …'

Patrick took my hand and we walked out into the middle of the dance floor. My heart was pounding and my hands were clammy but I was fizzing with energy. Our Charleston had gone brilliantly. Our tango – hmm, not so much, though it was definitely better than the first time we'd danced it. And now it was time for our show dance.

Leo and Alice, the other finalists, had already danced. They had both done amazing things.

Leo, the boyband member, had done a lot of gymnastics when he was a kid. His partner, a vibrant Eastern European dancer with bright red hair, had pulled out all the stops with her choreography producing a show dance that was athletic and energetic, and had the audience gasping with delight.

Alice's dance was my favourite, though. She was a very 'nice' TV presenter. Clean-cut, wholesome, pretty in a girl-next-door kind of way. She was always tramping through fields on telly, or riding a bike, or canoeing down a river. You know the kind of thing? And tonight she'd been transformed into a rock goddess. She danced a kind of tango/paso doble crossover to a Guns 'n'

Roses song. She wore a black leather catsuit that revealed an amazing body, and she was generally awesome. It was her we had to beat, I thought.

Patrick and our four backing dancers, who were all dressed in shirts and tailcoats, surrounded me, the lights went down, the band struck up 'Diamonds Are a Girl's Best Friend', and we were off.

We quickstepped our way round the floor, this way and that. I flicked up my toes and heels, we did our little running step perfectly. I almost turned the wrong way at one point but Patrick realized what was happening and managed to stop me.

'Stay calm,' he whispered in my ear. 'It's going great.'

As the music changed into Rihanna's 'Diamonds', the dancers surrounded me once again and in one swift move – with a bit of help from Patrick – I pulled my dress off, revealing the leotard underneath. Patrick yanked his shirt and took it off, too, showing the sparkly waistcoat he wore underneath. The other dancers stepped back, taking our discarded outfits with them, and we were alone on the dance floor.

During the Marilyn part of the dance, I'd felt like the audience were part of our efforts. They were cheering tricky steps and clapping and I was aware of them the whole time. But now it was different. The lights had changed, so we were in a spotlight with the trusty *Strictly Stars Dancing* glitterball spinning. The audience were quieter and because they were in darkness I couldn't see them anyway. I was dancing my favourite dance, to my favourite song, with my favourite man – it was heaven and I honestly didn't want it to end.

It was as though Patrick and I were one person as we swayed and sparkled on the dance floor. I felt like my breath was his breath, and his arms and legs were extensions of my own. I forgot it was a competition, I forgot we were trying to win – I just danced. And then it was over, and the audience were on their feet cheering and shouting, and I was crying. Of course.

'Don't cry,' said Patrick in my ear. 'You promised me there would be no tears.'

'But it was perfect,' I said. 'So perfect.'

He picked me up and spun me round.

'You're perfect,' he said. We gazed at each other for a minute, then Melissa was calling us over and we had to go and face the judges.

'I feel a bit emotional myself,' admitted the head judge, Frank. 'I think all our finalists have done themselves proud tonight …'

The audience roared their approval.

'Amy, you had a shaky start in this competition but you've worked so hard and I really think you deserve to win. I think everyone deserves to win.'

He was right, actually. Leo had come through alcoholism and bankruptcy and started a foundation to help kids pursue careers in music. And Alice had told me that she and her husband had been trying to start a family but she'd had several miscarriages and had decided to take part in the competition as a distraction.

'Oh, that would be nice,' said Melissa. 'But there's only going to be one winner – and it's the audience who decide tonight.'

We had a break while the phone votes were counted. Patrick disappeared somewhere – the loo probably – and I went to find Cora who was in the front row with Ginny, Natasha, and Natasha's eldest daughter.

Cora was in floods of tears.

'Oh, darling Amy, you did so well,' she gushed.

I gave her a hug.

'I went the wrong way during the quickstep,' I told her.

'No one noticed,' she said. 'Honestly, darling. It was wonderful.'

Ginny prodded me.

'When are you going to tell Patrick?' she said. 'Now?'

'No,' I said. 'Don't prod me. I'll tell him after the result.'

'Tell him now,' Ginny said. 'Have you practised?'

'Obviously,' I said. 'I've gone over and over it. He stayed over the night it snowed – on the sofa bed,' I added as I saw her face light up. 'And I couldn't sleep. Knowing he was just next door made me very edgy. I got it all straight in my head then.'

'And?' Ginny looked at me in expectation.

'I'm not going over it now,' I hissed, looking round in case Patrick was lurking. I spotted him on the other side of the room talking to a very excited Phil and Bertie. 'But it's about how he makes me feel, how I think we're good for each other. There are a few jokes in there. I've got it all memorized.'

'Really?' Ginny sounded doubtful.

'Really,' I said.

'Amy,' a voice said behind me. It was Babs.

'Ohmygod Babs,' I said. 'I didn't know you were coming. How did you get a ticket?'

'Oh, I pulled a few strings,' she said with a grin. She looked me up and down. 'You're pretty good at this,' she said. 'Have you ever thought of doing a musical?'

'Have you ever heard me sing?' I said.

'Bad?'

'I'm no Taylor Swift, let's just put it like that.'

'Maybe you could do that show where they get celebs to join a choir …' Babs said thoughtfully.

'Babs,' I said. 'No more reality TV.'

'Oh, I almost forgot,' she said. 'There's someone I want you to meet.'

She turned round and bustled forward a woman with wavy brown hair and a nice smile.

'Amy,' she said. 'This is Winnie Williams. She's the casting director at *Downton Abbey*.'

I gasped.

'It's so lovely to meet you,' I said, shaking her hand. 'I love that show.'

Winnie smiled at me.

'We love you,' she said. 'I'd like to have a chat about our next series. Can we meet next week?'

'Yes, please,' I said. I let out a little squeak of joy. I felt like I'd won already even if I didn't get to take the *Strictly Stars Dancing* trophy home.

Across the dance floor, Patrick was gesturing to me wildly. I bounded over to him.

'It's time for the results,' he said. 'Are you ready?'

We stood at one side of the dance floor, with Leo next to us, and Alice on the far side.

'Good luck,' I whispered at my fellow competitors and they all wished us luck, too. Patrick was holding my hand and I was super-aware of him. I hoped I'd be able to get him by himself for a while after the show, so I could make my little speech. And, of course, I hoped he'd feel the same way. I was completely excited about auditioning for *Downton*, but still I found I couldn't even imagine the next few weeks, months or years, even, without dancing – or Patrick.

There were runners zooming about all over the place and Melissa and Vicky were in a heated discussion with a man with a headset.

'I wish they'd hurry up,' Patrick said. 'I can't bear this waiting.'

'I've got an audition at *Downton*,' I said to distract him.

He swept me up into a hug.

'Well done, well done, well done,' he said. 'I am so proud of you.'

I wrapped my arms round his neck and found I didn't really want to let go.

'I'm proud of you, too,' I said.

We looked at each other for a moment and then we both spoke at once.

'I love you.'

I blinked in surprise.

'I love you, too,' we both said.

287

I felt a bubble of joy rise up inside me.

'You love me?' I said. 'Really?'

Patrick looked into my eyes.

'Really,' he said. 'Our show dance was basically my love letter to you.'

'I had a whole speech prepared,' I said in wonder. 'And it turned out I didn't need it after all.'

Patrick bent his head and kissed me on and on. I heard a thundering in my ears, which I thought was the sheer emotion of it all, until I realized it was the audience clapping and drumming their feet on the floor.

We broke apart and the crowd cheered.

Melissa was holding a card and standing in front of us, laughing.

'Ready?' she said.

'Going to live, in three, two, one …' said the producer. My heart began thumping, the crowd whooped again, and the band played.

'The votes have been counted and verified,' said Melissa.

The lights dimmed, and I caught my breath. Patrick squeezed my hand tightly.

'And the winner of *Strictly Stars Dancing* 2015 is …'

Epilogue

I was immensely proud of Amy. I watched her smiling and dancing her way round the wrap party. Chatting to everyone, laughing, posing for photos on people's phones – and all the time with Patrick stuck to her like glue. I was thrilled they'd finally got it together. She deserved a good'un like him, after all that business with Matty.

I wondered where Ginny had got to. She was supposed to be finding me a drink but she'd disappeared. I shifted in my seat. They were very uncomfortable, these studio chairs, but I couldn't stand up for much longer.

'Cora Devonshire as I live and breathe.'

I looked up. Standing in front of me was the head judge, Frank. Or Francis as I'd known him, back in the sixties.

'Francis,' I said, with a smile. 'I wondered when you'd track me down.'

He sat down next to me.

'It was Alice who told me you were around,' he said. 'She didn't know we were old friends, of course.'

He frowned.

'She told me what happened to your chap during the war.'

I lifted my chin.

'Long time ago now,' I said.

Frank nodded.

'My wife died,' he said. 'Twenty years gone now.'

'I'm sorry,' I said.

He looked at me.

'We had a good time, me and you,' he said, a hint of mischief in his brown eyes. 'Do you remember?'

'I remember.'

'Could I come and call on you one day next week?' Frank said.

I thought about what Amy had said about seizing my chance of happiness, too.

I smiled at Frank.

'I'd like that,' I said.

If you loved *A Step in Time* then don't
miss Kerry Barrett's other novel...

The Forgotten Girl

Chapter 1

2016

I was nervous. Not just a little bit wobbly. I was properly, squeaky-voiced, sweaty-palms, absolutely bloody terrified. And that was very unlike me.

The office was just up ahead – I could see it from where I stood, lurking behind my sunglasses in case anyone I knew spotted me and tried to speak to me. I wasn't ready for conversation yet. The building had a glass front, with huge blown-up magazine covers in its windows. In pride of place, right next to the revolving door, was the cover from the most recent issue of Mode.

I swallowed.

'It's fine,' I muttered to myself. 'They wouldn't have given you the job if they didn't think you were up to it. It's fine. You're fine. Better than fine. You're brilliant.'

I took a deep breath, straightened my back, threw back my shoulders and headed to the Starbucks opposite me.

I ordered an espresso and a soya latte, then I sat down to compose myself for a minute.

Today was my first day as editor of Mode. It was the job I'd wanted since I was a teenager. It had been my dream for so long,

I could barely believe it was happening, and I was determined to make a success of it.

Except here I was, ready to get started, and I'd been floored by these nerves.

Shaking slightly, I downed my espresso in one like it was a shot of tequila and checked the time on my phone. I was early, but that was no bad thing. I had lots of good luck messages – mostly from people hoping I'll give them a job, I thought wryly. I couldn't help noticing, as I scrolled through and deleted them, that there was nothing from my best friend, Jen. She was obviously still upset about the way I'd behaved when I'd got the job. And if I was honest, she had every right to be upset, but I didn't have time to worry about that now. I was sure she'd come round.

I stood up and straightened my clothes. I'd played it safe this morning with black skinny trousers, a fitted black shirt and funky leopard-print pumps. My naturally curly blonde hair was straightened and pulled into a sleek ponytail and I wore a slash of red lipstick. I looked good. I just hoped it was good enough for the editor of Mode.

A surge of excitement bubbled up inside me. I was the editor of Mode. Me. Fearne Summers. I picked up my latte and looped my arm through my Marc Jacobs tote.

'Right, Fearne,' I said out loud. 'Let's do this.'

I wasn't expecting a welcoming committee or a cheerleading squad waiting for me in reception (well, I was a bit) but I did think that the bored woman behind the desk could have at least cracked a smile. Or she could have tried to look a tiny bit impressed that I was the new editor of Mode. Mind you, if this office was anything like my old place – and I was pretty sure all magazine companies were the same – there would be a never-ending stream of celebrities, models, and strange PR stunts (last Christmas we'd had mince pies delivered by a llama wearing a Santa hat, and that was one of the more normal visitors). Perhaps a new editor was terribly run of the mill.

'Here's your pass,' she said, throwing it across the desk at me. 'The office is on the third floor, but you're to go up to fifth first of all to meet Lizzie.'

I was surprised. Lizzie was the chief-exec of Glam Media, the company that owned Mode along with lots of other magazines. I knew I'd have to catch up with her at some point today but I thought she'd give me time to meet my team, and find my office first.

Lizzie was waiting for me when I got out of the lift. The bored receptionist must have told her I was on my way.

She was in her early fifties, petite and stylishly dressed, with a cloud of dark hair. She was friendly and approachable, but she had a reputation of being ruthless in pursuit of profit for the company. She scared the bejeesus out of me if I was honest, but she'd been very nice when I met her at one of the many interviews I'd done to get the job. Now she smiled at me and shook my hand.

'Great to have you on board, Fearne' she said. 'This is a time of big change for Mode.'

'I've got loads of ideas,' I said, following her down the corridor to a meeting room. 'I can't wait to get started.'

She gave me a brief smile over her shoulder.

'Great,' she said again.

Except she didn't really mean great, I quickly discovered. She meant, *yeah good luck with that, Fearne.*

It turned out that Glam Media was worried about Mode. Really worried. I'd looked at the sales, of course, and seen they weren't as good as they could be but I hadn't really grasped just how much trouble the magazine was in.

'The problem is the competition has really raised its game,' Lizzie explained as I stared out of the big window in her office and tried to take in everything she was saying.

'Grace?' I said. It had been a fairly boring, unadventurous magazine called Home & Hearth until it was bought by a new company and had loads of money pumped into it. Now it had

295

a new name, it was exciting and fun, and it was stealing lots of Mode's readers.

'So the finance department have redone your budgets for this year,' said Lizzie. 'To reflect Mode's sales.'

She slid a piece of paper across her desk and I stared at the figures she'd put in front of me in horror.

'I can't run a glossy mag on this budget,' I said. 'How am I supposed to pay for fashion shoots? Or commission writers?'

Lizzie shrugged.

'Times are tough,' she said. 'That's all that's in the pot.'

'Can't I have some of the website budget?' I asked.

She shook her head.

'Digital budget is separate,' she said. 'The website's going very well. Advertising and readership are both up. It's the magazine that's in trouble.'

I looked at her, suddenly realizing where this was going, and why my predecessor had been so keen to leave her job.

'Are you going to close Mode?' I asked.

She stared back at me.

'Nothing's decided yet.'

'But it's possible?'

Lizzie looked at a point somewhere past my ear.

'Print isn't working,' she said.

'But Mode is an iconic brand,' I said desperately. 'It's been going since the sixties. It was the first ever young women's glossy. You can't close it.'

Lizzie still didn't look me in the eye, but she did at least assume a slightly sympathetic expression.

'We'd still have the website,' she said. 'It's not ending, it's just changing. Mode will still exist – just in a different form.'

'A glossy mag is a treat,' I said. 'People will pay for that.'

She shrugged.

'Would people lose their jobs?' I asked, suddenly realizing this didn't just affect me.

'That's also possible,' she said.

I put my head in my hands. This was a nightmare. My dream job was collapsing around my ears.

Lizzie took a breath.

'Fearne, we took you on for a reason,' she said. 'You're a great editor with a good reputation.'

I forced myself to raise my head and smile at her. That was nice to hear.

'But you're also known for being cut-throat,' she carried on. 'We all know you're single-minded and determined. That you don't let anything get in the way of success.'

I nodded slowly. I wasn't sure I'd use the word 'cut-throat' but I was definitely single-minded.

'We know you won't let emotions or sentiment get in the way of doing your job.'

Oh.

'You brought me here to close the magazine?' I said, as I worked it all out.

Lizzie had the grace to look slightly shame-faced.

'Well,' she said. 'Close it or make it work. Take back some of the sales we've lost to Grace.'

I looked at the budget again. With the figures she'd given me it was obvious which option she wanted. I could barely cover the staffing costs with this amount of money – and I had no chance of booking top photographers or paying for big-name writers. It was an impossible task.

'How long have I got?' I said. 'How long do I have to make Mode pay?'

Lizzie looked a bit confused. She'd clearly not considered this.

'Six months?'

I swallowed.

'Give me a year,' I said, wondering how on earth I managed to keep my voice steady when I was so terrified by the task that lay ahead. 'I need a year to have a proper go at this.'

Lizzie looked at something on the papers in front of her. She rubbed the bridge of her nose and sighed.

'Nine months?' she said.

I shrugged.

'Is that the best you can offer?' I said. She nodded.

'So if I can increase sales enough in that time, you'll let the magazine carry on?' I said.

Lizzie nodded again.

'If you can make it work on the new budget, then we'll reconsider,' she said, sounding incredulous that I was even thinking about it.

'Great,' I said, faking excitement when all I felt was despair. 'Nine months is more than enough.'

I gathered up my things and stood up, hoping she couldn't see my legs trembling. 'If you'll excuse me, I'm going to meet my team now.'

If you enjoyed *A Step In Time*, then why not try another gripping historical novel from HQ Digital?

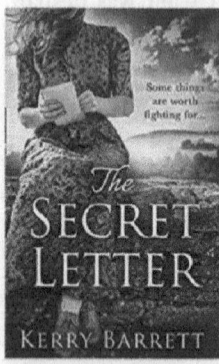

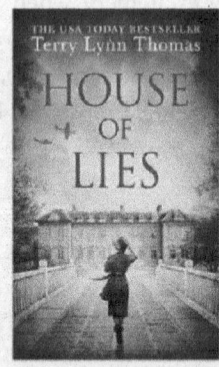

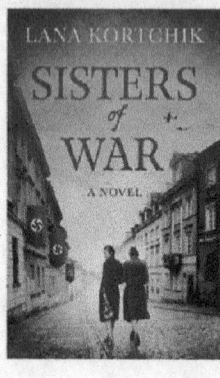